Cry, the
Beloved Country

CRY, The Beloved Country

ALAN PATON

LANDMARK BOOKS

ABC·CLIO

Santa Barbara, California
Oxford, England

First published 1948 in the United States by Scribner Book
Companies, Inc., and in Great Britain by Jonathan Cape,
Limited.

Published in Large Print 1987 by arrangement with Scribner Book Companies, Inc., and Jonathan Cape, Limited.

Library of Congress Cataloging-in-Publication Data
Paton, Alan.
  Cry, the beloved country.

  1. Large type books.   I. Title.
[PR9369.3.P37C7 1987]   [823]   86-32195

ISBN 1-55736-004-9
10 9 8 7 6 5 4 3 2 1

ABC-Clio, Inc.
2040 Alameda Padre Serra
Santa Barbara, California 93103-1788

Clio Press Ltd.
55 St. Thomas Street
Oxford, OX1 1JG, England

This book is smyth-sewn and printed on acid-free paper ∞.
Manufactured in the United States of America.

TO
Aubrey & Marigold Burns
of
Fairfax, California

Large print edition design by Terri Wright
Cover by Michael Mancarella, Communications,
Denver, Colorado
Composed in 16/18 pt. Plantin by QuadraType,
San Francisco, California
Printing and binding by Braun-Brumfield, Inc.,
Ann Arbor, Michigan

Foreword

One of the standard items of conventional wisdom in book publishing is that no worthwhile book ever comes in unsolicited—out of nowhere or, as publishers are likely to put it, over the transom. There is, of course, a mountain of sad but practical experience behind this principle, but as with all rules there are exceptions. One of the most dramatic of these was Alan Paton's novel *Cry, the Beloved Country*, which was mailed to Maxwell Perkins by an acquaintance of Paton's in California.

At that time, Alan Paton was the superintendent of a reformatory for native youths in South Africa and was visiting prisons in different parts of the world to study their methods and experiences. Perkins was very much impressed by this book with its strange title, *Cry, the Beloved Country*, but he did not live long after reading it, and few of us were aware of his enthusiasm although we knew that he had told Paton that one of the most important characters in the book was the land of South Africa itself.

When the book was published, it virtually exploded on the literary scene. Review after review heralded it as a literary classic, and sales began to climb at an extraordinary rate. Scribners noted that there was a "spontaneous chorus of praise" for the novel, and that was no exaggeration. The book became an instant best-seller and has sold thousands of copies every year in the forty years since its publication.

Cry, the Beloved Country is a classic work now and has found its place in school and college curriculums side by side with *Ethan Frome*; *The Great Gatsby*; and *The Old Man and the Sea*. It has also become a cultural force of great power and influence insofar as it has depicted the human tragedies of apartheid and brought readers all over the world to an understanding of the perversity and evil of that tragically misguided political system. A book of such unique beauty and power is, of course, an extremely rare event, still rarer when one considers the chain of circumstances that brought an unknown writer to world fame. How fortunate we are that the idea that such publishing events never happen proved to be magnificently wrong.

CHARLES SCRIBNER, JR.
SEPTEMBER 29, 1986

Preface

Cry, the Beloved Country, though it is a story about South Africa, was not written in that country at all. It was begun in Trondheim, Norway, in September 1946 and finished in San Francisco on Christmas Eve of that same year. It was first read by Aubrey and Marigold Burns of Fairfax, California, and they had it put into typescript and sent it to several American publishers, one of them being Charles Scribner's Sons. Scribners' senior editor, Maxwell Perkins, accepted it at once.

Perkins told me that one of the most important characters in the book was the land of South Africa itself. He was quite right. The title of the book confirms his judgment.

How did it get that title? After Aubrey and Marigold Burns had read it, they asked me what I would call it. We decided to have a little competition. We each took pen and paper and each of us wrote our proposed title. Each of us wrote "Cry, the Beloved Country."

Where did the title come from? It came from three or four passages in the book itself, each containing these words. I quote one of them:

Cry, the beloved country, for the unborn child that is the inheritor of our fear. Let him not love the earth too deeply. Let him not laugh too gladly when the water runs through his fingers, nor stand too silent when the setting sun makes red the veld with fire. Let him not be too moved when the birds of his land are singing, nor give too much of his heart to a mountain or a valley. For fear will rob him of all if he gives too much.

This passage was written by one who indeed had loved the earth deeply, by one who had been moved when the birds of his land were singing. The passage suggests that one can love a country too deeply, and that one can be too moved by the song of a bird. It is, in fact, a passage of poetic license. It offers no suggestion as to how one can prevent these things from happening.

What kind of a book is it? Many other people have given their own answers to this question, and I shall give my own, in words written in another book of mine, *For You Departed*, published, also by Charles Scribner's Sons, in 1969:

So many things have been written about this book that I would not add to them if I did not believe that I know best what kind of book it is. It is a song of love for one's far distant country, it is informed with longing for that land where they shall not hurt or destroy in all that holy mountain, for that unattainable and ineffable land where there shall be no more death, neither sorrow, nor crying, for the land that cannot be again, of hills and grass and bracken, the land where you were born. It is a story of the beauty and terror of human life, and it cannot be written again because it cannot be felt again. Just how good it is, I do not know and I do not care. All I know is that it changed our lives. It opened doors of the world to us, and we went through.

And that is true. The success of *Cry, the Beloved Country* changed our lives. To put it in materialistic terms, it has kept us alive ever since. It has enabled me to write books that cost more to write than their sales could ever repay. So I write this preface with pleasure and gratitude.

ALAN PATON
OCTOBER 13, 1986

(published in London by Jonathan Cape with the title *Kontakion for You Departed*).

Author's Note

IT is true that there is a lovely road that runs from Ixopo into the hills. It is true that it runs to Carisbrooke, and that from there, if there is no mist, you look down on one of the fairest scenes of Africa, the valley of the Umzimkulu. But there is no Ndotsheni there, and no farm called High Place. No person in this book is intended to be an actual person, except two, the late Professor Hoernle and Sir Ernest Oppenheimer; but nothing that is said about these two could be considered offensive. Professor Hoernle was Professor of Philosophy at the University of the Witwatersrand, and a great and courageous fighter for justice; in fact he was the prince of Kafferboetics. Sir Ernest Oppenheimer is the head of a very important mining group, a man of great influence, and able to do as much as any one man to arrest the process of deterioration described in this book. That does not mean of course that he can do everything.

Various persons are mentioned, not by name, but as the holders of this or that position. In no case is reference intended to any actual holder of any of these positions. Nor in any related event is reference intended to

any actual event; except that the accounts of the boycott of the buses, the erection of Shanty Town, the
finding of gold at Odendaalsrust, and the miners'
strike, are a compound of truth and fiction. In these respects therefore the story is not true, but considered as
a social record it is the plain and simple truth.

The book was begun in Trondheim and finished in
San Francisco. It was written in Norway, Sweden, England and the United States, for the most part in hotel-
rooms, during a tour of study of the penal and
correctional institutions of these countries. In San
Francisco I was invited to leave my hotel, and to stay at
the home of Mr. & Mrs. Aubrey Burns, of Fairfax,
California, whom I had met two days before. I accepted the invitation on condition that they read the
book. But I was not prepared for its reception. Mr.
Burns sat down and wrote letters to many publishers,
and when I was in Toronto (which fact they discovered) Mrs. Burns telephoned me to send the manuscript to California to be typed. They had received
some encouraging response to their letters, and were
now determined that I should have a typescript and
not a manuscript to present to the publisher, for I had
less than a week to spend in New York before sailing to
South Africa. I air-mailed the manuscript on a Tuesday, but owing to snowstorms no planes flew. The
package went by train, broke open and had to be re-
wrapped, and finally reached an intermediate Post Office on the Sunday, three days before I was due in New
York. My friends traced this package to this intermediate Post Office, and had the office opened and the
package delivered, by what means I do not know. In

the meantime they had friends standing by to do the typing, and they worked night and day, with the result that the first seventeen chapters arrived at the house of Scribner's on Wednesday, a few minutes before myself. On Thursday the next thirteen chapters arrived; and on Friday the last seven chapters, which I had kept with me, were delivered by the typing agency in the afternoon. There was only that afternoon left in which to decide, so it will readily be understood why I dedicate with such pleasure the American edition of this book to these two unselfish and determined friends.

For the benefit of readers I have appended a list of words at the end of the book, which includes by no means all the strange names and words that are used. But it contains those, a knowledge of the meaning and approximately correct pronunciation of which, should add to the reader's enjoyment.

I add too for this same purpose the information that the population of South Africa is about eleven millions, of these about two and a half million are white Afrikaans-speaking, and three-quarters of a million are white English-speaking. There are also about 250,000 Indians, mostly in Natal, and it is the question of their status that has brought South Africa into the lime-light of the world. The rest, except for one million colored people, by which we mean of mixed blood, are the black people of the African tribes. Johannesburg is referred to as the "great city"; this is judged by South African standards. Its population is about 700,000, but it is a fine modern city, to be compared with any American city except the very greatest. The Umzimkulu is called the "great river," but it is in fact a small river in a great valley. And lastly, a judge in South Africa presides over a Supreme Court; the presiding officer of a lower court is called a magistrate.

Second Author's Note

IT IS SOME eleven years since the first Author's Note was written. The population of South Africa today is estimated to be about 15,000,000, of whom 3,000,000 are white, 1¼ millions are colored people, nearly ½ million are Indians, and the rest are Africans. I did not mention the Indians in the first Author's Note largely because I did not want to confuse readers unnecessarily, but the existence of this minority is now much better known throughout the world because their position has become so desperate under apartheid legislation.

The City of Johannesburg has grown tremendously and today contains about 1¼ million people.

Sir Ernest Oppenheimer died in 1958, and his place has been taken by his very able son, Mr. Harry Oppenheimer.

OCTOBER 27, 1959
NATAL, SOUTH AFRICA

Introduction

Cry, the Beloved Country may be longer remembered than any other novel of 1948, but not because it fits into any pattern of the modern novel. It stands by itself; it creates rather than follows a tradition. It is at once unashamedly innocent and subtly sophisticated. It is a story; it is a prophecy; it is a psalm. It is passionately African, as no book before it had been; it is universal. It has in it elements of autobiography; yet it is selfless.

Let the reader discover the story for himself. Alan Paton tells something of its pre-publication history in his own author's introduction. The rest is still living history. In the United States, where it first saw print, the book had a small advance sale—3300 copies. It had no book-club fanfare in advance of publication; it never reached the top of the bestseller lists. But it made its way. People discovered it for themselves. They are still discovering it.

In South Africa it had a fantastic success. In that country of barely two million whites and nearly ten million mostly illiterate blacks, its present sale of thirty-odd thousand copies is the equivalent of a sale of more than two million copies in the United States. No other book in South African history ever stirred such an overwhelming response—and the aftermath of this response in the South African conscience is still to be written.

Alan Paton himself is a native son of South Africa, born in Pietermaritzburg in the east coast province of Natal in 1903. His father, a Scots Presbyterian and something of a poet, went out to South Africa as a civil servant just before the Boer War; his mother, though of English stock, was a third-generation South African. Alan Paton's entire schooling was South African. At college in Pietermaritzburg, he specialized in science and in off hours he wrote poetry. Until the European-American trip on which *Cry, the Beloved Country* came spilling out of his subconsciousness, he had been out of South Africa only once—at twenty-one, when he attended an Empire Students Conference in London, and followed that with a motorcycle trip through England and Scotland.

Just out of college, he wrote two novels—and almost immediately destroyed the manuscripts. He wrote some poetry. In his middle years he wrote serious essays—much such essays as Arthur Jarvis writes in the novel—for liberal South African magazines. It was life, rather than literature, which prepared Paton to write *Cry, the Beloved Country.*

After college Alan Paton taught in good schools— schools established for the sons of the rich, white minority in South Africa. One of them was in Ixopo (in Natal), in those grass-covered hills lovely beyond any singing of it, where the titihoya, the bird of the veld, sings in his book. It was there that he met Dorrie Francis, the girl he married, the mother of his two South-African schooled sons. She is also a born South African. Then he went to teach in Pietermaritzburg, and there, when he was about thirty, he suffered a severe attack of enteric fever. His illness gave him time to think. He did not, he decided, want to make a life career of teaching the sons of the rich.

South Africa was in one of its periods of fermenting change in 1934. One of the new reforms transferred all correctional institutions for young people under twenty-one from the Ministry of Justice to the Ministry of Education, and the Minister of Education at that time was one of South Africa's great men, Jan Hofmeyr. Had he lived, Hofmeyr might have succeeded to General Smuts' mantle (he became Deputy Prime Minister in 1939) and perhaps have changed the recent course of South African history. A Boer who dared to tell his fellow Afrikaners that they must give up "thinking with the blood," must "maintain the essential value of human personality as something independent of race or color," must supplant fear with faith, Hofmeyr was one of Alan Paton's heroes; as a boy Paton had gone camping with him. Later, the South African edition of *Cry, the Beloved Country* was dedicated to Jan Hofmeyr; it appeared three months before Hofmeyr's death. And the only poem which Alan Paton has published since his college days was a poem on the death of Hofmeyr.

So, recovering from his fever, Alan Paton wrote to Hofmeyr asking for a job. Somewhat to his horror, he got it—as principal of Diepkloof Reformatory, a huge prison school for delinquent black boys, set up in a sort of barbed-wire stockade on the edge of South Africa's greatest city, Johannesburg. It was a penitentiary, a place of locked cells and of despair. In ten years, under Hofmeyr's inspiring leadership, Alan Paton transformed the place. The barbed-wire vanished and gardens of geraniums took its place; the bars were torn down; the whole atmosphere changed. Some of these boys made good; and some, like Absalom in *Cry, the Beloved Country*, did not. You will find suggestions of Diepkloof in Alan Paton's novel, and there is a little of Paton himself in the anonymous young white man at the school, as well as in the character of Arthur Jarvis.

The "experiment" lasted more than ten years, a fertile interval, though Paton himself calls it a "period of aridity" in his literary life. He wrote serious articles but no poetry or fiction. Out of the experiment grew Paton's prison-study trip to Scandinavia, England and America which bore such unexpected fruit in *Cry, the Beloved Country*. Paton felt so profoundly that he needed a change that he sold his life insurance policies to finance the trip away from Africa.

In Sweden Paton read and was moved by John Steinbeck's *Grapes of Wrath*. Possibly the reading of that novel turned his mind back to his earlier interest in creative writing. He had at first no plan to write a novel of his own. But, not speaking Swedish, he passed many nights alone in his hotel; and, as in his bout with enteric fever, he had time to think and wonder. One dark afternoon a friendly stranger took him to see the rose window in the cathedral of Trondheim by torchlight. That somberly glowing experience set the mood.

Paton returned to his hotel, sat down at a desk and between five and seven, the whole first chapter of his novel poured out. He did not yet know what the rest of the story was to be. The theme was clear—he had been living it. The story seemed to form itself as he travelled. Parts were written in Stockholm, Trondheim, Oslo, London, and all the way across the United States; it was finished in San Francisco.

Then Paton went home to South Africa, and the book followed him, and changed his life. The next chapter in his life, it is safe to say, will involve more writing, and South Africa. It might involve him in an effort to recall South Africa to the vision of Jan Hofmeyr.

When Alan Paton flew to New York, in October, 1949, to see "Lost in the Stars," the musical play Maxwell Anderson wrote upon themes from *Cry, the Beloved Country,* he spoke to a Book and Author luncheon upon the South African background of his novel. It was an eloquent and revealing profession of faith. To attempt to condense or paraphrase it would be foolish, so, with a few modifications made with Mr. Paton's consent, I quote it at length.

"I was born," he said, "in that country known as the Union of South Africa. The heart of it is a great interior plateau that falls on all sides to the sea. But when one thinks of it and remembers it, one is aware not only of mountains and valleys, not only of the wide rolling stretches of the veld, but of solemn and deep undertones that have nothing to do with any mountain or any valley, but have to do with men. By some these are but vaguely heard and dimly understood; but for others they are never silent, they become ever more obtrusive and dominant, till the stretch of the sky and veld is nothing more than the backdrop against which is being played a great human drama in which I am deeply involved, my wife and my children, all men and their wives and children, of all colors and tongues, in which all Africa is involved, and all humanity and the world. For no country is now an island, of itself entire.

"There are eleven to twelve million people in the Union of South Africa. Of these only two and one-half million are white, three-fifths of these being Afrikaans-speaking, two-fifths English-speaking. There are one million of what we call 'colored' people, the descendants of the racial mixture which took place before white custom and law hardened against it, and forbade it, under the influence of the white man's intense determination to survive on a black continent. There are about one-quarter million Indians, whose forefathers were brought out by the English settlers to work on the sugar farms of Natal. And there are eight million black people, the people of the African tribes.

"The Afrikaans-speaking people are the descendants of the Dutch who first came to the Cape of Good Hope, which Francis Drake, the navigator, described as the fairest cape in all the circumference of the earth. These people did not come to Africa to settle, but the fertile valleys and great mountains of the Cape bound them with a spell.

"The primitive Bushmen and Hottentots could not stand up against this new thing that came out of Europe, and they melted away. But under the influence of the isolation of these vast spaces, and the hardships and loneliness of this patriarchal life, the people from Europe and the language from Holland changed. Something African entered into both people and language, and changed them. This the people themselves recognized and they called themselves the Afrikaners. Their new and simple and flexible and beautiful language they called Afrikaans; their love of this new country was profound and passionate.

"But still another change awaited them. As the Afrikaners moved yet further north they encountered the warlike tribes of the black African people. A long and bloody warfare ensued between them. The black men were numerous and savage and determined; the history of this encounter is one of terror and violence. The black people became truly a part of the white man's mind.

"Under the influence of this danger, the Afrikaner attitude toward black men hardened. The safety and survival of the small band of white people were seen as dependent on the rigid separation of white and black. It became the law that the relationship between white and black was to be that between master and servant; and it became the iron law that between white men and black women, between black men and white women, there was to be no other relationship but this. Land was set aside for the conquered tribes, but, as we see so clearly today, never enough.

"Yet another powerful influence entered into the making of the Afrikaner soul. In 1800 the English came to the Cape, during the Napoleonic Wars. They came initially, not as settlers, but as governors, officials, missionaries, teachers, traders, and fortune-seekers. Their attitude to the black man was different from that of the Afrikaner. The black man was not their enemy; he was their business. This fundamental incompatibility between two policies was to influence South African history for many years. It reached a climactic point in 1836, when many of the Afrikaner trekkers, abandoning all that they had so far gained, set out on the greatest trek of all, into the heart of the sub-continent, in order to escape the new and alien culture. There they set up the republics of the Transvaal and the Orange Free State. The position now was that the coastal regions of South Africa were English; the great interior plateau was Afrikaner; and on the fringes of both English and Afrikaner worlds lived the black men, doing the white man's work for him, steadily losing the dignity of their old ways of life.

"A new dramatic factor then entered the picture. In the interior of South Africa, in the very heart of the country to which the Afrikaner trekkers had gone to escape British rule, the richest gold of the world was discovered. The great modern, vigorous city of Johannesburg was born in a collection of tents and huts. Gold-seekers, many of them British, poured into the Transvaal. The Afrikaners watched with fear and anger and despair this new intrusion of the old enemy. The newcomers wanted the franchise; the Afrikaners dared not give it to them. And so a second great climax arrived, the Anglo-Boer War in 1899. The century-long incompatibility of a pastoral, agricultural, conservative community and a commercial, industrial, 'progressive' community exploded in war.

"In 1902 the Afrikaners capitulated. The British conscience, which was not to permit the British Crown ever again to engage in such a war, achieved the magnanimous settlement of 1906, by which self-government was restored to the defeated republics. A great wave of goodwill spread throughout the country, and four years later the Cape of Good Hope, the Orange Free State, the Transvaal and Natal came together to form the Union of South Africa, under the leadership of three defeated Afrikaner generals, General Botha, General Smuts and General Hertzog.

"But reconciliation was not so easily achieved. War, even when it is followed by magnanimity, leaves wounds not so easily healed. Twenty thousand Afrikaner women and children had died in the camps set up for their reception, mostly of typhoid fever. This was not easily forgotten. More important, the Afrikaner still feared that he and his world would be swallowed up and lost in the great British culture. He also saw a danger that the traditional English policy of laissez-faire toward the black people might lead to his engulfment.

"So the Afrikaner again set about to re-establish his separateness and distinctness. He established cultural societies for the protection of his customs, history and language. And he succeeded magnificently, largely because of his fiery independent spirit, and also because the ballot box had been put into his hands by his British enemy. Thus emerged what is today known as Afrikaner nationalism, the persistent and implacable urge that eventually, in 1948, defeated General Smuts, to the astonishment of every part of the civilized world.

"In the mean time the position of the black people had been changing beyond recognition. The cities of Johannesburg, Cape Town and Durban boomed; inevitably they attracted from the impoverished native reserves a never-ending stream of black people seeking work and city lights. They saw and envied the white man's world—his wealth, his comfort and his alien ways; meanwhile their own ancient tribal controls had been weakening. Their young men went astray; their old men were troubled and puzzled. Crime increased; the racial character deteriorated in the wretched hovels where the black men huddled in the slums of the white man's cities. This is the central theme of my novel, *Cry, the Beloved Country.*

"As the black men began to pour into the cities, the white people of South Africa became more and more reminded of the dangers of engulfment. This was one of the great reasons why white South Africans put the Nationalists in power. Afraid of the possible consequences of the laissez-faire policy of the Smuts government, they voted in favor of a party that advocated stern control and strict separation of the races as the 'only solution' of South Africa's ever more complicated and difficult problems.

"So South Africa returned, for the time at least, to the old policy of 'survival and separation.' It is the white settler on a black continent, aware of his precariousness of tenure, who speaks today through the mouthpiece of the Malan government.

"But one must not imagine that this white settler is motivated solely by fear. He too, is a human creature.

He has not lived upon the earth without being influenced by the great human ideas, notably by the ideas of Christianity. Therefore, he too is a divided creature, torn between his fears for his own safety and his desire for his own survival on the one hand, and on the other, by those ideas of justice and love which are at the very heart of his religion. We are witnessing today a struggle in the hearts of men, white men, between the claims of justice and of survival, of conscience and of fear.

"It is my own belief that the only power which can resist the power of fear is the power of love. It's a weak thing and a tender thing; men despise and deride it. But I look for the day when in South Africa we shall realize that the only lasting and worth-while solution of our grave and profound problems lies not in the use of power, but in that understanding and compassion without which human life is an intolerable bondage, condemning us all to an existence of violence, misery and fear."

Such is the beloved country of Alan Paton's faith, of his compassion, and his hope. In his novel, the music of its cry is a strangely blended folksong, with elements of Zulu and Xosa speech, and echoes of the rhythm of that Jewish-Christian Bible which speaks with such peculiar intimacy to black men in both America and South Africa. In *Cry, the Beloved Country* it sings with a new-old beauty to the whole world, with a faith that the dawn which brings light to the mountain-tops will also bring light to the valleys—a shining faith which is of the essence of the novel.

Cry, the Beloved Country stands alone. We have had many novels from statesmen and reformers, almost all bad; many novels from poets, almost all thin. In Alan Paton's *Cry, the Beloved Country* the statesman, the poet and the novelist meet in a unique harmony.

LEWIS GANNETT.

BOOK
I

1

THERE is a lovely road that runs from Ixopo into the hills. These hills are grass-covered and rolling, and they are lovely beyond any singing of it. The road climbs seven miles into them, to Carisbrooke; and from there, if there is no mist, you look down on one of the fairest valleys of Africa. About you there is grass and bracken and you may hear the forlorn crying of the titihoya, one of the birds of the veld. Below you is the valley of the Umzimkulu, on its journey from the Drakensberg to the sea; and beyond and behind the river, great hill after great hill; and beyond and behind them, the mountains of Ingeli and East Griqualand.

The grass is rich and matted, you cannot see the soil. It holds the rain and the mist, and they seep into the ground, feeding the streams in every kloof. It is well-tended, and not too many cattle feed upon it; not too many fires burn it, laying bare the soil. Stand unshod upon it, for the ground is holy, being even as it came from the Creator. Keep it, guard it, care for it, for it keeps men, guards men, cares for men. Destroy it and man is destroyed.

Where you stand the grass is rich and matted, you cannot see the soil. But the rich green hills break down. They fall to the valley below, and falling, change their nature. For they grow red and bare; they cannot hold the rain and mist, and the streams are dry in the kloofs. Too many cattle feed upon the grass, and too many fires have burned it. Stand shod upon it, for it is coarse and sharp, and the stones cut under the feet. It is not kept, or guarded, or cared for, it no longer keeps men, guards men, cares for men. The titihoya does not cry here any more.

The great red hills stand desolate, and the earth has torn away like flesh. The lightning flashes over them, the clouds pour down upon them, the dead streams come to life, full of the red blood of the earth. Down in the valleys women scratch the soil that is left, and the maize hardly reaches the height of a man. They are valleys of old men and old women, of mothers and children. The men are away, the young men and the girls are away. The soil cannot keep them any more.

2

THE small child ran importantly to the wood-and-iron church with the letter in her hand. Next to the church was a house and she knocked timidly on the door. The Reverend Stephen Kumalo looked up from the table where he was writing, and he called, Come in.

The small child opened the door, carefully like one who is afraid to open carelessly the door of so important a house, and stepped timidly in.

—I bring a letter, umfundisi.

—A letter, eh? Where did you get it, my child?

—From the store, umfundisi. The white man asked me to bring it to you.

—That was good of you. Go well, small one.

But she did not go at once. She rubbed one bare foot against the other, she rubbed one finger along the edge of the umfundisi's table.

—Perhaps you might be hungry, small one.

—Not very hungry, umfundisi.

—Perhaps a little hungry.

—Yes, a little hungry, umfundisi.

—Go to the mother then. Perhaps she has some food.

—I thank you, umfundisi.

She walked delicately, as though her feet might do harm in so great a house, a house with tables and chairs, and a clock, and a plant in a pot, and many books, more even than the books at the school.

Kumalo looked at his letter. It was dirty, especially about the stamp. It had been in many hands, no doubt. It came from Johannesburg; now there in Johannesburg were many of his own people. His brother John, who was a carpenter, had gone there, and had a business of his own in Sophiatown, Johannesburg. His sister Gertrude, twenty-five years younger than he, and the child of his parents' age, had gone there with her small son to look for the husband who had never come back from the mines. His only child Absalom had gone there, to look for his aunt Gertrude, and he had never returned. And indeed many other relatives were there, though none so near as these. It was hard to say from whom this letter came, for it was so long since any of these had written, that one did not well remember their writing.

He turned the letter over, but there was nothing to show from whom it came. He was reluctant to open it, for once such a thing is opened, it cannot be shut again.

He called to his wife, has the child gone?

—She is eating, Stephen.

—Let her eat then. She brought a letter. Do you know anything about a letter?

—How should I know, Stephen?

—No, that I do not know. Look at it.

She took the letter and she felt it. But there was nothing in the touch of it to tell from whom it might be. She read out the address slowly and carefully—

> Rev. Stephen Kumalo,
> St. Mark's Church.
> Ndotsheni.
> NATAL.

She mustered up her courage, and said, it is not from our son.

—No, he said. And he sighed. It is not from our son.

—Perhaps it concerns him, she said.

—Yes, he said. That may be so.

—It is not from Gertrude, she said.

—Perhaps it is my brother John.

—It is not from John, she said.

They were silent, and she said, How we desire such a letter, and when it comes, we fear to open it.

—Who is afraid, he said. Open it.

She opened it, slowly and carefully, for she did not open so many letters. She spread it out open, and read it slowly and carefully, so that he did not hear all that she said. Read it aloud, he said.

She read it aloud, reading as a Zulu who reads English.

The Mission House,
Sophiatown,
Johannesburg.
25/9/46.

MY DEAR BROTHER IN CHRIST,

I have had the experience of meeting a young woman here in Johannesburg. Her name is Gertrude Kumalo, and I understand she is the sister of the Rev. Stephen Kumalo, St. Mark's Church, Ndotsheni. This young woman is very sick, and therefore I ask you to come quickly to Johannesburg. Come to the Rev. Theophilus Msimangu, the Mission House, Sophiatown, and there I shall give you some advices. I shall also find accommodation for you, where the expenditure will not be very serious.

I am, dear brother in Christ,
Yours faithfully,
THEOPHILUS MSIMANGU.

They were both silent till at long last she spoke.
—Well, my husband?
—Yes, what is it?
—This letter, Stephen. You have heard it now.
—Yes, I have heard it. It is not an easy letter.
—It is not an easy letter. What will you do?
—Has the child eaten?
She went to the kitchen and came back with the child.
—Have you eaten, my child?
—Yes, umfundisi.

—Then go well, my child. And thank you for bringing the letter. And will you take my thanks to the white man at the store?

—Yes, umfundisi.

—Then go well, my child.

—Stay well, umfundisi. Stay well, mother.

—Go well, my child.

So the child went delicately to the door, and shut it behind her gently, letting the handle turn slowly like one who fears to let it turn fast.

When the child was gone, she said to him, what will you do, Stephen?

—About what, my wife?

She said patiently to him, about this letter, Stephen?

He sighed. Bring me the St. Chad's money, he said.

She went out, and came back with a tin, of the kind in which they sell coffee or cocoa, and this she gave to him. He held it in his hand, studying it, as though there might be some answer in it, till at last she said, it must be done, Stephen.

—How can I use it? he said. This money was to send Absalom to St. Chad's.

—Absalom will never go now to St. Chad's.

—How can you say that? he said sharply. How can you say such a thing?

—He is in Johannesburg, she said wearily. When people go to Johannesburg, they do not come back.

—You have said it, he said. It is said now. This money which was saved for that purpose will never be used for it. You have opened a door, and because you have opened it, we must go through. And *Tixo* alone knows where we shall go.

—It was not I who opened it, she said, hurt by his accusation. It has a long time been open, but you would not see.

—We had a son, he said harshly. Zulus have many children, but we had only one son. He went to Johannesburg, and as you said—when people go to Johannesburg, they do not come back. They do not even write any more. They do not go to St. Chad's to learn that knowledge without which no black man can live. They go to Johannesburg, and there they are lost, and no one hears of them at all. And this money. . . .

But she had no words for it, so he said, it is here in my hand.

And again she did not speak, so he said again, it is here in my hand.

—You are hurting yourself, she said.

—Hurting myself? hurting myself? I do not hurt myself, it is they who are hurting me. My own son, my own sister, my own brother. They go away and they do not write any more. Perhaps it does not seem to them that we suffer. Perhaps they do not care for it.

His voice rose into loud and angry words. Go up and ask the white man, he said. Perhaps there are letters. Perhaps they have fallen under the counter, or been hidden amongst the food. Look there in the trees, perhaps they have been blown there by the wind.

She cried out at him, You are hurting me also.

He came to himself and said to her humbly, that I may not do.

He held out the tin to her. Open it, he said.

With trembling hands she took the tin and opened it. She emptied it out over the table, some old and dirty notes, and a flood of silver and copper.

—Count it, he said.

She counted it laboriously, turning over the notes and the coins to make sure what they were.

—Twelve pounds, five shillings and seven pence.

—I shall take, he said, I shall take eight pounds, and the shillings and pence.

—Take it all, Stephen. There may be doctors, hospitals, other troubles. Take it all. And take the Post Office Book—there is ten pounds in it—you must take that also.

—I have been saving that for your stove, he said.

—That cannot be helped, she said. And that other money, though we saved it for St. Chad's, I had meant it for your new black clothes, and a new black hat, and new white collars.

—That cannot be helped either. Let me see, I shall go . . .

—Tomorrow, she said. From Carisbrooke.

—I shall write to the Bishop now, and tell him I do not know how long I shall be gone.

He rose heavily to his feet, and went and stood before her. I am sorry I hurt you, he said. I shall go and pray in the church.

He went out of the door, and she watched him through the little window, walking slowly to the door of the church. Then she sat down at his table, and put her head on it, and was silent, with the patient suffering of black women, with the suffering of oxen, with the suffering of any that are mute.

*   *   *   *   *

All roads lead to Johannesburg. Through the long nights the trains pass to Johannesburg. The lights of the swaying coach fall on the cutting-sides, on the grass and the stones of a country that sleeps. Happy the eyes that can close.

3

THE small toy train climbs up on its narrow gauge from the Umzimkulu valley into the hills. It climbs up to Carisbrooke, and when it stops there, you may get out for a moment and look down on the great valley from which you have come. It is not likely the train will leave you, for there are few people here, and every one will know who you are. And even if it did leave you, it would not much matter; for unless you are a cripple, or very old, you could run after it and catch it for yourself.

If there is mist here, you will see nothing of the great valley. The mist will swirl about and below you, and the train and the people make a small world of their own. Some people do not like it, and find it cold and gloomy. But others like it, and find in it mystery and fascination, and prelude to adventure, and an intimation of the unknown. The train passes through a world of fancy, and you can look through the misty panes at green shadowy banks of grass and bracken. Here in their season grow the blue agapanthus, the wild watsonia, and the red-hot poker, and now and then it happens that one may glimpse an arum in a dell. And always behind them the dim wall of the wattles, like ghosts in the mist.

It is interesting to wait for the train at Carisbrooke, while it climbs up out of the great valley. Those who know can tell you with each whistle where it is, at what road, what farm, what river. But though Stephen Kumalo has been there a full hour before he need, he does not listen to these things. This is a long way to go, and a lot of money to pay. And who knows how sick his sister may be, and what money that may cost? And if he has to bring her back, what will that cost too? And Johannesburg is a great city, with so many streets they say that a man can spend his days going up one and down another, and never the same one twice. One must catch buses too, but not as here, where the only bus that comes is the right bus. For there there is a multitude of buses, and only one bus in ten, one bus in twenty maybe, is the right bus. If you take the wrong bus, you may travel to quite some other place. And they say it is danger to cross the street, yet one must needs cross it. For there the wife of Mpanza of Ndotsheni, who had gone there when Mpanza was dying, saw her son Michael killed in the street. Twelve years and moved by excitement, he stepped out into danger, but she was hesitant and stayed at the curb. And under her eyes the great lorry crushed the life out of her son.

And the great fear too—the greatest fear since it was so seldom spoken. Where was their son? Why did he not write any more?

the eye can see. There are new names here, hard names for a Zulu who has been schooled in English. For they are in the language that was called Afrikaans, a language that he had never yet heard spoken.

—The mines, they cry, the mines. For many of them are going to work in the mines.

Are these the mines, those white flat hills in the distance? He can ask safely, for there is no one here who heard him yesterday.

—That is the rock out of the mines, umfundisi. The gold has been taken out of it.

—How does the rock come out?

—We go down and dig it out, umfundisi. And when it is hard to dig, we go away, and the white men blow it out with the fire-sticks. Then we come back and clear it away; we load it on to the trucks, and it goes up in a cage, up a long chimney so long that I cannot say it for you.

—How does it go up?

—It is wound up by a great wheel. Wait, and I shall show you one.

He is silent, and his heart beats a little faster, with excitement.

—There is the wheel, umfundisi. There is the wheel.

A great iron structure rearing into the air, and a great wheel above it, going so fast that the spokes play tricks with the sight. Great buildings, and steam blowing out of pipes, and men hurrying about. A great white hill, and an endless procession of trucks climbing upon it, high up in the air. On the ground, motor-cars, lorries, buses, one great confusion.

—Is this Johannesburg? he asks.

But they laugh confidently. Old hands some of them are.

—That is nothing, they say. In Johannesburg there are buildings, so high—but they cannot describe them.

—My brother, says one, you know the hill that stands so, straight up, behind my father's kraal. So high as that.

The other man nods, but Kumalo does not know that hill.

And now the buildings are endless, the buildings, and the white hills, and the great wheels, and streets without number, and cars and lorries and buses.

—This surely is Johannesburg, he says.

But they laugh again. They are growing a little tired. This is nothing, they say.

Railway-lines, railway-lines, it is a wonder. To the left, to the right, so many that he cannot count. A train rushes past them, with a sudden roaring of sound that makes him jump in his seat. And on the other side of them, another races beside them, but drops slowly behind. Stations, stations, more than he has ever imagined. People are waiting there in hundreds, but the train rushes past, leaving them disappointed.

The buildings get higher, the streets more uncountable. How does one find one's way in such a confusion? It is dusk, and the lights are coming on in the streets.

One of the men points for him.

—Johannesburg, umfundisi.

He sees great high buildings, there are red and green lights on them, almost as tall as the buildings. They go on and off. Water comes out of a bottle, till the glass is full. Then the lights go out. And when they come on again, lo the bottle is full and upright, and the glass empty. And there goes the bottle over again. Black and white, it says, black and white, though it is red and green. It is too much to understand.

He is silent, his head aches, he is afraid. There is this railway station to come, this great place with all its tunnels under the ground. The train stops, under a great roof, and there are thousands of people. Steps go down into the earth, and here is the tunnel under the ground. Black people, white people, some going, some coming, so many that the tunnel is full. He goes carefully that he may not bump anybody, holding tightly on to his bag. He comes out into a great hall, and the stream goes up the steps, and here he is out in the street. The noise is immense. Cars and buses one behind the other, more than he has ever imagined. The stream goes over the street, but remembering Mpanza's son, he is afraid to follow. Lights change from green to red, and back again to green. He has heard that. When it is green, you may go. But when he starts across, a great bus swings across the path. There is some law of it that he does not understand, and he retreats again. He finds himself a place against the wall, he will look as though he is waiting for some purpose.

His heart beats like that of a child, there is nothing to do or think to stop it. *Tixo*, watch over me, he says to himself. *Tixo*, watch over me.

*   *   *   *   *

A young man came to him and spoke to him in a language that he did not understand.

—I do not understand, he said.

—You are a Xosa, then, umfundisi?

—A Zulu, he said.

—Where do you want to go, umfundisi?

—To Sophiatown, young man.

—Come with me then and I shall show you.

He was grateful for this kindness, but half of him was afraid. He was glad the young man did not offer to carry his bag, but he spoke courteously, though in a strange Zulu.

The lights turned green, and his guide started across the street. Another car swung across the path, but the guide did not falter, and the car came to a stop. It made one feel confidence.

He could not follow the turnings that they made under the high buildings, but at last, his arm tired beyond endurance by the bag, they came to a place of many buses.

—You must stand in the line, umfundisi. Have you your money for the ticket?

Quickly, eagerly, as though he must show this young man that he appreciated his kindness, he put down his bag and took out his purse. He was nervous to ask how much it was, and took a pound from the purse.

—Shall I get your ticket for you, umfundisi? Then you need not lose your place in the line, while I go to the ticket office.

—Thank you, he said.

The young man took the pound and walked a short distance to the corner. As he turned it, Kumalo was afraid. The line moved forward and he with it, clutching his bag. And again forward, and again forward, and soon he must enter a bus, but still he had no ticket. As though he had suddenly thought of something he left the line, and walked to the corner, but there was no sign of the young man. He sought courage to speak to someone, and went to an elderly man, decently and cleanly dressed.

—Where is the ticket office, my friend?

—What ticket office, umfundisi?

—For the ticket for the bus.

—You get your ticket on the bus. There is no ticket office.

The man looked a decent man, and the parson spoke to him humbly. I gave a pound to a young man, he said, and he told me he would get my ticket at the ticket office.

—You have been cheated, umfundisi. Can you see the young man? No, you will not see him again. Look, come with me. Where are you going, Sophiatown?

—Yes, Sophiatown. To the Mission House.

—Oh yes. I too am an Anglican. I was waiting for

someone, but I shall wait no longer. I shall come with you myself. Do you know the Reverend Msimangu?

—Indeed, I have a letter from him.

They again took the last place in the line, and in due time they took their places in the bus. And it in its turn swung out into the confusion of the streets. The driver smoked carelessly, and it was impossible not to admire such courage. Street after street, light after light, as though they would never end, at times at such speed that the bus swayed from side to side, and the engine roared in the ears.

They alighted at a small street, and there were still thousands of people about. They walked a great distance, through streets crowded with people. His new friend helped to carry his bag, but he felt confidence in him. At last they stopped before a lighted house, and knocked.

The door opened and a young tall man in clerical dress opened to them.

—Mr. Msimangu, I bring a friend to you, the Reverend Kumalo from Ndotsheni.

—Come in, come in, my friends. Mr. Kumalo, I am glad to greet you. Is this your first visit to Johannesburg?

Kumalo could not boast any more. He had been safely guided and warmly welcomed. He spoke humbly. I am much confused, he said. I owe much to our friend.

—You fell into good hands. This is Mr. Mafolo, one of our big business men, and a good son of the Church.

—But not before he had been robbed, said the business man.

So the story had to be told, and there was much sympathy and much advice.

—And you are no doubt hungry, Mr. Kumalo. Mr. Mafolo, will you stay for some food?

But Mr. Mafolo would not wait. The door shut after him, and Kumalo settled himself in a big chair, and accepted a cigarette though it was not his custom to smoke. The room was light, and the great bewildering town shut out. He puffed like a child at his smoke, and was thankful. The long journey to Johannesburg was over, and he had taken a liking to this young confident man. In good time no doubt they would come to discuss the reason for this pilgrimage safely at an end. For the moment it was enough to feel welcome and secure.

5

—I HAVE a place for you to sleep, my friend, in the house of an old woman, a Mrs. Lithebe, who is a good member of our church. She is an Msutu, but she speaks Zulu well. She will think it an honour to have a priest in the house. It is cheap, only three shillings a week, and you can have your meals there with the people of the Mission. Now there is the bell. Would you like to wash your hands?

They washed their hands in a modern place, with a white basin, and water cold and hot, and towels worn but very white, and a modern lavatory too. When you were finished, you pressed a little rod, and the water rushed in as though something was broken. It would have frightened you if you had not heard of such things before.

They went into a room where a table was laid, and there he met many priests, both white and black, and they sat down after grace and ate together. He was a bit nervous of the many plates and knives and forks, but watched what others did, and used the things likewise.

He sat next to a young rosy-cheeked priest from

England, who asked him where he came from, and what it was like there. And another black priest cried out—I am also from Ixopo. My father and mother are still alive there, in the valley of the Lufafa. How is it there?

And he told them all about these places, of the great hills and valleys of that far country. And the love of them must have been in his voice, for they were all silent and listened to him. He told them too of the sickness of the land, and how the grass had disappeared, and of the dongas that ran from hill to valley, and valley to hill; how it was a land of old men and women, and mothers and children; how the maize grew barely to the height of a man; how the tribe was broken, and the house broken, and the man broken; how when they went away, many never came back, many never wrote any more. How this was true not only in Ndotsheni, but also in the Lufafa, and the Imhlavini, and the Umkomaas, and the Umzimkulu. But of Gertrude and Absalom he said nothing.

So they all talked of the sickness of the land, of the broken tribe and the broken house, of young men and young girls that went away and forgot their customs, and lived loose and idle lives. They talked of young criminal children, and older and more dangerous criminals, of how white Johannesburg was afraid of black crime. One of them went and got him a newspaper, the *Johannesburg Mail*, and showed him in bold black letters, OLD COUPLE ROBBED AND BEATEN IN LONELY HOUSE. FOUR NATIVES ARRESTED.

—That happens nearly every day, he said. And it is not only the Europeans who are afraid. We are also afraid, right here in Sophiatown. It was not long ago that a gang of these youths attacked one of our own African-girls; they took her bag, and her money, and would have raped her too but that people came running out of the houses.

—You will learn much here in Johannesburg, said the rosy-cheeked priest. It is not only in your place that there is destruction. But we must talk again. I want to hear again about your country, but I must go now.

So they broke up, and Msimangu said he would take his visitor to his own private room.

—We have much to talk about, he said.

They went to the room, and when Msimangu had shut the door and they had sat themselves down, Kumalo said to him, you will pardon me if I am hasty, but I am anxious to hear about my sister.

—Yes, yes, said Msimangu. I am sure you are anxious. You must think I am thoughtless. But you will pardon me if I ask you first, why did she come to Johannesburg?

Kumalo, though disturbed by this question, answered obediently. She came to look for her husband who was recruited for the mines. But when his time was up, he did not return, nor did he write at all. She did not know if he were dead perhaps. So she took her small child and went to look for him.

Then because Msimangu did not speak, he asked anxiously, is she very sick?

Msimangu said gravely, yes, she is very sick. But

it is not that kind of sickness. It is another, a worse kind of sickness. I sent for you firstly because she is a woman that is alone, and secondly because her brother is a priest. I do not know if she ever found her husband, but she has no husband now.

He looked at Kumalo. It would be truer to say, he said, that she has many husbands.

Kumalo said, *Tixo! Tixo!*

—She lives in Claremont, not far from here. It is one of the worst places in Johannesburg. After the police have been there, you can see the liquor running in the streets. You can smell it, you can smell nothing else, wherever you go in that place.

He leant over to Kumalo. I used to drink liquor, he said, but it was good liquor, such as our fathers made. But now I have vowed to touch no liquor any more. This is bad liquor here, made strong with all manner of things that our people have never used. And that is her work, she makes and sells it. I shall hide nothing from you, though it is painful for me. These women sleep with any man for their price. A man has been killed at her place. They gamble and drink and stab. She has been in prison, more than once.

He leant back in his chair and moved a book forward and backward on the table. This is terrible news for you, he said. Kumalo nodded dumbly, and Msimangu brought out his cigarettes. Will you smoke he said?

Kumalo shook his head. I do not really smoke, he said.

—Sometimes it quietens one to smoke. But there

should be another kind of quiet in a man, and then let him smoke to enjoy it. But in Johannesburg it is hard sometimes to find that kind of quiet.

—In Johannesburg? Everywhere it is so. The peace of God escapes us.

And they were both silent, as though a word had been spoken that made it hard to speak another. At last Kumalo said, where is the child?

—The child is there. But it is no place for a child. And that too is why I sent for you. Perhaps if you cannot save the mother, you can save the child.

—Where is this place?

—It is not far from here. I shall take you tomorrow.

—I have another great sorrow.

—You may tell me.

—I should be glad to tell you.

But then he was silent, and tried to speak and could not, so Msimangu said to him, Take your time, my brother.

—It is not easy. It is our greatest sorrow.

—A son, maybe. Or a daughter?

—It is a son.

—I am listening.

—Absalom was his name. He too went away, to look for my sister, but he never returned, nor after a while did he write any more. Our letters, his mother's and mine, all came back to us. And now after what you tell me, I am still more afraid.

—We shall try to find him, my brother. Perhaps your sister will know. You are tired, and I should take you to the room I have got for you.

—Yes, that would be better.

They rose, and Kumalo said, it is my habit to pray in the church. Maybe you will show me.

—It is on the way.

Kumalo said humbly, maybe you will pray for me.

—I shall do it gladly. My brother, I have of course my work to do, but so long as you are here, my hands are yours.

—You are kind.

Something in the humble voice must have touched Msimangu, for he said, I am not kind. I am a selfish and sinful man, but God put his hands on me, that is all.

He picked up Kumalo's bag, but before they reached the door Kumalo stopped him.

—I have one more thing to tell you.

—Yes.

—I have a brother also, here in Johannesburg. He too does not write any more. John Kumalo, a carpenter.

—Msimangu smiled. I know him, he said. He is too busy to write. He is one of our great politicians.

—A politician? My brother?

—Yes, he is a great man in politics.

Msimangu paused. I hope I shall not hurt you further. Your brother has no use for the Church any more. He says that what God has not done for South Africa, man must do. That is what he says.

—This is a bitter journey.

—I can believe it.

—Sometimes I fear—what will the Bishop say when he hears? One of his priests?

—What can a Bishop say? Something is happening that no Bishop can stop. Who can stop these things from happening? They must go on.

—How can you say so? How can you say they must go on?

—They must go on, said Msimangu gravely. You cannot stop the world from going on. My friend, I am a Christian. It is not in my heart to hate a white man. It was a white man who brought my father out of darkness. But you will pardon me if I talk frankly to you. The tragedy is not that things are broken. The tragedy is that they are not mended again. The white man has broken the tribe. And it is my belief—and again I ask your pardon—that it cannot be mended again. But the house that is broken, and the man that falls apart when the house is broken, these are the tragic things. That is why children break the law, and old white people are robbed and beaten.

He passed his hand across his brow.

—It suited the white man to break the tribe, he continued gravely. But it has not suited him to build something in the place of what is broken. I have pondered this for many hours, and I must speak it, for it is the truth for me. They are not all so. There are some white men who give their lives to build up what is broken.

—But they are not enough, he said. They are afraid, that is the truth. It is fear that rules this land.

He laughed apologetically. These things are too many to talk about now. They are things to talk over quietly and patiently. You must get Father Vincent to talk about them. He is a white man and can say what must be said. He is the one with the boy's cheeks, the one who wants to hear more about your country.

—I remember him.

—They give us too little, said Msimangu sombrely. They give us almost nothing. Come, let us go to the church.

*   *   *   *   *

—Mrs. Lithebe, I bring my friend to you. The Reverend Stephen Kumalo.

—Umfundisi, you are welcome. The room is small, but clean.

—I am sure of it.

—Goodnight, my brother. Shall I see you in the church tomorrow at seven?

—Assuredly.

—And after that I shall take you to eat. Stay well, my friend. Stay well, Mrs. Lithebe.

—Go well, my friend.

—Go well, umfundisi.

She took him to the small clean room and lit a candle for him.

—If there is anything, you will ask, umfundisi.

—I thank you.

—Sleep well, umfundisi.

—Sleep well, mother.

He stood a moment in the room. Forty-eight hours ago he and his wife had been packing his bag in far away Ndotsheni. Twenty-four hours ago the train, with the cage on its head, had been thundering through an unseen country. And now outside, the stir and movement of people, but behind them, through them, one could hear the roar of a great city. Johannesburg. Johannesburg.

Who could believe it?

6

IT is not far to Claremont. They lie together; Sophiatown, where any may own property, Western Native Township which belongs to the Municipality of Johannesburg, and Claremont, the garbage-heap of the proud city. These three are bounded on the West by the European district of Newlands, and on the East by the European district of Westdene.

—That is a pity, says Msimangu. I am not a man for segregation, but it is a pity that we are not apart. They run trams from the centre of the city, and part is for Europeans and part for us. But we are often thrown off the trams by young hooligans. And our hooligans are ready for trouble too.

—But the authorities, do they allow that?

—They do not. But they cannot watch every tram. And if a trouble develops, who can find how it began, and who will tell the truth? It is a pity we are not apart. Look, do you see that big building?

—I see it.

—That is the building of the *Bantu Press*, our newspaper. Of course there are Europeans in it too, and it is moderate and does not say all that could be said. Your brother John thinks little of the Bantu Press. He and his friends call it the Bantu Repress.

So they walked till they came to Claremont and Kumalo was shocked by its shabbiness and dirtiness, and the closeness of the houses, and the filth in the streets.

—Do you see that woman, my friend?

—I see her.

—She is one of the queens, the liquor sellers. They say she is one of the richest of our people in Johannesburg.

—And these children? Why are they not at school?

—Some because they do not care, and some because their parents do not care, but many because the schools are full.

They walked down Lily Street, and turned off into Hyacinth Street, for the names there are very beautiful.

—It is here, brother. Number eleven. Do you go in alone?

—It would be better.

—When you are ready, you will find me next door at Number thirteen. There is a woman of our church there, and a good woman who tries with her husband to bring up good children. But it is hard. Their eldest daughter whom I prepared for confirmation has run away, and lives in Pimville, with a young loafer of the streets. Knock there, my friend. You know where to find me.

There is laughter in the house, the kind of laughter of which one is afraid. Perhaps because one is afraid already, perhaps because it is in truth bad laughter. A woman's voice, and men's voices. But he knocks, and she opens.

—It is I, my sister.

Have no doubt it is fear in her eyes. She draws back a step, and makes no move towards him. She turns and says something that he cannot hear. Chairs are moved, and other things are taken. She turns to him.

—I am making ready, my brother.

They stand and look at each other, he anxious, she afraid. She turns and looks back into the room. A door closes, and she says, Come in, my brother.

Only then does she reach her hand to him. It is cold and wet, there is no life in it.

They sit down, she is silent upon her chair.

—I have come, he said.

—It is good.

—You did not write.

—No, I did not write.

—Where is your husband?

—I have not found him, my brother.

—But you did not write.

—That is true, indeed.

—Did you not know we were anxious?

—I had no money to write.

—Not two pennies for a stamp?

She does not answer him. She does not look at him.

—But I hear you are rich.

—I am not rich.

—I hear you have been in prison.

—That is true indeed.

—Was it for liquor?

A spark of life comes into her. She must do something, she cannot keep so silent. She tells him she was not guilty. There was some other woman.

—You stayed with this woman?

—Yes.

—Why did you stay with such a woman?

—I had no other place.

—And you helped her with her trade?

—I had to have money for the child.

—Where is the child?

She looks round vaguely. She gets up and goes to the yard. She calls, but the voice that was once so sweet has a new quality in it, the quality of the laughter that he heard in the house. She is revealing herself to him.

—I have sent for the child, she says.

—Where is it?

—It shall be fetched, she says.

There is discomfort in her eyes, and she stands fingering the wall. The anger wells up in him.

—Where shall I sleep, he asks?

The fear in her eyes is unmistakable. Now she will reveal herself, but his anger masters him, and he does not wait for it.

—You have shamed us, he says in a low voice, not wishing to make it known to the world. A liquor seller, a prostitute, with a child and you do not know where it is? Your brother a priest. How could you do this to us?

She looks at him sullenly, like an animal that is tormented.

—I have come to take you back. She falls on to the floor and cries; her cries become louder and louder, she has no shame.

—They will hear us, he says urgently.

She cries to control her sobs.

—Do you wish to come back?

She nods her head. I do not like Johannesburg, she says. I am sick here. The child is sick also.

—Do you wish with your heart to come back?

She nods her head again. She sobs too. I do not like Johannesburg, she says. She looks at him with eyes of distress, and his heart quickens with hope. I am a bad woman, my brother. I am no woman to go back.

His eyes fill with tears, his deep gentleness returns to him. He goes to her and lifts her from the floor to the chair. Inarticulately he strokes her face, his heart filled with pity.

—God forgives us, he says. Who am I not to forgive? Let us pray.

They knelt down, and he prayed, quietly so that the neighbors might not hear, and she punctuated his petitions with Amens. And when he had finished, she burst into a torrent of prayer, of self-denunciation, and urgent petition. And thus reconciled, they sat hand in hand.

—And now I ask you for help, he said.

—What is it, my brother?

—Our child, have you not heard of him?

—I did hear of him, brother. He was working at some big place in Johannesburg, and he lived in Sophiatown, but where I am not sure. But I know who will know. The son of our brother John and your son were often together. He will know.

—I shall go there. And now, my sister, I must see if Mrs. Lithebe has a room for you. Have you many things?

—Not many. This table and those chairs, and a bed. And some few dishes and pots. That is all.

—I shall find someone to fetch them. You will be ready?

—My brother, here is the child.

Into the room, shepherded by an older girl, came his little nephew. His clothes were dirty and his nose running, and he put his finger in his mouth, and gazed at his uncle out of wide saucer-like eyes.

Kumalo lifted him up, and wiped his nose clean, and kissed and fondled him.

—It will be better for the child, he said. He will go to a place where the wind blows, and where there is a school for him.

—It will be better, she agreed.

—I must go, he said. There is much to do.

He went out into the street, and curious neighbours stared at him. It was an umfundisi that was here. He found his friend, and poured out his news, and asked him where they could find a man to fetch his sister, her child and possessions.

—We shall go now, said Msimangu. I am glad for your sake, my friend.

—There is a great load off my mind, my friend. Please God the other will be as successful.

*   *   *   *   *

He fetched her with a lorry that afternoon, amidst a crowd of interested neighbours, who discussed the affair loudly and frankly, some with approval, and some with the strange laughter of the towns. He was glad when the lorry was loaded, and they left.

Mrs. Lithebe showed them their room, and gave the mother and child their food while Kumalo went down to the mission. And that night they held prayers in the diningroom, and Mrs. Lithebe and Gertrude punctuated his petitions with Amens. Kumalo himself was light-hearted and gay like a boy, more so than he had been for years. One day in Johannesburg, and already the tribe was being rebuilt, the house and the soul restored.

7

GERTRUDE'S dress, for all that she might once have been rich, was dirty, and the black greasy knitted cap that she wore on her head made him ashamed. Although his money was little, he bought her a red dress and a white thing that they called a turban for her head. Also a shirt, a pair of short trousers, and a jersey for the boy; and a couple of stout handkerchiefs for his mother to use on his nose. In his pocket was his Post Office Book, and there was ten pounds there that he and his wife were saving to buy the stove, for that, like any woman, she had long been wanting to have. To save ten pounds from a stipend of eight pounds a month takes much patience and time, especially for a parson, who must dress in good black clothes. His clerical collars were brown and frayed, but they must wait now a while. It was a pity about the ten pounds, that it would sooner or later have to be broken into, but the trains did not carry for nothing, and they would no doubt get a pound or two for her things. Strange that she had saved nothing from her sad employment, which brought in much money, it was said.

Gertrude was helping Mrs. Lithebe in the house, and he could hear her singing a little. The small boy was playing in the yard, with small pieces of brick and wood that a builder had left. The sun was shining, and even in this great city there were birds, small sparrows that chirped and flew about in the yard. But there was Msimangu coming up the street. He put aside the letter that he was writing to his wife, of the journey in the train, and the great city Johannesburg, and the young man who had stolen his pound, of his quick finding of Gertrude, and his pleasure in the small boy. And above all, that this day would begin the search for their son.

—Are you ready, my friend?

—Yes, I am ready. I am writing to my wife.

—Though I do not know her, send her my greetings.

They walked up the street, and down another, and up yet another. It was true what they said, that you could go up one street and down another till the end of your days, and never walk the same one twice.

—Here is your brother's shop. You see his name.

—Yes, I see it.

—Shall I come with you?

—Yes, I think it would be right.

His brother John was sitting there on a chair, talking to two other men. He had grown fat, and sat with his hands on his knees like a chief. His brother he did not recognize, for the light from the street was on the backs of his visitors.

—Good morning, my brother.

—Good morning, sir.

—Good morning, my own brother, son of our mother.

John Kumalo looked closely at him, and stood up with a great hearty smile.

—My own brother. Well, well, who can believe? What are you doing in Johannesburg?

Kumalo looked at the visitors. I come on business, he said.

—I am sure my friends will excuse us. My own brother, the son of our mother, has come.

The two men rose, and they all said stay well and go well.

—Do you know the Reverend Msimangu, my brother?

—Well, well, he is known to everybody. Everybody knows the Reverend Msimangu. Sit down, gentlemen. I think we must have some tea.

He went to the door and called into the place behind.

—Is your wife Esther well, my brother?

John Kumalo smiled his jolly and knowing smile. My wife Esther has left me these ten years, my brother.

—And have you married again?

—Well, well, not what the Church calls married, you know. But she is a good woman.

—You wrote nothing of this, brother.

—No, how could I write? You people in Ndotsheni do not understand the way life is in Johannesburg. I thought it better not to write.

—That is why you stopped writing.

—Well, well, that could be why I stopped. Trouble, brother, unnecessary trouble.

—But I do not understand. How is life different in Johannesburg?

—Well, that is difficult. Do you mind if I speak in English? I can explain these things better in English.

—Speak in English, then, brother.

—You see I have had an experience here in Johannesburg. It is not like Ndotsheni. One must live here to understand it.

He looked at his brother. Something new is happening here, he said.

He did not sit down, but began to speak in a strange voice. He walked about, and looked through the window into the street, and up at the ceiling, and into the corners of the room as though something were there, and must be brought out.

—Down in Ndotsheni I am nobody, even as you are nobody, my brother. I am subject to the chief, who is an ignorant man. I must salute him and bow to him, but he is an uneducated man. Here in Johannesburg I am a man of some importance, of some influence. I have my own business, and when it is good, I can make ten, twelve, pounds a week.

He began to sway to and fro, he was not speaking to them, he was speaking to people who were not there.

—I do not say we are free here. I do not say we are free as men should be. But at least I am free of the chief. At least I am free of an old and ignorant man, who is nothing but a white man's dog. He is a trick, a trick to hold together something that the white man desires to hold together.

He smiled his cunning and knowing smile, and for a moment addressed himself to his visitors.

—But it is not being held together, he said. It is breaking apart, your tribal society. It is here in Johannesburg that the new society is being built. Something is happening here, my brother.

He paused for a moment, then he said, I do not wish to offend you gentlemen, but the Church too is like the chief. You must do so and so and so. You are not free to have an experience. A man must be faithful and meek and obedient, and he must obey the laws, whatever the laws may be. It is true that the Church speaks with a fine voice, and that the Bishops speak against the laws. But this they have been doing for fifty years, and things get worse, not better.

His voice grew louder, and he was again addressing people who were not there. Here in Johannesburg it is the mines, he said, everything is the mines. These high buildings, this wonderful City Hall, this beautiful Parktown with its beautiful houses, all this is built with the gold from the mines. This wonderful hospital for Europeans, the biggest hospital south of the Equator, it is built with the gold from the mines.

There was a change in his voice, it became louder like the voice of a bull or a lion. Go to our hospital, he said, and see our people lying on the floors. They lie so close you cannot step over them. But it is they who dig the gold. For three shillings a day. We come

from the Transkei, and from Basutoland, and from
Bechuanaland, and from Swaziland, and from Zululand. And from Ndotsheni also. We live in the compounds, we must leave our wives and families
behind. And when the new gold is found, it is not
we who will get more for our labour. It is the white
man's shares that will rise, you will read it in all the
papers. They go mad when new gold is found. They
bring more of us to live in the compounds, to dig
under the ground for three shillings a day. They do
not think, here is a chance to pay more for our labour. They think only, here is a chance to build a
bigger house and buy a bigger car. It is important to
find gold, they say, for all South Africa is built on
the mines.

He growled, and his voice grew deep, it was like
thunder that was rolling. But it is not built on the
mines, he said, it is built on our backs, on our
sweat, on our labour. Every factory, every theatre,
every beautiful house, they are all built by us. And
what does a chief know about that? But here in Johannesburg they know.

He stopped, and was silent. And his visitors were
silent also, for there was something in this voice that
compelled one to be silent. And Stephen Kumalo
sat silent, for this was a new brother that he saw.

John Kumalo looked at him. The Bishop says it is
wrong, he said, but he lives in a big house, and his
white priests get four, five, six times what you get,
my brother.

He sat down, and took out a large red handkerchief to wipe his face.

—That is my experience, he said. That is why I no longer go to the Church.

—And that is why you did not write any more.

—Well, well, it could be the reason.

—That, and your wife Esther?

—Yes, yes, both perhaps. It is hard to explain in a letter. Our customs are different here.

And Msimangu said, are there any customs here?

John Kumalo looked at him. There is a new thing growing here, he said. Stronger than any church or chief. You will see it one day.

—And your wife? Why did she leave?

—Well, well, said John Kumalo with his knowing smile. She did not understand my experience.

—You mean, said Msimangu coldly, that she believed in fidelity?

John looked at him suspiciously. Fidelity, he said. But Msimangu was quick to see that he did not understand.

—Perhaps we should speak Zulu again, he said.

The angry veins stood out on the great bull neck, and who knows what angry words might have been spoken, but Stephen Kumalo was quick to intervene.

—Here is the tea, my brother. That is kind of you.

The woman was not introduced, but took round the tea humbly. When she had gone, Kumalo spoke to his brother.

—I have listened attentively to you, my brother. Much of what you say saddens me, partly because of the way you say it, and partly because much of it is true. And now I have something to ask of you. But I must tell you first that Gertrude is with me here. She is coming back to Ndotsheni.

—Well, well, I shall not say it is a bad thing. Johannesburg is not a place for a woman alone. I myself tried to persuade her, but she did not agree, so we did not meet any more.

—And now I must ask you. Where is my son?

There is something like discomfort in John's eyes. He takes out his handkerchief again.

—Well, you have heard no doubt he was friendly with my son.

—I have heard that.

—Well, you know how these young men are. I do not blame them altogether. You see, my son did not agree well with his second mother. What it was about I could never discover. Nor did he agree with his mother's children. Many times I tried to arrange matters, but I did not succeed. So he said he would leave. He had good work so I did not stop him. And your son went with him.

—Where, my brother?

—I do not rightly know. But I heard that they had a room in Alexandra. Now wait a minute. They were both working for a factory. I remember. Wait till I look in the telephone book.

He went to a table and there Kumalo saw the telephone. He felt a little pride to be the brother of a man who had such a thing.

—There it is. Doornfontein Textiles Company, 14 Krause St. I shall write it down for you, my brother.

—Can we not telephone them? asked Kumalo hesitantly.

His brother laughed. What for? he asked. To ask if Absalom Kumalo is working there? Or to ask if they will call him to the telephone? Or to ask if they will give his address? They do not do such things for a black man, my brother.

—It does not matter, said Msimangu. My hands are yours, my friend.

They said their farewells and went out into the street.

Huh, there you have it.

—Yes, we have it there.

—He is a big man, in this place, your brother. His shop is always full of men, talking as you have heard. But they say you must hear him at a meeting, he and Dubula and a brown man named Tomlinson. They say he speaks like a bull, and growls in his throat like a lion, and could make men mad if he would. But for that they say he has not enough courage, for he would surely be sent to prison.

—I shall tell you one thing, Msimangu continued. Many of the things that he said are true.

He stopped in the street and spoke quietly and earnestly to his companion. Because the white man has power, we too want power, he said. But when a black man gets power, when he gets money, he is a great man if he is not corrupted. I have seen it often. He seeks power and money to put right what is wrong, and when he gets them, why, he enjoys the power and the money. Now he can gratify his lusts, now he can arrange ways to get white man's liquor, he can speak to thousands and hear them clap their hands. Some of us think when we have power, we shall revenge ourselves on the white man who has had power, and because our desire is corrupt, we are corrupted, and the power has no heart in it. But most white men do not know this truth about power, and they are afraid lest we get it.

He stood as though he was testing his exposition. Yes, that is right about power, he said. But there is only one thing that has power completely, and that is love. Because when a man loves, he seeks no power, and therefore he has power. I see only one hope for our country, and that is when white men and black men, desiring neither power nor money, but desiring only the good of their country, come together to work for it.

He was grave and silent, and then he said sombrely, I have one great fear in my heart, that one day when they are turned to loving, they will find we are turned to hating.

—This is not the way to get to Doornfontein, he said. Come, let us hurry.

And Kumalo followed him silently, oppressed by the grave and sombre words.

*　　*　　*　　*　　*

But they were not successful at Doornfontein, although the white men treated them with consideration. Msimangu knew how to arrange things with white men, and they went to a great deal of trouble, and found that Absalom Kumalo had left them some twelve months before. One of them remembered that Absalom had been friendly with one of their workmen, Dhlamini, and this man was sent for from his work. He told them that when he had last heard, Absalom was staying with a Mrs. Ndlela, of End St., Sophiatown, the street that separates Sophiatown from the European suburb of Westdene. He was not sure, but he thought that the number of the house was 105.

So they returned to Sophiatown, and indeed found Mrs. Ndlela at 105 End Street. She received them with a quiet kindness, and her children hid behind her skirts, and peeped out at the visitors. But Absalom was not there, she said. But wait, she had had a letter from him, asking about the things he had left behind. So while Kumalo played with her children, and Msimangu talked to her husband, she brought out a big box full of papers and other belongings, and looked for the letter. And while she was searching, and Msimangu was watching her kind and tired face, he saw her stop in her search for a moment, and look at Kumalo for a moment, half curiously, and half with pity. At last she found the letter, and she showed them the address, c/o Mrs. Mkize, 79 Twenty-third Avenue, Alexandra.

Then they must drink a cup of tea, and it was dark before they rose to leave, and the husband stepped out with Kumalo into the street.

—Why did you look at my friend with pity? asked Msimangu of the woman.

She dropped her eyes, then raised them again. He is an umfundisi, she said.

—Yes.

—I did not like his son's friends. Nor did my husband. That is why he left us.

—I understand you. Was there anything worse than that?

—No. I saw nothing. But I did not like his friends.

Her face was honest and open, and she did not drop her eyes again.

—Goodnight, mother.

—Goodnight, umfundisi.

Out in the street they said farewell to the husband, and set off back to the Mission House.

—Tomorrow, said Msimangu, we go to Alexandra.

Kumalo put his hand on his friend's arm. The things are not happy that brought me to Johannesburg, he said, but I have found much pleasure in your company.

—Huh, said Msimangu, huh, we must hurry or we shall be late for our food.

8

THE next morning, after they had eaten at the Mission House, Msimangu and Kumalo set off for the great wide road where the buses run.

—Every bus is here the right bus, said Msimangu.

Kumalo smiled at that, for it was a joke against him and his fear of catching the wrong bus.

—All these buses go to Johannesburg, said Msimangu. You need not fear to take a wrong bus here.

So they took the first bus that came. and it set them down at the place where Kumalo had lost his pound. And then they walked, through many streets full of cars and buses and people, till they reached the bus rank for Alexandra. But here they met an unexpected obstacle, for a man came up to them and said to Msimangu, are you going to Alexandra, umfundisi?

—Yes, my friend.

—We are here to stop you, umfundisi. Not by force, you see—he pointed—the police are there to prevent that. But by persuasion. If you use this bus you are weakening the cause of the black people. We have determined not to use these buses until the fare is brought back again to fourpence.

—Yes, indeed, I have heard of it.

He turned to Kumalo.

—I was very foolish, my friend. I had forgotten that there were no buses; at least I had forgotten the boycott of the buses.

—Our business is very urgent, said Kumalo humbly.

—This boycott is also urgent, said the man politely. They want us to pay sixpence, that is one shilling a day. Six shillings a week, and some of us only get thirty-five or forty shillings.

—Is it far to walk? asked Kumalo.

—It is a long way, umfundisi. Eleven miles.

—That is a long way, for an old man.

—Men as old as you are doing it every day, umfundisi. And women, and some that are sick, and some crippled, and children. They start walking at four in the morning, and they do not get back till eight at night. They have a bite of food, and their eyes are hardly closed on the pillow before they must stand up again, sometimes to start off with nothing but hot water in their stomachs. I cannot stop you taking a bus, umfundisi, but this is a cause to fight for. If we lose it, then they will have to pay more in Sophiatown and Claremont and Kliptown and Pimville.

—I understand you well. We shall not use the bus.

The man thanked them and went to another would-be traveller.

—That man has a silver tongue, said Kumalo.

—That is the famous Dubula, said Msimangu quietly. A friend of your brother John. But they say—excuse me, my friend—that Tomlinson has the brains, and your brother the voice, but that this man has the heart. He is the one the Government is afraid of, because he himself is not afraid. He seeks nothing for himself. They say he has given up his own work to do this picketing of the buses, and his wife pickets the other bus rank at Alexandra.

—That is something to be proud of. Johannesburg is a place of wonders.

—They were church people, said Msimangu regretfully, but are so no longer. Like your brother, they say the church has a fine voice, but no deeds. Well, my friend, what do we do now?

—I am willing to walk.

—Eleven miles, and eleven miles back. It is a long journey.

—I am willing. You understand I am anxious, my friend. This Johannesburg—it is no place for a boy to be alone.

—Good. Let us begin then.

So they walked many miles through the European city, up Twist Street to the Clarendon Circle, and down Louis Botha towards Orange Grove. And the cars and the lorries never ceased, going one way or the other. After a long time a car stopped and a white man spoke to them.

—Where are you two going? he asked.

—To Alexandra, sir, said Msimangu, taking off his hat.

—I thought you might be. Climb in.

That was a great help to them, and at the turn-off to Alexandra they expressed their thanks.

—It is a long journey, said the white man. And I know that you have no buses.

They stood to watch him go on, but he did not go on. He swung round, and was soon on the road back to Johannesburg.

—Huh, said Msimangu, that is something to marvel at.

It was still a long way to Twenty-third Avenue, and as they passed one avenue after the other, Msimangu explained that Alexandra was outside the boundaries of Johannesburg, and was a place where a black man could buy land and own a house. But the streets were not cared for, and there were no lights, and so great was the demand for accommodation that every man if he could, built rooms in his yard and sublet them to others. Many of these rooms were the hide-outs for thieves and robbers, and there was much prostitution and brewing of illicit liquor.

—These things are so bad, said Msimangu, that the white people of Orange Grove and Norwood and Highlands North got up a great petition to do away with the place altogether. One of our young boys snatched a bag there from an old white woman, and she fell to the ground, and died there of shock and fear. And there was a terrible case of a white woman who lived by herself in a house not far from here, and because she resisted some of our young men who broke in, they killed her. Sometimes too white men and women sit in their cars in the dark under the trees on the Pretoria Road; and some of our young men sometimes rob and assault them, sometimes even the women. It is true that they are often bad women, but that is the one crime we dare not speak of.

—It reminds me, he said, of a different case on the other side of Johannesburg. One of my friends lives there in a house that stands by itself on the Potchefstroom road. It was a cold winter's night, and it was still far from morning when there was a knock on the door. It was a woman knocking, a white woman, with scarcely a rag to cover her body. Those she had were torn, and she held them with her hands to hide her nakedness, and she was blue with the cold. A white man had done this to her, taken her in his car, and when he had satisfied himself—or not, I cannot say, I was not there—he threw her out into the cold, with these few rags, and drove back to Johannesburg. Well my friend and his wife found an old dress for her, and an old coat, and boiled water for tea, and wrapped her in blankets. The children were awake, and asking questions, but my friends told them to sleep, and would not let them come in to see. Then my friend went off in the dark to the house of a white farmer not very far away. The dogs were fierce and he was afraid, but he persisted, and when the white man came he told him of the trouble, and that it was the kind of thing to be settled quietly. The white man said, Huh, I will come. He brought out his car, and they went back to my friend's house. The white woman would have shown her thanks with money, but she had no

money. My friend and his wife both told her it was
not a matter for money. The white man said to my
friend, he said it twice, *Jy is 'n goeie Kaffer,* you are
a good Kaffir. Something touched him, and he said
it in the words that he had.

—I am touched also.

—Well, I was telling you about this petition. Our
white friends fought against this petition, for they
said that the good things of Alexandra were more
than the bad. That it was something to have a place
of one's own, and a house to bring up children in,
and a place to have a voice in, so that a man is something in the land where he was born. Professor
Hoernle—he is dead, God rest his soul—he was the
great fighter for us. Huh, I am sorry you cannot
hear him. For he had Tomlinson's brains, and your
brother's voice, and Dubula's heart, all in one man.
When he spoke, there was no white man that could
speak against him. Huh, I remember it even now.
He would say that this is here, and that is there, and
that yonder is over there yonder, and there was no
man that could move these things by so much as an
inch from the places where he put them. English-
man or Afrikaner, they could move nothing from
the places where he put them.

He took out his handkerchief and wiped his face.
I have talked a great deal, he said, right up to the
very house we are seeking.

A woman opened the door to them. She gave
them no greeting, and when they stated their business, it was with reluctance that she let them in.

—You say the boy has gone, Mrs. Mkize?

—Yes, I do not know where he is gone.

—When did he go?

—These many months. A year it must be.

—And had he a friend?

—Yes, another Kumalo. The son of his father's brother. But they left together.

—And you do not know where they went?

—They talked of many places. But you know how these young men talk.

—How did he behave himself, this young man Absalom, Kumalo asked her?

Have no doubt it is fear in her eyes. Have no doubt it is fear now in his eyes also. It is fear, here in this house.

—I saw nothing wrong, she said.

—But you guessed there was something wrong.

—There was nothing wrong, she said.

—Then why are you afraid?

—I am not afraid, she said.

—Then why do you tremble? asked Msimangu.

—I am cold, she said.

She looked at them sullenly, watchfully.

—We thank you, said Msimangu. Stay well.

—Go well, she said.

Out in the street Kumalo spoke.

—There is something wrong, he said.

—I do not deny it. My friend, two of us are too many together. Turn left at the big street and go up the hill, and you will find a place for refreshment. Wait for me there.

Heavy-hearted the old man went, and Msimangu followed him slowly till he turned at the corner.

Then he turned back himself, and returned to the house.

She opened again to him, as sullen as before; now that she had recovered, there was more sullenness than fear.

—I am not from the police, he said. I have nothing to do with the police. I wish to have nothing to do with them. But there is an old man suffering because he cannot find his son.

—That is a bad thing, she said, but she spoke as one speaks who must speak so.

—It is a bad thing, he said, and I cannot leave you until you have told what you would not tell.

—I have nothing to tell, she said.

—You have nothing to tell because you are afraid. And you do not tremble because it is cold.

—And why do I tremble? she asked.

—That I do not know. But I shall not leave you till I discover it. And if it is necessary, I shall go to the police after all, because there will be no other place to go.

—It is hard for a woman who is alone, she said resentfully.

—It is hard for an old man seeking his son.

—I am afraid, she said.

—He is afraid also. Could you not see he is afraid?

—I could see it, umfundisi.

—Then tell me, what sort of life did they lead here, these two young men? But she kept silent, with the fear in her eyes, and tears near to them. He could see she would be hard to move.

—I am a priest. Would you not take my word? But she kept silent.

—Have you a Bible?

—I have a Bible.

—Then I will swear to you on the Bible.

But she kept silent till he said again, I will swear to you on the Bible. So getting no peace, she rose irresolute, and went to a room behind, and after some time she returned with the Bible.

—I am a priest, he said. My yea has always been yea, and my nay, nay. But because you desire it, and because an old man is afraid, I swear to you on this Book that no trouble will come to you of this, for we seek only a boy. So help me *Tixo*.

—What sort of life did they lead? he asked.

—They brought many things here, umfundisi, in the late hours of the night. They were clothes, and watches, and money, and food in bottles, and many other things.

—Was there ever blood on them?

—I never saw blood on them, umfundisi.

—That is something. Only a little, but something.

—And why did they leave? he asked.

—I do not know, umfundisi. But I think they were near to being discovered.

—And they left when?

—About a year since, umfundisi. Indeed as I told you.

—And here on this Book you will swear you do not know where they are gone?

She reached for the Book, but, it does not matter, he said. He said farewell to her, and hurried out after his friend. But she called after him:

—They were friendly with the taxi-driver Hlabeni. Near the bus rank he lives. Everyone knows him.

—For that I give you thanks. Stay well, Mrs. Mkize.

At the refreshment stall he found his friend.

—Did you find anything further? asked the old man eagerly.

—I heard of a friend of theirs, the taxi-driver Hlabeni. Let me first eat, and we shall find him out.

When Msimangu had eaten, he went to ask a man where he could find Hlabeni, the taxi-driver. There he is on the corner sitting in his taxi, said the man. Msimangu walked over to the taxi, and said to the man sitting in it, Good afternoon, my friend.

—Good afternoon, umfundisi.

—I want a taxi, my friend. What do you charge to Johannesburg? For myself and a friend?

—For you, umfundisi, I should charge eleven shillings.

—It is a lot of money.

—Another taxi would charge fifteen or twenty shillings.

—My companion is old and tired. I shall pay you eleven shillings.

The man made to start his engine, but Msimangu stopped him. I am told, he said, that you can help me to find a young man Absalom Kumalo.

Have no doubt too that this man is afraid. But

Msimangu was quick to reassure him. I am not here for trouble, he said. I give you my word that I am seeking trouble neither for you nor for myself. But my companion, the old man who is tired, is the father of this young man, and he has come from Natal to find him. Everywhere we go, we are told to go somewhere else, and the old man is anxious.

—Yes, I knew this young man.

—And where is he now, my friend?

—I heard he was gone to Orlando, and lives there amongst the squatters in Shanty Town. But further than that I do not know.

—Orlando is a big place, said Msimangu.

—Where the squatters live is not so big, umfundisi. It should not be hard to find him. There are people from the Municipality working amongst the squatters, and they know them all. Could you not ask one of those people?

—There you have helped me, my friend. I know some of those people. Come, we shall take your taxi.

He called Kumalo, and told him they were returning by taxi. They climbed in, and the taxi rattled out of Alexandra on to the broad high road that runs from Pretoria to Johannesburg. The afternoon was late now, and the road was crowded with traffic, for at this time it pours both into and out of Johannesburg on this road.

—You see the bicycles, my friend. These are the thousands of Alexandra people returning home after their work, and just now we shall see the thousands of them walking, because of the boycott of the buses.

And true, they had not gone far before the pavements were full of the walking people. There were so many that they overflowed into the streets, and the cars had to move carefully. And some were old, and some tired, and some even crippled as they had been told, but most of them walked resolutely, as indeed they had been doing now these past few weeks. Many of the white people stopped their cars, and took in the black people, to help them on their journey to Alexandra. Indeed, at one robot where they stopped, a traffic officer was talking to one of these white men, and they heard the officer asking whether the white man had a license to carry the black people. I am asking no money, said the white man. But you are carrying passengers on a bus route, said the officer. Then take me to court, said the white man. But they heard no more than that, for they had to move on because the light was green.

—I have heard of that, said Msimangu. I have heard that they are trying to prevent the white people from helping with their cars, and that they are even ready to take them to the courts.

It was getting dark now, but the road was still thick with the Alexandra people going home. And there were still cars stopping to give them lifts, especially to the old people, and the women, and the cripples. Kumalo's face wore the smile, the strange smile not known in other countries, of a black man when he sees one of his people helped in public by a white man, for such a thing is not lightly done. And so immersed was he in the watching that he was astonished when Msimangu suddenly burst out:

—It beats me, my friend, it beats me.

—What beats you, this kindness?

—No, no. To tell the truth I was not thinking of it.

He sat up in the taxi, and hit himself a great blow across the chest.

—Take me to court, he said. He glared fiercely at Kumalo and hit himself again across the chest. Take me to court, he said.

Kumalo looked at him bewildered.

—That is what beats me, Msimangu said.

9

ALL roads lead to Johannesburg. If you are white or if you are black they lead to Johannesburg. If the crops fail, there is work in Johannesburg. If there are taxes to be paid, there is work in Johannesburg. If the farm is too small to be divided further, some must go to Johannesburg. If there is a child to be born that must be delivered in secret, it can be delivered in Johannesburg.

The black people go to Alexandra or Sophiatown or Orlando, and try to hire rooms or to buy a share of a house.

—Have you a room that you could let?

—No, I have no room.

—Have you a room that you could let?

—It is let already.

—Have you a room that you could let?

Yes, I have a room that I could let, but I do not want to let it. I have only two rooms, and there are six of us already, and the boys and girls are growing up. But school books cost money, and my husband is ailing, and when he is well it is only thirty-five shillings a week. And six shillings of that is for the rent, and three shillings for travelling, and a shilling that we may all be buried decently, and a shilling for the books, and three shillings is for clothes and that is little enough, and a shilling for my husband's beer, and a shilling for his tobacco, and these I do not grudge for he is a decent man and does not gamble or spend his money on other women, and a shilling for the Church, and a shilling for sickness. And that leaves seventeen shillings for food for six, and we are always hungry. Yes I have a room but I do not want to let it. How much would you pay?

—I could pay three shillings a week for the room.

—And I would not take it.

—Three shillings and sixpence.

—Three shillings and sixpence. You can't fill your stomach on privacy. You need privacy when your children are growing up, but you can't fill your stomach on it. Yes, I shall take three shillings and sixpence.

The house is not broken, but it is overflowing. Ten people in two rooms, and only one door for the entrance, and people to walk over you when you go to sleep. But there is a little more food for the children, and maybe once a month a trip to the pictures.

I do not like this woman, nor the way she looks at my husband. I do not like this boy, nor the way he looks at my daughter. I do not like this man, I do not like the way he looks at me, I do not like the way he looks at my daughter.

—I am sorry, but you must go now.

—We have no place to go to.

—I am sorry, but the house is too full. It cannot hold so many.

—We have put our name down for a house. Can you not wait till we get a house?

—There are people in Orlando who have been waiting five years for a house.

—I have a friend who waited only one month for a house.

—I have heard of such. They say you can pay a bribe.

—We have no money for a bribe.

—I am sorry, but the house is full.

Yes, this house is full, and that house is full. For everyone is coming to Johannesburg. From the Transkei and the Free State, from Zululand and Sekukuniland. Zulus and Swazis, Shangaans and Bavenda, Bapedi and Basuto, Xosas and Tembus, Pondos and Fingos, they are all coming to Johannesburg.

I do not like this woman. I do not like this boy. I do not like this man. I am sorry, but you must go now.

—Another week, that is all I ask.

—You may have one more week.

*   *   *   *   *

—Have you a room to let?

—No, I have no room to let.

—Have you a room to let?

—It is let already.

—Have you a room to let?

Yes, I have a room to let, but I do not want to let it. For I have seen husbands taken away by women, and wives taken away by men. I have seen daughters corrupted by boys, and sons corrupted by girls. But my husband gets only thirty-four shillings a week—

*   *   *   *   *

—What shall we do, those who have no houses?

—You can wait five years for a house, and be no nearer getting it than at the beginning.

—They say there are ten thousand of us in Orlando alone, living in other people's houses.

—Do you hear what Dubula says? That we must put up our own houses here in Orlando?

—And where do we put up the houses?

—On the open ground by the railway line, Dubula says.

—And of what do we build the houses?

—Anything you can find. Sacks and planks and grass from the veld and poles from the plantations.

—And when it rains?

—Siyafa. Then we die.

—No, when it rains, they will have to build us houses.

—It is foolishness. What shall we do in the Winter?

Six years waiting for a house. And full as the houses are, they grow yet fuller, for the people still come to Johannesburg. There has been a great war raging in Europe and North Africa, and no houses are being built.

—Have you a house for me yet?

—There is no house yet.

—Are you sure my name is on the list?

—Yes, your name is on the list.

—What number am I on the list?

—I cannot say, but you must be about number six thousand on the list.

Number six thousand on the list. That means I shall never get a house, and I cannot stay where I am much longer. We have quarrelled about the stove, we have quarrelled about the children, and I do not like the way the man looks at me. There is the open ground by the railway line, but what of the rain and the winter? They say we must go there, all go together, fourteen days from today. They say we must get together the planks and the sacks and the tins and the poles, and all move together. They say we must all pay a shilling a week to the Committee, and they will move all our rubbish and put up lavatories for us, so that there is no sickness. But what of the rain and the winter?

—Have you a house for me yet?

—There is no house yet.

—But I have been two years on the list.

—You are only a child on the list.

—Is it true that if you pay money—?

But the man does not hear me, he is already busy with another. But a second man comes to me from what place I do not see, and what he says bewilders me.

—I am sorry they have no house, Mrs. Seme. By the way, my wife would like to discuss with you the work of the Committee. Tonight at seven o'clock, she said. You know our house, No. 17852, near the Dutch Reformed Church. Look, I shall write down the number for you. Good morning, Mrs. Seme.

But when I make to answer him, he is already gone.

—Ho, but this man bewilders me. Who is his wife, I do not know her. And what is this committee, I know of no committee.

—Ho, but you are a simple woman. He wants to discuss with you the money you are willing to pay for a house.

Well, I shall go there then. I hope he does not ask too much, one cannot pay too much on thirty-seven shillings a week. But a house we must have. I am afraid of the place where we are. There is too much coming and going, when all decent people are asleep. Too many young men coming and going, that seem never to sleep, and never to work. Too much clothing, good clothing, white people's clothing. There will be trouble one day, and my husband and I have never been in trouble. A house we must have.

*   *   *   *   *

—Five pounds is too much. I have not the money.

—Five pounds is not too much for a house, Mrs. Seme.

—What, just to put my name higher on the list?

—But it is dangerous. The European manager has said that he will deal severely with any who tamper with the list.

—Well I am sorry. But I cannot pay the money.

But before I can go, his wife comes into the room with another woman.

—There must be a mistake, my husband. I do not know this woman. She is not on the Committee.

—Ho, I am sorry, my wife. I am sorry, Mrs. Seme. I thought you were on the committee. Go well, Mrs. Seme.

But I do not say stay well. I do not care if they stay well or ill. And nothing goes well with me. I am tired and lonely. Oh my husband, why did we leave the land of our people? There is not much there, but it is better than here. There is not much food there, but it is shared by all together. If all are poor, it is not so bad to be poor. And it is pleasant by the river, and while you wash your clothes the water runs over the stones, and the wind cools you. Two weeks from today, that is the day of the moving. Come my husband, let us get the planks and the tins and the sacks and the poles. I do not like the place where we are.

There are planks at the Baragwanath Hospital, left there by the builders. Let us go tonight and carry them away. There is corrugated iron at the Reformatory, they use it to cover the bricks. Let us go tonight and carry it away. There are sacks at the Nancefield Station, lying neatly packed in bundles. Let us go tonight and carry them away. There are trees at the Crown Mines. Let us go tonight and cut a few poles quietly.

*　　*　　*　　*　　*

This night they are busy in Orlando. At one house after another the lights are burning. I shall carry the iron, and you my wife the child, and you my son two poles, and you small one, bring as many sacks as you are able, down to the land by the railway lines. Many people are moving there, you can hear the sound of digging and hammering already. It is good that the night is warm, and there is no rain. Thank you, Mr. Dubula, we are satisfied with this piece of ground. Thank you, Mr. Dubula, here is our shilling for the Committee.

Shanty Town is up overnight. What a surprise for the people when they wake in the morning. Smoke comes up through the sacks, and one or two have a chimney already. There was a nice chimney-pipe lying there at the Kliptown Police Station, but I was not such a fool as to take it.

Shanty Town is up overnight. And the newspapers are full of us. Great big words and pictures. See, that is my husband, standing by the house. Alas, I was too late for the picture. Squatters, they call us. We are the squatters. This great village of sack and plank and iron, with no rent to pay, only a shilling to the Committee.

Shanty Town is up overnight. The child coughs badly, and her brow is as hot as fire. I was afraid to move her, but it was the night for the moving. The cold wind comes through the sacks. What shall we do in the rain, in the winter? Quietly my child, your mother is by you. Quietly my child, do not cough any more, your mother is by you.

*   *   *   *   *

The child coughs badly, her brow is hotter than fire. Quietly my child, your mother is by you. Outside there is laughter and jesting, digging and hammering, and calling in languages that I do not know. Quietly my child, there is a lovely valley where you were born. The water sings over the stones, and the wind cools you. The cattle come down to the river, they stand there under the trees. Quietly my child, oh God make her quiet. God have mercy upon us. Christ have mercy upon us. White man, have mercy upon us.

*   *   *   *   *

—Mr. Dubula, where is the doctor?

—We shall get the doctor in the morning. You need not fear, the Committee will pay for him.

—But the child is like to die. Look at the blood.

—It is not long till morning.

—It is long when the child is dying, when the heart is afraid. Can we not get him now, Mr. Dubula?

—I shall try, mother. I shall go now and try.

—I am grateful, Mr. Dubula.

*   *   *   *   *

Outside there is singing, singing round a fire. It is *Nkosi sikelel' iAfrika* that they sing, God Save

Africa. God save this piece of Africa that is my own, delivered in travail from my body, fed from my breast, loved by my heart, because that is the nature of women. Oh lie quietly, little one. Doctor, can you not come?

* * * * *

—I have sent for the doctor, mother. The Committee has sent a car for the doctor. A black doctor, one of our own.

—I am grateful, Mr. Dubula.

—Shall I ask them to be quiet, mother?

—It does not matter, she does not know.

Perhaps a white doctor would have been better, but any doctor if only he come. Does it matter if they are quiet, these sounds of an alien land? I am afraid, my husband. She burns my hand like fire.

* * * * *

We do not need the doctor any more. No white doctor, no black doctor, can help her any more. Oh child of my womb and fruit of my desire, it was pleasure to hold the small cheeks in the hands, it was pleasure to feel the tiny clutching of the fingers, it was pleasure to feel the little mouth tugging at the breast. Such is the nature of woman. Such is the lot of women, to carry, to bear, to watch, and to lose.

* * * * *

The white men come to Shanty Town. They take photographs of us, and moving photographs for the pictures. They come and wonder what they can do, there are so many of us. What will the poor devils do in the rain? What will the poor devils do in the winter? Men come, and machines come, and they start building rough houses for us. That Dubula is a clever man, this is what he said they would do. And no sooner do they begin to build for us, than there come in the night other black people, from Pimville and Alexandra and Sophiatown, and they too put up their houses of sack and grass and iron and poles. And the white men come again, but this time it is anger, not pity. The police come and drive the people away. And some that they drive away are from Orlando itself. They go back to the houses that they left, but of some the rooms are already taken, and some will not have them any more.

You need not be ashamed that you live in Shanty Town. It is in the papers, and that is my husband standing by the house. A man here has a paper from Durban, and my husband is there too, standing by the house. You can give your address as Shanty Town, Shanty Town alone, everyone knows where it is, and give the number that the committee has given you.

What shall we do in the rain? in the winter? Already some of them are saying, look at those houses over the hill. They are not finished, but the roofs are on. One night we shall move there and be safe from the rain and the winter.

10

WHILE Kumalo was waiting for Msimangu to take him to Shanty Town, he spent the time with Gertrude and her child. But it was rather to the child, the small serious boy, that he turned for his enjoyment; for he had been a young man in the twenties when his sister was born, and there had never been great intimacy between them. After all he was a parson, sober and rather dull no doubt, and his hair was turning white, and she was a young woman still. Nor could he expect her to talk with him about the deep things that were here in Johannesburg; for it was amongst these very things that saddened and perplexed him, that she had found her life and occupation.

Here were heavy things indeed, too heavy for a woman who had not gone beyond the fifth standard of her country school. She was respectful to him, as it behooved her to be to an elder brother and a parson, and they exchanged conventional conversation; but never again did they speak of the things that had made her fall on the floor with crying and weeping.

But the good Mrs. Lithebe was there, and she and

Gertrude talked long and simply about things dear to the heart of women, and they worked and sang together in the performance of the daily tasks.

Yes, it was to the small serious boy that he turned for his enjoyment. He had bought the child some cheap wooden blocks, and with these the little one played endlessly and intently, with a purpose obscure to the adult mind, but completely absorbing. Kumalo would pick the child up, and put his hand under the shirt to feel the small warm back, and tickle and poke him, till the serious face relaxed into smiles, and the smiles grew into uncontrollable laughter. Or he would tell him of the great valley where he was born, and the names of hills and rivers, and the school that he would go to, and the mist that shrouded the tops above Ndotsheni. Of this the child understood nothing; yet something he did understand, for he would listen solemnly to the deep melodious names, and gaze at his uncle out of wide and serious eyes. And this to the uncle was pleasure indeed, for he was homesick in the great city; and something inside him was deeply satisfied by this recital. Sometimes Gertrude would hear him and come to the door and stand shyly there, and listen to the tale of the beauties of the land where she was born. This enriched his pleasure, and sometimes he would say to her, do you remember, and she would answer, yes, I remember, and be pleased that he had asked her.

But there were times, some in the very midst of satisfaction, when the thought of his son would come to him. And then in one fraction of time the hills with the deep melodious names stood out waste and desolate beneath the pitiless sun, the streams ceased to run, the cattle moved thin and listless over the red and rootless earth. It was a place of old women and mothers and children, from each house something was gone. His voice would falter and die away, and he would fall silent and muse. Perhaps it was that, or perhaps he clutched suddenly at the small listening boy, for the little one would break from the spell, and wriggle in his arms to be put down, to play again with his blocks on the floor. As though he was searching for something that would put an end to this sudden unasked-for pain, the thought of his wife would come to him, and of many a friend that he had, and the small children coming down from the hills, dropping sometimes out of the very mist, on their way to the school. These things were so dear to him that the pain passed, and he contemplated them in quiet, and some measure of peace.

Who indeed knows the secret of the earthly pilgrimage? Who indeed knows why there can be comfort in a world of desolation? Now God be thanked that there is a beloved one who can lift up the heart in suffering, that one can play with a child in the face of such misery. Now God be thanked that the name of a hill is such music, that the name of a river can heal. Aye, even the name of a river that runs no more.

Who indeed knows the secret of the earthly pilgrimage? Who knows for what we live, and struggle, and die? Who knows what keeps us living and struggling, while all things break about us? Who knows why the warm flesh of a child is such comfort, when one's own child is lost and cannot be recovered? Wise men write many books, in words too hard to understand. But this, the purpose of our lives, the end of all our struggle, is beyond all human wisdom. Oh God, my God, do not Thou forsake me. Yea, though I walk through the valley of the shadow of death, I shall fear no evil, if Thou art with me. . . .

But he stood up. That was Msimangu talking at the door. It was time to continue the search.

*   *   *   *   *

—And this is Shanty Town, my friend.

Even here the children laugh in the narrow lanes that run between these tragic habitations. A sheet of iron, a few planks, hessian and grass, an old door from some forgotten house. Smoke curls from vents cunningly contrived, there is a smell of food, there is a sound of voices, not raised in anger or pain, but talking of ordinary things, of this one that is born and that one that has died, of this one that does so well at school and that one who is now in prison. There is drought over the land, and the sun shines warmly down from the cloudless sky. But what will they do when it rains, what will they do when it is winter?

—It is sad for me to see.

—Yet see them building over there. And that they have not done for many a year. Some good may come of this. And this too is Dubula's work.

—He is everywhere, it seems.

—See, there is one of our nurses. Does she not look well in her red and white, and her cap upon her head?

—She looks well indeed.

—The white people are training more and more of them. It is strange how we move forward in some things, and stand still in others, and go backward in yet others. Yet in this matter of nurses we have many friends amongst the white people. There was a great outcry when it was decided to allow some of our young people to train as doctors at the European University of the Witwatersrand. But our friends stood firm, and they will train there until we have a place of our own. Good morning, nurse.

—Good morning, umfundisi.

—Nurse, have you been working here long?

—Yes, as long as the place is here.

—And did you ever know a young man, Absalom Kumalo?

—Yes, that I did. But he is not here now. And I can tell where he stayed. He stayed with the Hlatshwayos, and they are still here. Do you see the place where there are many stones so that they cannot build? See, there is a small boy standing there.

—Yes, I see it.

—And beyond it the house with the pipe, where the smoke is coming out?

—Yes, I see it.

—Go down that lane, and you will find the Hlatshwayos in the third or fourth house, on the side of the hand that you eat with.

—Thank you, nurse, we shall go.

Her directions were so clear that they had no difficulty in finding the house.

—Good morning, mother.

The woman was clean and nice-looking, and she smiled at them in a friendly way.

—Good morning, umfundisi.

—Mother, we are looking for a lad, Absalom Kumalo.

—He stayed with me, umfundisi. We took pity on him because he had no place to go. But I am sorry to tell you that they took him away, and I heard that the magistrate had sent him to the reformatory.

—The reformatory?

—Yes, the big school over there, beyond the soldiers' hospital. It is not too far to walk.

—I must thank you, mother. Stay well. Come, my friend. They walked on in silence, for neither of them had any words. Kumalo would have stumbled, though the road was straight and even, and Msimangu took his arm.

—Have courage, my brother.

He glanced at his friend, but Kumalo's eyes were on the ground. Although Msimangu could not see his face, he could see the drop that fell on the ground, and he tightened his grip on the arm.

—Have courage, my brother.

—Sometimes it seems that I have no more courage.

—I have heard of this reformatory. Your friend

the priest from England speaks well of it. I have heard him say that if any boy wishes to amend, there is help for him there. So take courage.

—I was afraid of this.

—Yes, I too was afraid of it.

—Yes, I remember when you first became afraid. The day at Alexandra, when you sent me on, and you returned to speak again to the woman.

—I see that I cannot hide from you.

—That is not because I am so wise. Only because it is my son.

They walked out of Shanty Town into Orlando, and out along the tarred street that leads to the high road to Johannesburg, to the place where the big petrol station of the white people stands at the gates of Orlando; for the black people are not allowed to have petrol stations in Orlando.

—What did the woman say to you, my friend?

—She said that these two young men were in some mischief. Many goods, white people's goods, came to the house.

—This reformatory, can they reform there?

—I do not know it well. Some people say one thing, some the other. But your friend speaks well of it.

And after a long while, during which Msimangu's thoughts had wandered elsewhere, Kumalo said again, It is my hope that they can reform there.

—It is my hope also, my brother.

After a walk of about one hour, they came to the road that led up to the reformatory. It was midday when they arrived, and from all directions there

came boys marching, into the gates of the reformatory. From every place they came, until it seemed
that the marching would never end.

—There are very many here, my friend.

—Yes, I did not know there would be so many.

One of their own people, a pleasant fellow with a
smiling face, came up to them and asked them what
they wanted, and they told him they were searching
for one Absalom Kumalo. So this man took them to
an office, where a young white man enquired of
them in Afrikaans what was their business.

—We are looking, sir, for the son of my friend,
one Absalom Kumalo, said Msimangu in the same
language.

—Absalom Kumalo. Yes, I know him well.
Strange, he told me he had no people.

—Your son told him, my friend, that he had no
people, said Msimangu in Zulu.

—He was no doubt ashamed, said Kumalo. I am
sorry, he said to Msimangu in Zulu, that I speak no
Afrikaans. For he had heard that sometimes they do
not like black people who speak no Afrikaans.

—You may speak what you will, said the young
man. Your son did well here, he said. He became
one of our senior boys, and I have great hope for his
future.

—You mean, sir, that he is gone?

—Gone, yes, only one month ago. We made an
exception in his case, partly because of his good be-
haviour, partly because of his age, but mainly because there was a girl who was pregnant by him. She
came here to see him, and he seemed fond of her,

and anxious about the child that would be born. And the girl too seemed fond of him, so with all these things in mind, and with his solemn undertaking that he would work for his child and its mother, we asked the Minister to let him go. Of course we do not succeed in all these cases, but where there seems to be real affection between the parties, we take the chance, hoping that good will come of it. One thing is certain that if it fails, there is nothing that could have succeeded.

—And is he now married, sir?

—No, umfundisi, he is not. But everything is arranged for the marriage. This girl has no people, and your son told us he had no people, so I myself and my native assistant have arranged it.

—That is good of you, sir. I thank you for them.

—It is our work. You must not worry too much about this matter, and the fact that they were not married, the young man said kindly. The real question is whether he will care for them, and lead a decent life.

—That I can see, although it is a shock to me.

—I understand that. Now I can help you in this matter. If you will sit outside while I finish my work, I will take you to Pimville, where Absalom and this girl are living. He will not be there, because I have found work for him in the town, and they have given me good reports of him. I persuaded him to open a Post Office book, and he already has three or four pounds in it.

—Indeed I cannot thank you, sir.

—It is our work, said the young man. Now if you

will leave me, I shall finish what I have to do, and then take you to Pimville.

Outside the pleasant-faced man came and spoke to them and hearing their plans, invited them to his house, where he and his wife had a number of boys in their charge, boys who had left the big reformatory building and were living outside in these free houses. He gave them some tea and food, and he too told them that Absalom had become a head-boy, and had behaved well during his stay at the reformatory. So they talked about the reformatory, and the children that were growing up in Johannesburg without home or school or custom, and about the broken tribe and the sickness of the land, until a messenger came from the young man to say that he was ready.

It was not long before the motorcar had reached Pimville, which is a village of half-tanks used as houses, set up many years before in emergency, and used ever since. For there have never been houses enough for all the people who came to Johannesburg. At the gate they asked permission to enter, for a white man may not go into these places without permission.

They stopped at one of these half-tank houses, and the young white man took them in, where they were greeted by a young girl, who herself seemed no more than a child.

—We have come to enquire after Absalom, said the young white man. This umfundisi is his father.

—He went on Saturday to Springs, she said, and he has not yet returned.

The young man was silent awhile, and he frowned in perplexity or anger.

—But this is Tuesday, he said. Have you heard nothing from him?

—Nothing, she said.

—When will he return? he asked.

—I do not know, she said.

—Will he ever return? he asked, indifferently, carelessly.

—I do not know, she said. She said it tonelessly, hopelessly, as one who is used to waiting, to desertion. She said it as one who expects nothing from her seventy years upon the earth. No rebellion will come out of her, no demands, no fierceness. Nothing will come out of her at all save the children of men who will use her, leave her, forget her. And so slight was her body, and so few her years, that Kumalo for all his suffering was moved to compassion.

—What will you do? he said.

—I do not know, she said.

—Perhaps you will find another man, said Msimangu bitterly. And before Kumalo could speak, to steal away the bitterness and hide it from her—I do not know, she said.

And again before Kumalo could speak, Msimangu turned his back on the girl, and spoke to him privately.

—You can do nothing here, he said. Let us go.

—My friend. . . . . . .

—I tell you, you can do nothing. Have you not troubles enough of your own? I tell you there are thousands such in Johannesburg. And were your back as broad as heaven, and your purse full of gold, and did your compassion reach from here to hell itself, there is nothing you can do.

Silently they withdrew. All of them were silent, the young white man heavy with failure, the old man with grief, Msimangu still bitter with his words. Kumalo stood at the car though the others were already seated.

—You do not understand, he said. The child will be my grandchild.

—Even that you do not know, said Msimangu angrily. His bitterness mastered him again. And if he were, he said, how many more such have you? Shall we search them out, day after day, hour after hour? Will it ever end?

Kumalo stood in the dust like one who has been struck. Then without speaking any more he took his seat in the car.

Again they stopped at the gate of the village, and the young white man got out and went into the office of the European Superintendent. He came back, his face set and unhappy.

—I have telephoned the factory, he said. It is true. He has not been at work this week.

At the gates of Orlando, by the big petrol station, they stopped yet again.

—Would you like to get out here? the young man asked. They climbed out, and the young man spoke to Kumalo.

—I am sorry for this, he said.

—Yes, it is very heavy. As if his English had left him, he spoke in Zulu to Msimangu.

—I am sorry too for this end to his work, he said.

—He too is sorry for this end to your work, said Msimangu in Afrikaans.

—Yes, it is my work, but it is his son. He turned to Kumalo and spoke in English. Let us not give up all hope, he said. It has happened sometimes that a boy is arrested, or is injured and taken to hospital, and we do not know. Do not give up hope, umfundisi. I will not give up the search.

They watched him drive away. He is a good man, said Kumalo. Come, let us walk.

But Msimangu did not move. I am ashamed to walk with you, he said. His face was twisted, like that of a man much distressed.

Kumalo looked at him astonished.

—I ask your forgiveness for my ugly words, said Msimangu.

—You mean about the search?

—You understood, then?

—Yes, I understood.

—You are quick to understand.

—I am old, and have learnt something. You are forgiven.

—Sometimes I think I am not fit to be a priest. I could tell you—

—It is no matter. You have said you are a weak and selfish man, but God put his hands upon you. It is true, it seems.

—Huh, you comfort me.

—But I have something to ask of you.

Msimangu looked at him, searching his face, and then he said, it is agreed.

—What is agreed?

—That I should take you again to see this girl.

—You are clever too, it seems.

—Huh, it is not good that only one should be clever.

Yet they were not really in the mood for jesting. They walked along the hot road to Orlando, and both fell silent, each no doubt with many things in mind.

11

—I HAVE been thinking, said Msimangu, as they were sitting in the train that would take them back to Sophiatown, that it is time for you to rest for a while.

Kumalo looked at him. How can I rest? he said.

—I know what you mean. I know you are anxious, but the young man at the reformatory will do better at this searching than you or I could do. Now this is Tuesday; the day after tomorrow I must go to Ezenzeleni, which is the place of our blind, to hold a service for them, and to attend to our own people. And that night I shall sleep there, and return the day after. I shall telephone to the superintendent, and ask if you may come with me. While I work, you can rest. It is a fine place there; there is a chapel there, and the ground falls away from one's feet to the valley below. It will lift your spirits to see what the white people are doing for our blind. Then we can return strengthened for what is still before us.

—What about your work, my friend?

—I have spoken to my superiors about the work.

They are agreed that I must help you till the young man is found.

—They are indeed kind. Good, we shall go then.

*   *   *   *   *

It was a pleasant evening at the Mission House. Father Vincent, the rosy-cheeked priest, was there, and they talked about the place where Kumalo lived and worked. And the white man in his turn spoke about his own country, about the hedges and the fields, and Westminster Abbey, and the great cathedrals up and down the land. Yet even this pleasure was not to be entire, for one of the white priests came in from the city with the *Evening Star*, and showed them the bold black lines. MURDER IN PARKWOLD. WELL-KNOWN CITY ENGINEER SHOT DEAD. AS-SAILANTS THOUGHT TO BE NATIVES.

—This is a terrible loss for South Africa, said the white priest. For this Arthur Jarvis was a courageous young man, and a great fighter for justice. And it is a terrible loss for the Church too. He was one of the finest of all our young laymen.

—Jarvis? It is indeed a terrible thing, said Msimangu. He was the President of the African Boys' Club, here in Claremont, in Gladiolus Street.

—Perhaps you might have known him, said Father Vincent to Kumalo. It says that he was the only child of Mr. James Jarvis, of High Place, Carisbrooke.

—I know the father, said Kumalo sorrowfully. I

mean I know him well by sight and name, but we have never spoken. His farm is in the hills above Ndotsheni, and he sometimes rode past our church. But I did not know the son.

He was silent, then he said, yet I remember, there was a small bright boy, and he too sometimes rode on his horse past the church. A small bright boy, I remember, though I do not remember it well.

And he was silent again, for who is not silent when someone is dead, who was a small bright boy?

—Shall I read this? said Father Vincent:

At 1:30 P.M. today Mr. Arthur Jarvis, of Plantation Road, Parkwold, was shot dead in his house by an intruder, thought to be a native. It appears that Mrs. Jarvis and her two children were away for a short holiday, and that Mr. Jarvis had telephoned his partners to say that he would be staying at home with a slight cold. It would seem that a native, probably with two accomplices, entered by the kitchen, thinking no doubt that there would be no one in the house. The native servant in the kitchen was knocked unconscious, and it would appear that Mr. Jarvis heard the disturbance and came down to investigate. He was shot dead at short range in the passageway leading from the stairs into the kitchen. There were no signs of any struggle.

Three native youths were seen lounging in Plantation Road shortly before the tragedy occurred, and a strong force of detectives was immediately sent to the scene. Exhaustive inquiries are being made, and the plantations on Parkwold Ridge are being combed. The native servant, Richard Mpiring, is lying unconscious in the Non-European Hospital, and it is hoped that when he regains consciousness he will be able to furnish the police with important information. His condition is serious however.

The sound of the shot was heard by a neighbour, Mr. Michael Clarke, who investigated promptly and made the tragic discovery. The police were on the scene within a few minutes. On the table by the bed of the murdered man was found an unfinished manuscript on "The Truth about Native Crime," and it would appear that he was engaged in writing it when he got up to go to his death. The bowl of a pipe on the table was found still to be warm.

Mr. Jarvis leaves a widow, a nine-year-old son, and a five-year-old daughter. He was the only son of Mr. James Jarvis, of High Place Farm, Carisbrooke, Natal, and a partner in the city engineering firm of Davis, van der Walt and Jarvis. The dead man was well known for his interest in social problems, and for his efforts for the welfare of the non-European sections of the community.

There is not much talking now. A silence falls upon them all. This is no time to talk of hedges and fields, or the beauties of any country. Sadness and fear and hate, how they well up in the heart and mind, whenever one opens the pages of these messengers of doom. Cry for the broken tribe, for the law and the custom that is gone. Aye, and cry aloud for the man who is dead, for the woman and children bereaved. Cry, the beloved country, these things are not yet at an end. The sun pours down on the earth, on the lovely land that man cannot enjoy. He knows only the fear of his heart.

*　　　*　　　*　　　*　　　*

Kumalo rose. I shall go to my room, he said. Goodnight to you all.

—I shall walk with you, my friend.

They walked to the gate of the little house of Mrs. Lithebe. Kumalo lifted to his friend a face that was full of suffering.

—This thing, he said. This thing. Here in my heart there is nothing but fear. Fear, fear, fear.

—I understand. Yet it is nevertheless foolish to fear that one thing in this great city, with its thousands and thousands or people.

—It is not a question of wisdom and foolishness. It is just fear.

—The day after tomorrow we go to Ezenzeleni. Perhaps you will find something there.

—No doubt, no doubt. Anything but what I most desire.

—Come and pray.

—There is no prayer left in me. I am dumb here inside. I have no words at all.

—Good night, my brother.

—Good night.

Msimangu watched him go up the little path. He looked very old. He himself turned and walked back to the Mission. There are times, no doubt, when God seems no more to be about the world.

12

I HAVE no doubt it is fear in the land. For what can men do when so many have grown lawless? Who can enjoy the lovely land, who can enjoy the seventy years, and the sun that pours down on the earth, when there is fear in the heart? Who can walk quietly in the shadow of the jacarandas, when their beauty is grown to danger? Who can lie peacefully abed, while the darkness holds some secret? What lovers can lie sweetly under the stars, when menace grows with the measure of their seclusion?

There are voices crying what must be done, a hundred, a thousand voices. But what do they help if one seeks for counsel, for one cries this, and one cries that, and another cries something that is neither this nor that.

*   *   *   *   *

It's a crying scandal, ladies and gentlemen, that we get so few police. This suburb pays more in taxes than most of the suburbs of Johannesburg, and what do we get for it? A third-class police station, with one man on the beat, and one at the telephone. This is the second outrage of its kind in six months, and we must demand more protection.

(Applause).

Mr. McLaren, will you read us your resolution?

*   *   *   *   *

I say we shall always have native crime to fear until the native people of this country have worthy purposes to inspire them and worthy goals to work for. For it is only because they see neither purpose nor goal that they turn to drink and crime and prostitution. Which do we prefer, a law-abiding, industrious and purposeful native people, or a lawless, idle and purposeless people? The truth is that we do not know, for we fear them both. And so long as we vacillate, so long will we pay dearly for the dubious pleasure of not having to make up our minds. And the answer does not lie, except temporarily, in more police and more protection.   *(Applause).*

*   *   *   *   *

—And you think, Mr. de Villiers, that increased schooling facilities would cause a decrease in juvenile delinquency amongst native children?

—I am sure of it, Mr. Chairman.

—Have you the figures for the percentage of children at school, Mr. de Villiers?

—In Johannesburg, Mr. Chairman, not more than four out of ten are at school. But of those four not even one will reach his sixth standard. Six are being educated in the streets.

—May I ask Mr. de Villiers a question, Mr. Chairman?

—By all means, Mr. Scott.

—Who do you think should pay for this schooling, Mr. de Villiers?

—We should pay for it. If we wait till native parents can pay for it, we will pay more heavily in other ways.

—Don't you think, Mr. de Villiers, that more schooling simply means cleverer criminals?

—I am sure that is not true.

—Let me give you a case. I had a boy working for me who had passed Standard Six. Perfect gentleman, bow-tie, hat to the side, and the latest socks. I treated him well and paid him well. Now do you know, Mr. de Villiers, that this self-same scoundrel . . . . .

*   *   *   *   *

—They should enforce the pass laws, Jackson.

—But I tell you the pass laws don't work.

—They'd work if they were enforced.

—But I tell you they're unenforceable. Do you know that we send one hundred thousand natives every year to prison, where they mix with real criminals?

—That's not quite true, Jackson. I know they're trying road camps, and farm-labour, and several other things.

—Well, perhaps you know. But it doesn't alter my argument at all, that the pass laws are unenforceable. You can send 'em to road-camps or farms or anywhere else you damn well please, but you can't tell me it's a healthy thing even to convict one hundred thousand people.

—What would you do then?

—Well now you're asking. I don't know what I'd do. But I just know the pass laws don't work.

*   *   *   *   *

—We went to the Zoo Lake, my dear. But it's quite impossible. I really don't see why they can't have separate days for natives.

—I just don't go there any more on a Sunday, my dear. We take John and Penelope on some other day. But I like to be fair. Where can these poor creatures go?

—Why can't they make recreation places for them?

—When they wanted to make a recreation centre on part of the Hillside Golf Course, there was such a fuss that they had to drop it.

—But my dear, it would have been impossible. The noise would have been incredible.

—So they stay on the pavements and hang about the corners. And believe me, the noise is just as incredible there too. But that needn't worry you where you live.

—Don't be catty, my dear. Why can't they put

up big recreation centres somewhere, and let them all go free on the buses?

—Where, for example?

—You do persist, my dear. Why not in the City?

—And how long will it take them to get there? And how long to get back? How many hours do you give your servants off on a Sunday?

—Oh, it's too hot to argue. Get your racquet, my dear, they're calling us. Look, it's Mrs. Harvey and Thelma. You've got to play like a demon, do you hear?

*   *   *   *   *

And some cry for the cutting up of South Africa without delay into separate areas, where white can live without black, and black without white, where black can farm their own land and mine their own minerals and administer their own laws. And others cry away with the compound system, that brings men to the towns without their wives and children, and breaks up the tribe and the house and the man, and they ask for the establishment of villages for the labourers in mines and industry.

And the churches cry too. The English-speaking churches cry for more education, and more opportunity, and for a removal of the restrictions on native labour and enterprise. And the Afrikaans-speaking churches want to see the native people given opportunity to develop along their own lines, and remind their own people that the decay of family religion, where the servants took part in family devotions, has contributed in part to the moral decay of the native people. But there is to be no equality in church or state.

*   *   *   *   *

Yes, there are a hundred, and a thousand voices crying. But what does one do, when one cries this thing, and one cries another? Who knows how we shall fashion a land of peace where black outnumbers white so greatly? Some say that the earth has bounty enough for all, and that more for one does not mean less for another, that the advance of one does not mean the decline of another. They say that poor-paid labour means a poor nation, and that better-paid labour means greater markets and greater scope for industry and manufacture. And others say that this is a danger, for better-paid labour will not only buy more but will also read more, think more, ask more, and will not be content to be forever voiceless and inferior.

Who knows how we shall fashion such a land? For we fear not only the loss of our possessions, but the loss of our superiority and the loss of our whiteness. Some say it is true that crime is bad, but would this not be worse? Is it not better to hold what we have, and to pay the price of it with fear? And others say, can such fear be endured? For is it not this fear that drives men to ponder these things at all?

*   *   *   *   *

We do not know, we do not know. We shall live
from day to day, and put more locks on the doors,
and get a fine fierce dog when the fine fierce bitch
next door has pups, and hold on to our handbags
more tenaciously; and the beauty of the trees by
night, and the raptures of lovers under the stars,
these things we shall forego. We shall forego the
coming home drunken through the midnight
streets, and the evening walk over the star-lit yield.
We shall be careful, and knock this off our lives, and
knock that off our lives, and hedge ourselves about
with safety and precaution. And our lives will
shrink, but they shall be the lives of superior beings;
and we shall live with fear, but at least it will not be a
fear of the unknown. And the conscience shall be
thrust down; the light of life shall not be extin-
guished, but be put under a bushel, to be preserved
for a generation that will live by it again, in some
day not yet come; and how it will come, and when it
will come, we shall not think about at all.

*   *   *   *   *

They are holding a meeting in Parkwold tonight,
as they held one last night in Turffontein, and will
hold one tomorrow night in Mayfair. And the people
will ask for more police, and for heavier sentences for
native housebreakers, and for the death penalty for
all who carry weapons when they break in. And
some will ask for a new native policy, that will show

the natives who is the master, and for a curb on the activities of Kafferboeties and Communists.

And the Left Club is holding a meeting too, on "A Longterm Policy for Native Crime," and has invited both European and non-European speakers to present a symposium. And the Cathedral Guild is holding a meeting too, and the subject is "The Real Causes of Native Crime." But there will be a gloom over it, for the speaker of the evening, Mr. Arthur Jarvis, has just been shot dead in his house at Parkwold.

*   *   *   *   *

Cry, the beloved country, for the unborn child that is the inheritor of our fear. Let him not love the earth too deeply. Let him not laugh too gladly when the water runs through his fingers, nor stand too silent when the setting sun makes red the veld with fire. Let him not be too moved when the birds of his land are singing, nor give too much of his heart to a mountain or a valley. For fear will rob him of all if he gives too much.

*   *   *   *   *

—Mr. Msimangu?

—Ah, it is Mrs. Ndlela, of End St.

—Mr. Msimangu, the police have been to me.

—The police?

—Yes, they want to know about the son of the old umfundisi. They are looking for him.

—For what, mother?

—They did not say, Mr. Msimangu.

—Is it bad, mother?

—It looks as if it were bad.

—And then, mother?

—I was frightened, umfundisi. So I gave them the address. Mrs. Mkize, 79 Twenty-third Avenue, Alexandra. And one said yes, this woman was known to deal in heavy matters.

—You gave them the address?

He stood silent in the door.

—Did I do wrong, umfundisi?

—You did no wrong, mother.

—I was afraid.

—It is the law, mother. We must uphold the law.

—I am glad, umfundisi.

He thanks the simple woman, and tells her to go well. He stands for a moment, then turns swiftly and goes to his room. He takes out an envelope from a drawer, and takes paper money from it. He looks at it ruefully, and then with decision puts it into his pocket, with decision takes down his hat. Then dressed, with indecision looks out of the window to the house of Mrs. Lithebe, and shakes his head. But he is too late, for as he opens his door, Kumalo stands before him.

—You are going out, my friend?

Msimangu is silent. I was going out, he says at last.

—But you said you would work in your room today.

And Msimangu would have said, can I not do as I

wish, but something prevented him. Come in, he said.

—I would not disturb you, my friend.

—Come in, said Msimangu, and he shut the door. My friend, I have just had a visit from Mrs. Ndlela, at the house we visited in End Street, here in Sophiatown.

Kumalo hears the earnest tones. There is news? he asks, but there is fear, not eagerness, in his voice.

—Only this, said Msimangu, that the police came to her house, looking for the boy. She gave them the address, Mrs. Mkize, at 79 Twenty-third Avenue in Alexandra.

—Why do they want the boy? asked Kumalo in a low and trembling voice.

—That we do not know. I was ready to go there when you came.

Kumalo looked at him out of sad and grateful eyes, so that the resentment of the other died out of him. You were going alone? the old man asked.

—I was going alone, yes. But now that I have told you, you may come also.

—How were you going, my friend? There are no buses.

—I was going by taxi. I have money.

—I too have money. No one must pay but me.

—It will take a great deal of money.

Kumalo opened his coat, and took out his purse eagerly. Here is my money, he said.

—We shall use it then. Come, let us look for a taxi.

*   *   *   *   *

—Mrs. Mkize!

She drew back, hostile.

—Have the police been here?

—They have been, not long since.

—And what did they want?

—They wanted the boy.

—And what did you say?

—I said it was a year since he left here.

—And where have they gone?

—To Shanty Town. She draws back again, remembering.

—To the address you did not know, he said coldly.

She looks at him sullenly. What could I do, she said. It was the police.

—No matter. What was the address?

—I did not know the address. Shanty Town, I told them. Some fire came into her. I told you I did not know the address, she said.

*   *   *   *   *

—Mrs. Hlatshwayo!

The pleasant-faced woman smiled at them, and drew aside for them to enter the hessian house.

—We shall not come in. Have the police been here?

—They were here, umfundisi.

—And what did they want?

—They wanted the boy, umfundisi.

—For what, mother?

—I do not know, umfundisi.

—And where have they gone?

—To the school, umfundisi.

—Tell me, he said privately, did it seem heavy?

—I could not say, umfundisi.

—Stay well, Mrs. Hlatshwayo.

—Go well, umfundisi.

*   *   *   *   *

—Good morning, my friend.

—Good morning, umfundisi, said the native assistant.

—Where is the young white man?

—He is in the town. It was now, now, that he went.

—Have the police been here?

—They have been here. It was now, now, that they left.

—What did they want?

—They wanted the boy, Absalom Kumalo, the son of the old man there in the taxi.

—Why did they want him?

—I do not know. I had other work, and went out while they came in with the white man.

—And you do not know what they wanted?

—I truly do not know, umfundisi.

Msimangu was silent. Did it seem heavy? he asked at last.

—I do not know. I really could not say.

—Was the young white man—well, disturbed?

—He was disturbed.

—How did you know?

The assistant laughed. I know him, he said.

—And where did they go?

—To Pimville, umfundisi. To the home of the girl.

—Now, now, you said.

—Now, now, indeed.

—We shall go then. Stay well. And tell the white man we came.

—Go well, umfundisi. I shall tell him.

   *   *   *   *   *

—My child!

—Umfundisi.

—Have the police been here?

—They have been here, now, now, they were here.

—And what did they want?

—They wanted Absalom, umfundisi.

—And what did you tell them?

—I told them I had not seen him since Saturday, umfundisi.

—And why did they want him? cried Kumalo in torment.

She drew back frightened. I do not know, she said.

—And why did you not ask? he cried.

The tears filled her eyes. I was afraid, she said.

—Did no one ask?

—The women were about. Maybe one of them asked.

—What women? said Msimangu. Show us the women.

So she showed them the women, but they too did not know.

—They would not tell me, said a woman.

Msimangu turned privately to her. Did it seem heavy? he asked.

—It seemed heavy, umfundisi. What is the trouble? she asked.

—We do not know.

—The world is full of trouble, she said.

He went to the taxi, and Kumalo followed him. And the girl ran after them, as one runs who is with child.

—They told me I must let them know if he comes.

Her eyes were full of trouble. What shall I do? she said.

—That is what you ought to do, said Msimangu. And you will let us know also. Wait, you must go to the Superintendent's office and ask him to telephone to the Mission House in Sophiatown. I shall write the number here for you. 49–3041.

—I shall do it, umfundisi.

—Tell me, did the police say where they would go?

—They did not say, umfundisi. But I heard them say, *die spoor loop dood*, the trail runs dead.

—Stay well, my child.

—Go well, umfundisi. She turned to say go well to the other, but he was already in the taxi, bowed over his stick.

* * * * *

—How much is your charge, my friend? asks Msimangu.

—Two pounds and ten shillings, umfundisi.

Kumalo feels with shaking hands for his purse.

—I should like to help you in this, says Msimangu. It would be my joy to help you. You are kind, says Kumalo trembling, but no one must pay but me. And he draws the notes from the dwindling store.

—You are trembling, my friend.

—I am cold, very cold.

Msimangu looks up at the cloudless sky, from which the sun of Africa is pouring down upon the earth. Come to my room, he says. We shall have a fire and make you warm again.

13

IT was a silent journey to Ezenzeleni, and though Msimangu tried to converse with his friend during the walk from the station to the place of the blind, the older man was little inclined for speech, and showed little interest in anything about him.

—What will you do while I am here? asked Misimangu.

—I should like to sit in one of these places that you told me of, and perhaps when you are finished you will show me round this Ezenzeleni.

—You shall do what you will.

—You must not be disappointed in me.

—I understand everything. There is no need to talk of it again.

So he introduced Kumalo to the European Superintendent, who called him Mr. Kumalo, which is not the custom. And Msimangu must have spoken privately to the Superintendent, for they did not worry him to come with them; instead the Superintendent led him to the place where the ground fell away, and told him they would call him when it was time for food.

For some hours he sat there in the sun, and whether it was the warmth of it, or the sight of the wide plain beneath stretching away to blue and distant mountains, or the mere passage of time, or the divine providence for the soul that is distressed, he could not say; but there was some rising of the spirit, some lifting of the fear.

Yes, it was true what Msimangu had said. Why fear the one thing in a great city where there were thousands upon thousands of people? His son had gone astray in the great city, where so many others had gone astray before him, and where many others would go astray after him, until there was found some great secret that as yet no man had discovered. But that he should kill a man, a white man! There was nothing that he could remember, nothing, nothing at all, that could make it probable.

His thoughts turned to the girl, and to the unborn babe that would be his grandchild. Pity that he a priest should have a grandchild born in such a fashion. Yet that could be repaired. If they were married, then he could try to rebuild what had been broken. Perhaps his son and the girl would go back with him to Ndotsheni, perhaps he and his wife could give to the child what they had failed to give to their own. Yet where had they failed? What had they done, or left undone, that their son had become a thief, moving like a vagabond from place to place, living with a girl who was herself no more than a child, father of a child who would have had no name? Yet, he comforted himself, that was Johannesburg. And yet again, and the fear smote him as grievously as ever, his son had left the girl and the unborn child, left the work that the young white man had got for him, and was vagabond again. And what did vagabonds do? Did they not live without law or custom, without faith or purpose, might they not then lift their hand against any other, any man who stood between them and the pitiful gain that they were seeking?

What broke in a man when he could bring himself to kill another? What broke when he could bring himself to thrust down the knife into the warm flesh, to bring down the axe on the living head, to cleave down between the seeing eyes, to shoot the gun that would drive death into the beating heart?

With a shudder he turned from contemplation of so terrible a thing. Yet the contemplation of it reassured him. For there was nothing, nothing in all the years at Ndotsheni, nothing in all the years of the boyhood of his son, that could make it possible for him to do so terrible a deed. Yes, Msimangu was right. It was the suspense, the not-knowing, that made him fear this one thing, in a great city where there were thousands upon thousands of people.

He turned with relief to the thought of rebuilding, to the home that they would fashion, he and his wife, in the evening of their lives, for Gertrude and her son, and for his son and the girl and the child. After seeing Johannesburg he would return with a deeper understanding to Ndotsheni. Yes, and with a greater humility, for had his own sister not been a prostitute? And his son a thief? And might not he himself be grandfather to a child that would have no name? This he thought without bitterness, though with pain. One could go back knowing better the things that one fought against, knowing better the kind of thing that one must build. He would go back with a new and quickened interest in the school, not as a place where children learned to read and write and count only, but as a place where they must be prepared for life in any place to which they might go. Oh for education for his people, for schools up and down the land, where something might be built that would serve them when they went away to the towns, something that would take the place of the tribal law and custom. For a moment he was caught up in a vision, as man so often is when he sits in a place of ashes and destruction.

Yes—it was true, then. He had admitted it to himself. The tribe was broken, and would be mended no more. He bowed his head. It was as though a man borne upward into the air felt suddenly that the wings of miracle dropped away from him, so that he looked down upon the earth, sick with fear and apprehension. The tribe was broken, and would be mended no more. The tribe that had nurtured him, and his father and his father's father, was broken. For the men were away, and the young men and the girls were away, and the maize hardly reached to the height of a man.

—There is food for us, my brother.

—Already?

—You have been here a long time.

—I did not know it.

—And what have you found?

—Nothing.

—Nothing?

—No, nothing. Only more fear and more pain. There is nothing in the world but fear and pain.

—My brother . . . . .

—What is it?

—I hesitate to speak to you.

—You have a right to speak. More right than any.

—Then I say that it is time to turn. This is madness, that is bad enough. But it is also sin, which is worse. I speak to you as a priest.

Kumalo bowed his head. You are right, father, he said. I must sit here no longer.

*   *   *   *   *

It was a wonderful place, this Ezenzeleni. For here the blind, that dragged out their days in a world they could not see, here they had eyes given to them. Here they made things that he for all his sight could never make. Baskets stout and strong, in osiers of different colours, and these osiers ran through one another by some magic that he did not understand, coming together in patterns, the red with the red, the blue with the blue, under the seeing and sightless hands. He talked with the people, and the blind eyes glowed with something that could only have been fire in the soul. It was white men who did this work of mercy, and some of them spoke English and some spoke Afrikaans. Yes, those who spoke English and those who spoke Afrikaans came together to open the eyes of black men that were blind.

His friend Msimangu would preach this afternoon, in the chapel that he had seen. But because they were not all of one church here, there was no altar with a cross upon it, but the cross was in the wall itself, two open clefts that had been left open and not filled in by the bricks. And Msimangu would not wear the vestments that he would wear at Sophiatown; those he would wear early the next morning, when he ministered to his own people.

*   *   *   *   *

Msimangu opened the book, and read to them first from the book. And Kumalo had not known that his friend had such a voice. For the voice was of gold, and the voice had love for the words it was reading. The voice shook and beat and trembled, not as the voice of an old man shakes and beats and trembles, nor as a leaf shakes and beats and trembles, but as a deep bell when it is struck. For it was not only a voice of gold, but it was the voice of a man whose heart was golden, reading from a book of golden words. And the people were silent, and Kumalo was silent, for when are three such things found in one place together?

I the Lord have called thee in righteousness
and will hold thine hand and will keep thee
and give thee for a covenant of the people
for a light of the Gentiles

To open the blind eyes
to bring out the prisoners from the prison
And them that sit in darkness
out of the prison house.

And the voice rose, and the Zulu tongue was
lifted and transfigured, and the man too was lifted,
as is one who comes to something that is greater
than any of us. And the people were silent, for were
they not the people of the blind eyes? And Kumalo
was silent, knowing the blind man for whom Msimangu was reading these words:

And I will bring the blind by a way they knew not
I will lead them in paths that they have not known.
I will make darkness light before them
and crooked things straight.
These things I will do unto them
and not forsake them.

*   *   *   *   *

Yes, he speaks to me, there is no doubt of it. He
says we are not forsaken. For while I wonder for
what we live and struggle and die, for while I wonder what keeps us living and struggling, men are
sent to minister to the blind, white men are sent to
minister to the black blind. Who gives, at this one
hour, a friend to make darkness light before me?
Who gives, at this one hour, wisdom to one so
young, for the comfort of one so old? Who gives to
me compassion for a girl my son has left?

Yes, he speaks to me, in such quiet and such simple words. We are grateful for the saints, he says, who lift up the heart in the days of our distress. Would we do less? For do we less, there are no saints to lift up any heart. If Christ be Christ he says, true Lord of Heaven, true Lord of Men, what is there that we would not do no matter what our suffering may be?

I hear you, my brother. There is no word I do not hear.

He is finishing. I can hear it in his voice. One can know that what is said, is said, is rounded, finished, it is perfection. He opens the book and reads again. He reads to me:

> *Hast thou not known, hast thou not heard*
> *that the everlasting God, the Lord,*
> *the Creator of the ends of the earth*
> *fainteth not, neither is weary?*

And the voice rises again, and the Zulu tongue is lifted and transfigured, and the man too is lifted . . . . .

> *Even the youths shall faint and be weary*
> *and the young men shall utterly fall.*
> *But they that wait upon the Lord*
> *shall renew their strength,*
> *they shall mount up with wings as eagles,*
> *they shall run and not be weary*
> *and they shall walk and not faint.*

*   *   *   *   *

The people sigh, and Kumalo sighs, as though this is a great word that has been spoken. And indeed this Msimangu is known as a preacher. It is good for the Government, they say in Johannesburg, that Msimangu preaches of a world not made by hands, for he touches people at the hearts, and sends them marching to heaven instead of to Pretoria. And there are white people who marvel and say, what words to come from the son of a barbarian people, who not long since plundered and slaughtered, in thousands and tens of thousands, under the most terrible chief of all.

Yet he is despised by some, for this golden voice that could raise a nation, speaks always thus. For this place of suffering, from which men might escape if some such voice could bind them all together, is for him no continuing city. They say he preaches of a world not made by hands, while in the streets about him men suffer and struggle and die. They ask what folly it is that can so seize upon a man, what folly is it that seizes upon so many of their people, making the hungry patient, the suffering content, the dying at peace? And how fools listen to him, silent, enrapt, sighing when he is done, feeding their empty bellies on his empty words.

Kumalo goes to him.

—Brother, I am recovered.

Msimangu's face lights up, but he talks humbly, there is no pride or false constraint.

—I have tried every way to touch you, he says, but I could not come near. So give thanks and be satisfied.

14

ON the day of their return from Ezenzeleni, Kumalo ate his midday meal at the Mission, and returned to Mrs. Lithebe's to play with Gertrude's
son. There was great bargaining going on, for Mrs.
Lithebe had found a buyer for Gertrude's table and
chairs, and for the pots and pans. Everything was
sold for three pounds, which was not a bad sum for
a table that was badly marked and discoloured, with
what he did not ask. And the chairs too were weak,
so that one had to sit carefully upon them. Indeed
the price was paid for the pots and pans, which were
of the stuff called aluminum. Now the black people
do not buy such pots and pans, but his sister said
that they were the gift of a friend, and into that too
he did not enquire.

With the money she intended to buy some shoes,
and a coat against the rain that was now beginning
to fall; and this he approved, for her old coat and
shoes went ill with the red dress and the white turban that he had bought for her.

When the last thing had been loaded, and the
money paid, and the lorry had gone, he would have

played with the small boy, but he saw, with the fear catching at him suddenly with a physical pain, Msimangu and the young white man walking up the street towards the house. With the habit born of experience, he forced himself to go to the gate, and noted with dread their set faces and the low tones in which they spoke.

—Good afternoon, umfundisi. Is there a place where we can talk? asked the young man.

—Come to my room, he said, hardly trusting to his voice.

In the room he shut the door, and stood not looking at them.

—I have heard what you fear, said the young man. It is true.

And Kumalo stood bowed, and could not look at them. He sat down in his chair and fixed his eyes upon the floor.

Well, what does one say now? Does one put an arm about the shoulders, touch a hand maybe? As though they did not not know, Msimangu and the young man talked in low voices, as one talks in a room where someone is dead.

The young man shrugged his shoulders. This will be bad for the reformatory, he said more loudly, even indifferently.

And Kumalo nodded his head, not once, nor twice, but three or four times, as though he too would say, Yes, it will be bad for the reformatory.

—Yes, said the young man, it will be bad for us. They will say we let him out too soon. Of course, he said, there is one thing. The other two were not reformatory boys. But it was he who fired the shot.

—My friend, said Msimangu, in as ordinary a voice as he could find, one of the two others is the son of your brother.

And so Kumalo nodded his head again, one, two, three, four times. And when that was finished, he began again, as though he too was saying, one of the two others is the son of my brother.

Then he stood up, and looked round the room, and they watched him. He took his coat from a nail, and put it on, and he put his hat on his head, and took his stick in his hand. And so dressed he turned to them, and nodded to them again. But this time they did not know what he said.

—You are going out? my friend.

—Do you wish to come to the prison, umfundisi? I have arranged it for you.

And Kumalo nodded. He turned and looked round the room again, and found that his coat was already on him, and his hat; he touched both coat and hat, and looked down at the stick that was in his hand.

—My brother first, he said, if you will show me the way only.

—I shall show you the way, my friend.

—And I shall wait at the Mission, said the young man.

As Msimangu put his hand to the door, Kumalo halted him. I shall walk slowly up the street, he said. You must tell them—he pointed with his hand.

—I shall tell them, my friend.

So he told them, and having told them, closed the front door on the wailing of the women, for such is their custom. Slowly he followed the bent figure up the street, saw him nodding as he walked, saw the people turning. Would age now swiftly overtake him? Would this terrible nodding last now for all his days, so that men said aloud in his presence, it is nothing, he is old and does nothing but forget? And would he nod as though he too were saying, Yes, it is nothing, I am old and do nothing but forget? But who would know that he said, I do nothing but remember?

Msimangu caught him up at the top of the hill, and took his arm, and it was like walking with a child or with one that was sick. So they came to the shop. And at the shop Kumalo turned, and closed his eyes, and his lips were moving. Then he opened his eyes and turned to Msimangu.

—Do not come further, he said. It is I who must do this.

And then he went into the shop.

Yes, the bull voice was there, loud and confident. His brother John was sitting there on a chair talking to two other men, sitting there like a chief. His brother he did not recognize, for the light from the street was on the back of the visitor.

—Good afternoon, my brother.

—Good afternoon, sir.

—Good afternoon, my own brother, son of our mother.

—Ah my brother, it is you. Well, well, I am glad to see you. Will you not come and join us?

Kumalo looked at the visitors. I am sorry, he said, but I come again on business, urgent business.

—I am sure my friends will excuse us. Excuse us, my friends.

So they all said stay well, and go well, and the two men left them.

—Well, well, I am glad to see you, my brother. And your business, how does it progress? Have you found the prodigal? You will see I have not forgotten my early teaching altogether.

And he laughed at that, a great bull laugh. But we must have tea, he said, and he went to the door and called into the place behind.

—It is still the same woman, he said. You see, I also have my ideas of—how do you say it in English? And he laughed his great laugh again, for he was only playing with his brother. Fidelity, that was the word. A good word, I shall not easily forget it. He is a clever man, our Mr. Msimangu. And now the prodigal, have you found him?

—He is found, my brother. But not as he was found in the early teaching. He is in prison, arrested for the murder of a white man.

—Murder? The man does not jest now. One does not jest about murder. Still less about the murder of a white man.

—Yes, murder. He broke into a house in a place that they call Parkwold, and killed the white man who would have prevented him.

—What? I remember! Only a day or two since? On Tuesday?

—Yes.

—Yes, I remember.

Yes, he remembers. He remembers too that his own son and his brother's son are companions. The veins stand out on the bull neck, and the sweat forms on the brow. Have no doubt it is fear in the eyes. He wipes his brow with a cloth. There are many questions he could ask before he need come at it. All he says is, yes, indeed, I do remember. His brother is filled with compassion for him. He will try gently to bring it to him.

—I am sorry, my brother.

What does one say? Does one say, of course you are sorry? Does one say, of course, it is your son? How can one say it, when one knows what it means? Keep silent then, but the eyes are upon one. One knows what they mean.

—You mean . . . .? he asked.

—Yes. He was there also.

John Kumalo whispers *Tixo, Tixo*. And again, *Tixo, Tixo*. Kumalo comes to him and puts his hand on his shoulders.

—There are many things I could say, he said.

—There are many things you could say.

—But I do not say them. I say only that I know what you suffer.

—Indeed, who could know better?

—Yes, that is one of the things I could say. There is a young white man at the Mission House, and he is waiting to take me now to the prison. Perhaps he would take you also.

—Let me get my coat and hat, my brother.

They do not wait for the tea, but set out along the

street to the Mission House. Msimangu, watching anxiously for their return sees them coming. The old man walks now more firmly, it is the other who seems bowed and broken.

Father Vincent, the rosy-cheeked priest from England, takes Kumalo's hand in both his own. Anything, he says, anything. You have only to ask. I shall do anything.

*   *   *   *   *

They pass through the great gate in the grim high wall. The young man talks for them, and it is arranged. John Kumalo is taken to one room, and the young man goes with Stephen Kumalo to another. There the son is brought to them.

They shake hands, indeed the old man takes his son's hand in both his own, and the hot tears fall fast upon them. The boy stands unhappy, there is no gladness in his eyes. He twists his head from side to side, as though the loose clothing is too tight for him.

—My child, my child.

—Yes, my father.

—At last I have found you.

—Yes, my father.

—And it is too late.

To this the boy makes no answer. As though he may find some hope in this silence, the father presses him. Is it not too late? he asks. But there is no answer. Persistently, almost eagerly, is it not too late? he asks. The boy turns his head from side to side, he meets the eyes of the young white man, and his own retreat swiftly. My father, it is what my father says, he answers.

—I have searched in every place for you.

To that also no answer. The old man loosens his hands, and his son's hand slips from them lifelessly. There is a barrier here, a wall, something that cuts off one from the other.

—Why did you do this terrible thing, my child?

The young white man stirs watchfully, the white warder makes no sign, perhaps he does not know this tongue. There is a moisture in the boy's eyes, he turns his head from side to side, and makes no answer.

—Answer me, my child.

—I do not know, he says.

—Why did you carry a revolver?

The white warder stirs too, for the word in Zulu is like the word in English and in Afrikaans. The boy too shows a sign of life.

—For safety, he says. This Johannesburg is a dangerous place. A man never knows when he will be attacked.

—But why take it to this house?

And this again cannot be answered.

—Have they got it, my child?

—Yes, my father.

—They have no doubt it was you?

—I told them, my father.

—What did you tell them?

—I told them I was frightened when the white man came. So I shot him. I did not mean to kill him.

—And your cousin. And the other?

—Yes, I told them. They came with me, but it was I who shot the white man.

—Did you go there to steal?

And this again cannot be answered.

—You were at the reformatory, my child?

The boy looked at his boot, and pushed it forward along the ground. I was there, he said.

—Did they treat you well?

Again there is a moisture in the eyes, again he turns his head from side to side, drops his eyes again to the boot pushing forward and backward on the ground. They treated me well, he said.

—And this is your repayment, my child?

And this again cannot be answered. The young white man comes over, for he knows that this does nothing, goes nowhere. Perhaps he does not like to see these two torturing each other.

—Well, Absalom?

—Sir?

—Why did you leave the work that I got for you?

And you too, young man, can get no answer. There are no answers to these things.

—Why did you leave it, Absalom?

There are no answers to these things.

—And your girl. The one we let you go to, the girl you worried over, so that we took pity on you.

And again the tears in the eyes. Who knows if he weeps for the girl he has deserted? Who knows if he weeps for a promise broken? Who knows if he weeps for another self, that would work for a woman, pay his taxes, save his money, keep the laws, love his children, another self that has always been defeated? Or does he weep for himself alone, to be let be, to be let alone, to be free of the merciless rain of questions, why, why, why, when he knows not why. They do not speak with him, they do not jest with him, they do not sit and let him be, but they ask, ask, ask, why, why, why,—his father, the white man, the prison officers, the police, the magistrates,—why, why, why.

The young white man shrugs his shoulders, smiles indifferently. But he is not indifferent, there is a mark of pain between his eyes.

—So the world goes, he says.

—Answer me one thing, my child. Will you answer me?

—I can answer, father.

—You wrote nothing, sent no message. You went with bad companions. You stole and broke in and—yes, you did these things. But why?

The boy seizes upon the word that is given him. It was bad companions, he said.

—I need not tell you that is no answer, said Kumalo. But he knows he will get no other this way. Yes, I see, he said, bad companions. Yes, I understand. But for you, yourself, what made you yourself do it?

How they torture one another. And the boy, tortured, shows again a sign of life.

—It was the devil, he said.

Oh boy, can you not say you fought the devil, wrestled with the devil, struggled with him night and day, till the sweat poured from you and no strength was left? Can you not say that you wept for your sins, and vowed to make amends, and stood upright, and stumbled, and fell again? It would be some comfort for this tortured man, who asks you, desperately, why did you not struggle against him?

And the boy looks down at his feet again, and says, I do not know.

The old man is exhausted, the boy is exhausted, and the time is nearly over. The young white man comes to them again. Does he still wish to marry the girl? he asks Kumalo.

—Do you wish to marry this girl, my son?

—Yes, my father.

—I shall see what I can do, says the young man. I think it is time for us to go.

—May we come again?

—Yes, you may come again. We shall ask the hours at the gate.

—Stay well, my child.

—Go well, my father.

—My child, I think you may write letters here. But do not write to your mother till I see you again. I must first write to her.

—It is good, my father.

They go, and outside the gate they meet John Kumalo. He is feeling better, the big bull man. Well, well, he says, we must go at once and see a lawyer.

—A lawyer, my brother. For what should we spend such money? The story is plain, there cannot be doubt about it.

—What is the story? asks John Kumalo.

—The story? These three lads went to a house

that they thought was empty. They struck down the servant. The white man heard a noise and he came to see. And then . . . and then . . . my son . . . mine, not yours . . . shot at him. He was afraid, he says.

—Well, well, says John Kumalo, that is a story. He seems reassured. Well, well, he says, that is a story. And he told you this in front of the others?

—Why not, if it is the truth?

John Kumalo seems reassured. Perhaps you do not need a lawyer, he said. If he shot the white man, there is perhaps nothing more to be said.

—Will you have a lawyer then?

John Kumalo smiles at his brother. Perhaps I shall need a lawyer, he says. For one thing, a lawyer can talk to my son in private.

He seems to think, then he says to his brother, You see, my brother, there is no proof that my son or this other young man was there at all.

Yes, John Kumalo smiles at that, he seems quite recovered.

—Not there at all? But my son—

—Yes, yes, John Kumalo interrupts him, and smiles at him. Who will believe your son? he asks.

He says it with meaning, with cruel and pitiless meaning. Kumalo stands bereft, and the young white man climbs into the car. Kumalo looks to him for guidance, but the young man shrugs his shoulders. Do what you will, he says indifferently. It is not my work to get lawyers. But if you wish to go back to Sophiatown, I shall take you.

Kumalo, made still more nervous by this indifference, stands outside irresolute. His irresolution seems to anger the young white man, who leans out of the window and speaks loudly.

—It is not my work to get lawyers, he says. It is my work to reform, to help, to uplift.

With his hand he makes an angry gesture of uplifting, and then draws back his head into the car and makes as if to start. But he changes his plan and leans out again.

—It is a wonderful work, he says, a wonderful work, a noble work.

He withdraws again, then leans out again and talks to Kumalo.

—You must not think a parson's work is nobler, he says.

Perhaps he is speaking too loudly, for he lowers his voice and speaks through tight and angry lips.

—You save souls, he says, as though it is a grim jest to save souls. But I save souls also. You see people come into the world and you see them go out. And so do I. I saw this Absalom born into a new world and now I shall see him go out.

He looks at Kumalo fiercely. We shall see him go out, he says. He draws back again, and grips the wheel as though he would break it. Are you coming to Sophiatown? he asks.

But Kumalo shakes his head, for how shall he climb into the car with this stranger? The young man looks at John Kumalo and he puts out his head again and says to him, you are a clever man, he says, but thank God you are not my brother. He starts the car with a great noise, and goes off with a great sound of sliding wheels, still speaking angrily to himself.

Kumalo looks at his brother, but his brother does not look at him. Indeed he walks away. Wearily, wearily, he goes from the great gate in the wall to the street. *Tixo*, he says, *Tixo*, forsake me not. Father Vincent's words come back to him, anything, anything, he said, you have only to ask. Then to Father Vincent he will go.

15

KUMALO returned to Mrs. Lithebe's tired and dispirited. The two women were silent, and he had no desire to speak to them, and none to play with his small nephew. He withdrew into his room, and sat silent there, waiting till he could summon strength enough to go to the Mission House. But while he sat, there was a knock at his door, and Mrs. Lithebe stood there with the young white man. Fresh from the pain of their encounter, Kumalo shrank from him; and at that sign, the young man frowned, and spoke to Mrs. Lithebe in Sesuto, so that she withdrew.

Kumalo stood up, an old bowed man. He sought for humble and pleading words, but none came to him. And because he could not look at the young man, he fixed his eyes on the floor.

—Umfundisi.

—Sir?

The young man looked angrier than ever. I am sorry, umfundisi, that I spoke such angry words, he said. I have come to speak to you about this matter of a lawyer.

—Sir?

Indeed it was hard to speak to a man who stood thus before one. Umfundisi, do you wish me to speak to you?

Kumalo struggled within himself. For it is thus with a black man, who has learned to be humble and who yet desires to be something that is himself.

—Sir, he said again.

—Umfundisi, said the young man patiently, I know how it is. Will you not sit down?

So Kumalo sat down, and the young man, still frowning angrily, stood and talked to him.

—I spoke like that because I was grieved and because I try to give myself to my work. And when my work goes wrong, I hurt myself and I hurt others also. But then I grow ashamed, and that is why I am here.

And then because Kumalo was still silent, he said, do you understand?

And Kumalo said, yes, I understand. He turned his face so that the young man could see that the hurt was gone out of it. I understand completely, he said.

The young man stopped frowning. About this lawyer, he said. I think you must have a lawyer. Not because the truth must not be told, but because I do not trust your brother. You can see what is in his mind. His plan is to deny that his son and the third man were with your son. Now you and I do not know whether that will make matters worse or not, but a lawyer would know. And another thing also, Absalom says that he fired the revolver because he was afraid, with no intention of killing the white man. It needs a lawyer to make the court believe that that is true.

—Yes, I see that.

—Do you know of any lawyer, of your Church maybe?

—No, sir, I do not. But it was my plan to go to see Father Vincent at the Mission House, when I had rested for a while.

—Are you rested now?

—Your visit has put a fresh heart into me, sir. I felt. . . .

—Yes, I know.

The young man frowned and said, as if to himself, it is my great fault. Shall we go then?

So they walked to the Mission House, and were shown into Father Vincent's room, and there they talked for a long time with the rosy-cheeked priest from England.

—I think I could get a good man to take the case, said Father Vincent. I think we are all agreed that it is to be the truth and nothing but the truth, and that the defense will be that the shot was fired in fear and not to kill. Our lawyer will tell us what to do about this other matter, the possibility, my friend, that your nephew and the other young man will deny that they were there. For it appears that it is only your son who states that they were there. For us it is to be the truth, and nothing but the truth, and indeed, the man I am thinking of would not otherwise take the case. I shall see him as soon as possible.

—And what about the marriage? asked the young man.

—I shall ask him about that also. I do not know if it can be arranged, but I should gladly marry them if it can be.

So they rose to separate, and Father Vincent put his hand on the old man's arm. Be of good courage, he said. Whatever happens, your son will be severely punished, but if his defence is accepted, it will not be extreme punishment. And while there is life, there is hope for amendment of life.

—That is now always in my mind, said Kumalo. But my hope is little.

—Stay here and speak with me, said Father Vincent.

—And I must go, said the young white man. But umfundisi, I am ready to help if my help is needed.

When the young man had gone, Kumalo and the English priest sat down, and Kumalo said to the other, you can understand that this has been a sorrowful journey.

—I understand that, my friend.

—At first it was a search. I was anxious at first, but as the search went on, step by step, so did the anxiety turn to fear, and this fear grew deeper step by step. It was at Alexandra that I first grew afraid, but it was here in your House, when we heard of the murder, that my fear grew into something too great to be borne.

The old man paused and stared at the floor, remembering, indeed quite lost in remembering. He stared at it a long time and then he said, Msimangu said to me, why fear this one thing in a city where there are thousands upon thousands of people?

—That comforted me, he said.

And the way in which he said, that comforted me, was to Father Vincent so unendurable, that he sat there rigid, almost without breathing, hoping that this would soon be finished.

—That comforted me, said Kumalo, yet it did not comfort me. And even now I can hardly believe that this thing, which happens one time in a thousand, has happened to me. Why, sometimes, for a moment or two, I can even believe that it has not happened, that I shall wake and find it has not happened. But it is only for a moment or two.

—To think, said Kumalo, that my wife and I lived out our lives in innocence, there in Ndotsheni, not knowing that this thing was coming, step by step.

—Why, he said, if one could only have been told, this step is taken, and this step is about to be taken. If only one could have been told that.

—But we were not told, continued Kumalo. Now we can see, but we could not see then. And yet others saw it. It was revealed to others to whom it did not matter. They saw it, step by step. They said, this is Johannesburg, this is a boy going wrong, as other boys have gone wrong in Johannesburg. But to us, for whom it was life and death, it was not revealed.

Father Vincent put his hand over his eyes, to hide them from the light, to hide them from the sight of the man who was speaking. He would himself have spoken, to break the painful spell that was being woven about him, but something told him to leave it. What was more, he had no words to say.

—There is a man sleeping in the grass, said Kumalo. And over him is gathering the greatest storm of all his days. Such lightning and thunder will come there as have never been seen before, bringing death and destruction. People hurry home past him, to places safe from danger. And whether they do not see him there in the grass, or whether they fear to halt even a moment, but they do not wake him, they let him be.

After that Kumalo seemed to have done with speaking, and they were silent a long time. Father Vincent tried a dozen sentences, but none seemed fitting. But he did say, my friend, and although he said nothing more, he hoped that Kumalo would take it as a signal that other words would follow, and himself say nothing more.

So he said again, my friend.

—Father?

—My friend, your anxiety turned to fear, and your fear turned to sorrow. But sorrow is better than fear. For fear impoverishes always, while sorrow may enrich.

Kumalo looked at him, with an intensity of gaze that was strange in so humble a man, and hard to encounter.

—I do not know that I am enriched, he said.

—Sorrow is better than fear, said Father Vincent doggedly. Fear is a journey, a terrible journey, but sorrow is at least an arriving.

—And where have I arrived? asked Kumalo.

—When the storm threatens, a man is afraid for his house, said Father Vincent in that symbolic language that is like the Zulu tongue. But when the house is destroyed, there is something to do. About a storm he can do nothing, but he can rebuild a house.

—At my age? asked Kumalo. Look what has happened to the house that I built when I was young and strong. What kind of house shall I build now?

—No one can comprehend the ways of God, said Father Vincent desperately.

Kumalo looked at him, not bitterly or accusingly or reproachfully.

—It seems that God has turned from me, he said.

—That may seem to happen, said Father Vincent. But it does not happen, never, never, does it happen.

—I am glad to hear you, said Kumalo humbly.

—We spoke of amendment of life, said the white priest. Of the amendment of your son's life. And because you are a priest, this must matter to you more than all else, more even than your suffering and your wife's suffering.

—That is true. Yet I cannot see how such a life can be amended.

—You cannot doubt that. You are a Christian. There was a thief upon the cross.

—My son was not a thief, said Kumalo harshly. There was a white man, a good man, devoted to his wife and children. And worst of all—devoted to our people. And this wife, these children, they are bereaved because of my son. I cannot suppose it to be less than the greatest evil I have known.

—A man may repent him of any evil.

—He will repent, said Kumalo bitterly. If I say to him, do you repent, he will say, it is as my father says. If I say to him, was this not evil, he will say, it is evil. But if I speak otherwise, putting no words in his mouth, if I say, what will you do now, he will say, I do not know, or he will say, it is as my father says.

Kumalo's voice rose as though some anguish compelled him.

—He is a stranger, he said, I cannot touch him, I cannot reach him. I see no shame in him, no pity for those he has hurt. Tears come out of his eyes, but it seems that he weeps only for himself, not for his wickedness, but for his danger.

The man cried out, can a person lose all sense of evil? A boy, brought up as he was brought up? I see only his pity for himself, he who has made two children fatherless. I tell you, that whosoever offends one of these little ones, it were better. . . .

—Stop, cried Father Vincent. You are beside yourself. Go and pray, go and rest. And do not judge your son too quickly. He too is shocked into silence, maybe. That is why he says to you, it is as my father wishes, and yes that is so, and I do not know.

Kumalo stood up. I trust that is so, he said, but I have no hope any more. What did you say I must do? Yes, pray and rest.

There was no mockery in his voice, and Father Vincent knew that it was not in this man's nature to speak mockingly. But so mocking were the words that the white priest caught him by the arm, and said to him urgently, sit down, I must speak to you as a priest.

When Kumalo had sat down, Father Vincent said to him, yes, I said pray and rest. Even if it is only words that you pray, and even if your resting is only a lying on a bed. And do not pray for yourself, and do not pray to understand the ways of God. For they are secret. Who knows what life is, for life is a secret. And why you have compassion for a girl, when you yourself find no compassion, that is a secret. And why you go on, when it would seem better to die, that is a secret. Do not pray and think about these things now, there will be other times. Pray for Gertrude, and for her child, and for the girl that is to be your son's wife, and for the child that will be your grandchild. Pray for your wife and all at Ndotsheni. Pray for the woman and the children that are bereaved. Pray for the soul of him who was killed. Pray for us at the Mission House, and for those at Ezenzeleni, who try to rebuild in a place of destruction. Pray for your own rebuilding. Pray for all white people, those who do justice, and those who would do justice if they were not afraid. And do not fear to pray for your son, and for his amendment.

—I hear you, said Kumalo humbly.

—And give thanks where you can give thanks. For nothing is better. Is there not your wife, and Mrs. Lithebe, and Msimangu, and this young white man at the reformatory? Now, for your son and his amendment, you will leave this to me and

Msimangu; for you are too distraught to see God's will. And now my son, go and pray, go and rest.

He helped the old man to his feet, and gave him his hat. And when Kumalo would have thanked him, he said, we do what is in us, and why it is in us, that is also a secret. It is Christ in us, crying that men may be succoured and forgiven, even when He Himself is forsaken.

He led the old man to the door of the Mission and there parted from him.

—I shall pray for you, he said, night and day. That I shall do and anything more that you ask.

16

THE next day Kumalo, who was learning to find his way about the great city, took train to Pimville to see the girl who was with child by his son. He chose this time so that Msimangu would not be able to accompany him, not because he was offended, but because he felt he would do it better alone. He thought slowly and acted slowly, no doubt because he lived in the slow tribal rhythm; and he had seen that this could irritate those who were with him, and he had felt also that he could reach his goal more surely without them.

He found the house not without difficulty, and knocked at the door, and the girl opened to him. And she smiled at him uncertainly, with something that was fear, and something that was child-like and welcoming.

—And how are you, my child?

—I am well, umfundisi.

He sat down on the only chair in the room, sat down carefully on it, and wiped his brow.

—Have you heard of your husband? he asked. Only the word does not quite mean husband.

The smile went from her face. I have not heard, she said.

—What I have to say is heavy, he said. He is in prison.

—In prison, she said.

—He is in prison, for the most terrible deed that a man can do.

But the girl did not understand him. She waited patiently for him to continue. She was surely but a child.

—He has killed a white man.

—Au! The exclamation burst from her. She put her hands over her face. And Kumalo himself could not continue, for the words were like knives, cutting into a wound that was still new and open. She sat down on a box, and looked at the floor, and the tears started to run slowly down her cheeks.

—I do not wish to speak of it, my child. Can you read? The white man's newspaper?

—A little.

—Then I shall leave it with you. But do not show it to others.

—I shall not show it to others, umfundisi.

—I do not wish to speak of it any more. I have come to speak with you of another matter. Do you wish to marry my son?

—It is as the umfundisi sees it.

—I am asking you, my child.

—I can be willing.

—And why would you be willing?

She looked at him, for she could not understand such a question.

—Why do you wish to marry him? he persisted.

She picked little strips of wood from the box, smiling in her perplexedness. He is my husband, she said, with the word that does not quite mean husband.

—But you did not wish to marry him before?

The questions embarrassed her; she stood up, but there was nothing to do, and she sat down again, and fell to picking at the box.

—Speak, my child.

—I do not know what to say, umfundisi.

—Is it truly your wish to marry him?

—It is truly my wish, umfundisi.

—I must be certain. I do not wish to take you into my family if you are unwilling.

At those words she looked up at him eagerly. I am willing, she said.

—We live in a far place, he said, there are no streets and lights and buses there. There is only me and my wife, and the place is very quiet. You are a Zulu?

—Yes, umfundisi.

—Where were you born?

—In Alexandra.

—And your parents?

—My father left my mother, umfundisi. And my second father I could not understand.

—Why did your father leave?

—They quarreled, umfundisi. Because my mother was so often drunk.

—So your father left. And he left you also?

—He left us, my two brothers and me, my younger brothers.

—And your two brothers, where are they?

—One is in the school, umfundisi, the school where Absalom was sent. And one is in Alexandra. But he is disobedient, and I have heard that he too may go to the school.

—But how could your father have left you so?

She looked at him with strange innocence. I do not know, she said.

—And you did not understand your second father? So what did you do?

—I left that place.

—And what did you do?

—I lived in Sophiatown.

—Alone?

—No, not alone.

—With your first husband? he asked coldly.

—With my first, she agreed, not noticing his coldness.

—How many have there been?

She laughed nervously, and looked down at the hand picking at the box. She looked up, and finding his eyes upon her, was confused. Only three, she said.

—And what happened to the first?

—He was caught, umfundisi.

—And the second?

—He was caught also.

—And now the third is caught also.

He stood up, and a wish to hurt her came into him. Although he knew it was not seemly, he yielded to it, and he said to her, yes, your third is caught also, but now it is for murder. Have you had a murderer before?

He took a step toward her, and she shrank away on the box, crying, no, no. And he, fearing that those outside might overhear, spoke more quietly to her and told her not to be afraid, and took a step backwards. But no sooner had she recovered than he wished to hurt her again. And he said to her, will you now take a fourth husband? And desperately she said, No, no, I want no husband any more.

And a wild thought came to Kumalo in his wild and cruel mood.

—Not even, he asked, if I desired you?

—You, she said, and shrank from him again.

—Yes, I, he said.

She looked round and about her, as one that was trapped. No, no, she said, it would not be right.

—Was it right before?

—No, it was not right.

—Then would you be willing?

She laughed nervously, and looked about her, and picked strips of wood from the box. But she felt his eyes upon her, and she said in a low voice, I could be willing.

He sat down and covered his face with his hands; and she, seeing him, fell to sobbing, a creature shamed and tormented. And he, seeing her, and the frailty of her thin body, was ashamed also, but for his cruelty, not her compliance.

He went over to her and said, how old are you, my child?

—I do not know, she sobbed, but I think I am sixteen.

And the deep pity welled up in him, and he put his hand on her head. And whether it was the priestly touch, or whether the deep pity flowed into the fingers and the palm, or whether it was some other reason—but the sobbing was quietened, and he could feel the head quiet under his hand. And he lifted her hands with his other, and felt the scars of her meaningless duties about this forlorn house.

—I am sorry, he said. I am ashamed that I asked you such a question.

—I did not know what to say, she said.

—I knew that you would not know. That is why I am ashamed. Tell me, do you truly wish to marry my son?

She clutched at his hands. I wish it, she said.

—And to go to a quiet and far-off place, and be our daughter?

There was no mistaking the gladness of her voice. I wish it, she said.

—Greatly?

—Greatly, she said.

—My child?

—Umfundisi?

—I must say one more hard thing to you.

—I am listening, umfundisi.

—What will you do in this quiet place when the

desire is upon you? I am a parson, and live at my
church, and our life is quiet and ordered. I do not
wish to ask you something that you cannot do.

—I understand, umfundisi. I understand completely. She looked at him through her tears. You
shall not be ashamed of me. You need not be afraid
for me. You need not be afraid because it is quiet.
Quietness is what I desire.

And the word, the word desire, quickened her to
brilliance. That shall be my desire, she said, that is
the desire that will be upon me, so that he was
astonished.

—I understand you, he said. You are cleverer than
I thought.

—I was clever at school, she said eagerly.

He was moved to sudden laughter, and stood
wondering at the strangeness of its sound.

—What church are you?

—Church of England, umfundisi . . . this too,
eagerly.

He laughed again at her simplicity, and was as
suddenly solemn. I want one promise from you, he
said, a heavy promise.

And she too was solemn. Yes, umfundisi?

—If you should ever repent of this plan, either
here or when we are gone to my home, you must
not shut it up inside you, or run away as you did
from your mother. You will promise to tell me that
you have repented.

—I promise, she said gravely, and then eagerly, I
shall never repent.

And so he laughed again, and let go her hands,

everything is ready for the marriage. Have you clothes?

—I have some clothes, umfundisi. I shall prepare them.

—And you must not live here. Shall I find you a place near me?

—I would wish that, umfundisi. She clapped her hands like a child. Let it be soon, she said, and I shall give up my room at this house.

—Stay well, then, my child.

—Go well, umfundisi.

He went out of the house, and she followed him to the little gate. When he turned back to look at her, she was smiling at him. He walked on like a man from whom a pain has lifted a little, not altogether, but a little. He remembered too that he had laughed, and that it had pained him physically, as it pains a man who is ill and should not laugh. And he remembered too, with sudden and devastating shock, that Father Vincent had said, I shall pray, night and day. At the corner he turned, and looking back, saw that the girl was still watching him.

17

THERE are few people that do not let their rooms, and Mrs. Lithebe is one. Her husband was a builder, a good and honest man, but they were not blessed with children. He built her this fine big house, it has a room to eat and live in, and three rooms to sleep in. And one she has for herself, and one for the priest that she is glad to have, for it is good to have a priest, it is good to have prayers in the house. And one she has for Gertrude and the child, for do they not belong to the priest? But strangers she will not have at all, she has money enough.

It is sad about the priest, it is sad about this Gertrude and the child, it is saddest of all about his son. But about his goodness she has no doubt at all. He is kind and gentle, and treats her with courtesy and respect, and uses the house as if it were his. And she admires him for what he has done, for saving Gertrude and the child, for getting his sister a new dress and a clean white cloth for her head, for getting shirt and jersey and trousers for the child. According to the custom she has thanked him for these gifts.

And it is pleasant having Gertrude and the child in the house. The girl is helpful and clean, though there is a strange carelessness about her, and she talks too easily to strangers, especially if they are men. For Mrs. Lithebe knows that she is a married woman, and Gertrude knows that the old woman is strict with her house, and she understands and is obedient.

But it is saddest of all about the son, and after their custom they have wept and wailed for him. She and Gertrude talk endlessly about it, indeed it is the only thing they talk about now. The old man is silent, and his face has fallen into a mould of suffering. But she hears it all in his prayers, and feels for him in her heart. And though he sits long hours in the chair, and stares in front of him out of tragic eyes, he will stir to life when she speaks to him, and his smile lifts his face out of the mould of its suffering, and he is never otherwise than gentle and courteous towards her. Indeed when he plays with the child, there is something that comes out of him so that he is changed. Yet even then sometimes there is a silence, and she hears the child asking and asking unanswered, and she looks through the door, and he is sitting there silent, alone with his thoughts, his face in the mould of its suffering.

* * * * *

—Mrs. Lithebe.
—Umfundisi?

—Mrs. Lithebe, you have been so kind, and I have another kindness to ask you.

—Perhaps it can be done.

—Mrs. Lithebe, you have heard of this girl who is with child by my son.

—I have heard of her.

—She lives in Pimville, in a room in the house of other people. She wishes to marry my son, and I believe it can be arranged. Then—whatever may happen—she will go with me to Ndotsheni, and bear her child there in a clean and decent home. But I am anxious to get her away from this place, and I wondered. . . . I do not like to trouble you, mother.

—You would like to bring her here, umfundisi?

—Indeed, that would be a great kindness.

—I will take her, said Mrs. Lithebe. She can sleep in the room where we eat. But I have no bed for her.

—That would not matter. It is better for her to sleep on the floor of a decent house, than to . . .

—Indeed, indeed.

—Mother, I am grateful. Indeed you are a mother to me.

—Why else do we live? she said.

And after that he was cheerful, and called to the little boy, and sat him upon his knee, and moved him up and down quickly as a man moves on a horse. But it is not a good game, for an old man gets tired and a child does not. So they brought out the blocks, and built tall buildings like the buildings in Johannesburg, and sent them toppling over to destruction with noise and laughter.

—And now I must go, said Kumalo. I have a new sister to bring to you.

He counted out his money. There were only one or two notes left. Soon he would have to break into the money in the Post Office Book. He sighed a little, and put on his coat and his hat and took up his stick. His wife would have to wait longer for her stove, and he would have to wait longer for his new black clothes, and for the collars that a parson wears.

* * * * *

The girl is not like Gertrude. She is openly glad to be in this house. Her clothes are few but clean, for she has prepared them with care, and of other belongings she has almost none at all. She opens the doors and looks into the rooms, and she is glad, not having lived before in such a house. She calls Mrs. Lithebe mother, and that pleases the good woman; and she is pleased too because the girl can speak Sesuto after a broken fashion. Gertrude too welcomes her, for it is no doubt dull for her in this house. They will talk much together.

Indeed Mrs. Lithebe comes upon them, when they have been laughing together. They fall silent, Gertrude with some amusement in her eyes, and the girl confused. But Mrs. Lithebe does not like this laughter, it is the careless laughter that she does not like. She calls the girl to the kitchen to help her, and she says she does not like it.

—You are in a decent home, my child.

—Yes, mother, says the girl with downcast eyes.

—And you are brought here by a good and kindly man, so good that there is no word for it.

The girl looked up at her eagerly. I know it, she said.

—Then if you are content to be brought by him, you will not laugh so carelessly.

—Yes, mother.

—You are but a child, and laughter is good for a child. But there is one kind of laughter, and there is another.

—Yes, mother.

—You understand what I mean?

—I understand you completely.

—This old man has been hurt greatly. Do you understand what I mean?

—I understand you completely.

—And he shall not be hurt any more, not in my house.

—I understand you.

—Then go, my child. But do not speak of what we have spoken.

—I understand you.

—My child, are you content to be brought here?

The girl looks at her fully. She spread out her hands, seeking some gesture to convey her conviction. I am content, she said. I desire to be nowhere but where I am. I desire no father but the umfundisi. I desire nothing that is not here.

—I see you are content. And one thing more, my child. When the little one plays with you, do not let him press so against you. It is your time to be careful.

—I understand you.

—Go then, my child. This home is your home.

So there was no more of the careless laughter, and the girl was quiet and obedient. And Gertrude saw that she was a child, and left her alone and was indifferent and amused after her own fashion.

*   *   *   *   *

He passed again through the great gate in the grim high wall, and they brought the boy to him. Again he took the lifeless hand in his own, and was again moved to tears, this time by the dejection of his son.

—Are you in health, my son?

The son stood and moved his head to one side, and looked for a while at the one window, and then moved and looked at the other, but not at his father.

—I am in health, my father.

—I have some business for you, my son. Are you certain that you wish to marry this girl?

—I can marry her?

—There is a friend of mine, a white priest, and he will see if it can be arranged, and he will see the Bishop to see if it can be done quickly. And he will get a lawyer for you.

There is a spark of life in the eyes, of some hope maybe.

—You would like a lawyer?

—They say one can be helped by a lawyer.

—You told the police that these other two were with you?

—I told them. And now I have told them again.

—And then?

—And then they sent for them and fetched them from their cells.

—And then?

—And then they were angry with me, and cursed me in front of the police, and said that I was trying to bring them into trouble.

—And then?

—And then they asked what proof I had. And the only proof I had was that it was true, it was these two and no other and they stood there with me in the house, I here and they yonder.

He showed his father with his hands, and the tears came into his eyes, and he said, Then they cursed me again, and stood. looking angrily at me, and said one to the other, How can he lie so about us?

—They were your friends?

—Yes, they were my friends.

—And they will leave you to suffer alone?

—Now I see it.

—And until this, were they friends you could trust?

—I could trust them.

—I see what you mean. You mean they were the kind of friends that a good man could choose, up-right, hard-working, obeying the law?

Old man, leave him alone. You lead him so far and then you spring upon him. He looks at you sul-lenly, soon he will not answer at all.

—Tell me, were they such friends?

But the boy made no answer.

—And now they leave you alone?

Silence, then—I see it.

—Did you not see it before?

Reluctantly the boy said, I saw it. The old man was tempted to ask, then why, why did you continue with them? But the boy's eyes were filled with tears, and the father's compassion struggled with the temptation and overcame it. He took his son's hands, and this time they were not quite lifeless, but there was some feeling in them, and he held them strongly and comfortingly.

—Be of courage, my son. Do not forget there is a lawyer. But it is only the truth you must tell him.

—I shall tell him only the truth, my father.

He opened his mouth as though there were something he would say, but he did not say it.

—Do not fear to speak, my son.

—He must come soon, my father.

He looked at the window, and his eyes filled again with tears. He tried to speak carelessly. Or it may be too late, he said.

—Have no fear of that. He will come soon. Shall I go now to see when he will come?

—Go now, soon, soon, my father.

—And Father Vincent will come to see you, so that you can make confession, and be absolved, and amend your life.

—It is good, my father.

—And the marriage, that will be arranged if we can arrange it. And the girl—I had not told you—

she is living with me in Sophiatown. And she will come back with me to Ndotsheni, and the child will be born there.

—It is good, my father.

—And you may write now to your mother.

—I shall write, my father.

—And wipe away your tears.

The boy stood up and wiped his eyes with the cloth that his father gave him. And they shook hands, and there was some life now in the hand of the boy. The warder said to the boy, you may stay here, there is a lawyer to see you. You, old man, you must go.

So Kumalo left him, and at the door stood a white man, ready to come in. He was tall and grave, like a man used to heavy matters, and the warder knew him and showed him much respect. He looked like a man used to great matters, much greater than the case of a black boy who has killed a man, and he went gravely into the room, even as a chief would go.

*   *   *   *   *

Kumalo returned to the Mission House, and there had tea with Father Vincent. After the tea was over there was a knock at the door, and the tall grave man was shown into the room. And Father Vincent treated him also with respect, and called him sir, and then Mr. Carmichael. He introduced Kumalo to him, and Mr. Carmichael shook hands with him, and called him Mr. Kumalo, which is not the custom. They had more tea, and fell to discussing the case.

—I shall take it for you, Mr. Kumalo, said Mr. Carmichael. I shall take it pro deo, as we say. It is a simple case, for the boy says simply that he fired because he was afraid, not meaning to kill. And it will depend entirely on the judge and his assessors, for I think we will ask for that, and not for a jury. But with regard to the other two boys, I do not know what to say. I hear, Mr. Kumalo, that your brother had found another lawyer for them, and indeed I could not defend them, for I understand that their defence will be that they were not there at all, and that your son is for reasons of his own trying to implicate them. Whether that is true or not will be for the Court to decide, but I incline to the opinion that your son is speaking the truth, and has no motive for trying to implicate them. It is for me to persuade the Court that he is speaking the whole truth, and that he speaks the whole truth when he says that he fired because he was afraid, and therefore I obviously could not defend these two who maintain that he is not speaking the truth. Is that clear, Mr. Kumalo?

—It is clear, sir.

—Now I must have all the facts about your son, Mr. Kumalo, when and where he was born, and what sort of child he was, and whether he was obedient and truthful, and when and why he left home, and what he has done since he came to Johannesburg. You understand?

—I understand, sir.

—I want this as soon as I can, Mr. Kumalo, for the case will probably be heard at the next sessions. You must find out what he has done, not only from him, but from others. You must check the one account against the other, you understand, and if there are differences, you must give them also. And I shall do the same on my own account. Do you understand?

—I understand, sir.

—And now, Father Vincent, could you and I go into this matter of the school?

—With pleasure, sir. Mr. Kumalo, will you excuse us?

He took Kumalo to the door, and standing outside it, shut it.

—You may thank God that we have got this man, he said. He is a great man, and one of the greatest lawyers in South Africa, and one of the greatest friends of your people.

—I do thank God, and you too, father. But tell me. I have one anxiety, what will it cost? My little money is nearly exhausted.

—Did you not hear him say he would take the case pro deo? Ah yes, you have not heard of that before. It is Latin, and it means for God. So it will cost you nothing, or at least very little.

—He takes it for God?

—That is what it meant in the old days of faith, though it has lost much of that meaning. But it still means that the case is taken for nothing.

Kumalo stammered. I have never met such kindness, he said. He turned away his face, for he wept easily in those days. Father Vincent smiled at him. Go well, he said, and went back to the lawyer who was taking the case for God.

BOOK
II

18

THERE is a lovely road that runs from Ixopo into the hills. These hills are grass-covered and rolling, and they are lovely beyond any singing of it. The road climbs seven miles into them, to Carisbrooke; and from there, if there is no mist, you look down on one of the fairest valleys of Africa. About you there is grass and bracken and the forlorn crying of the titihoya, one of the birds of the veld. Below you is the valley of the Umzimkulu, on its journey from the Drakensberg to the sea; and beyond and behind the river, great hill after great hill; and beyond and behind them, the mountains of Ingeli and East Griqualand.

The grass is rich and matted, you cannot see the sod. It holds the rain and the mist, and they seep into the ground, feeding the streams in every kloof. It is well tended, and not too many cattle feed upon it, and not too many fires burn it, laying bare the soil.

Up here on the tops is a small and lovely valley, between two hills that shelter it. There is a house there, and flat ploughed fields; they will tell you that it is one of the finest farms of this countryside. It is called High Place, the farm and dwelling-place of James Jarvis, Esquire, and it stands high above Ndotsheni, and the great valley of the Umzimkulu.

*   *   *   *   *

Jarvis watched the ploughing with a gloomy eye. The hot afternoon sun of October poured down on the fields, and there was no cloud in the sky. Rain, rain, there was no rain. The clods turned up hard and unbroken, and here and there the plough would ride uselessly over the iron soil. At the end of the field it stopped, and the oxen stood sweating and blowing in the heat.

—It is no use, umnumzana.

—Keep at it, Thomas. I shall go up to the tops and see what there is to see.

—You will see nothing, umnumzana. I know because I have looked already.

Jarvis grunted, and calling his dog, set out along the kaffir path that led up to the tops. There was no sign of drought there, for the grass was fed by the mists, and the breeze blew coolingly on his sweating face. But below the tops the grass was dry, and the hills of Ndotsheni were red and bare, and the farmers on the tops had begun to fear that the desolation of them would eat back, year by year, mile by mile, until they too were overtaken.

Indeed they talked about it often, for when they visited one another and sat on the long cool verandahs drinking their tea, they must needs look out over the barren valleys and the bare hills that were stretched below them. Some of their labour was drawn from Ndotsheni, and they knew how year by year there was less food grown in these reserves. There were too many cattle there, and the fields were eroded and barren; each new field extended the devastation. Something might have been done, if these people had only learned how to fight erosion, if they had built walls to save the soil from washing, if they had ploughed along the contours of the hills. But the hills were steep, and indeed some of them were never meant for ploughing. And the oxen were weak, so that it was easier to plough downwards. And the people were ignorant, and knew nothing about farming methods.

Indeed it was a problem almost beyond solution. Some people said there must be more education, but a boy with education did not want to work on the farms, and went off to the towns to look for more congenial occupation. The work was done by old men and women, and when the grown men came back from the mines and the towns, they sat in the sun and drank their liquor and made endless conversation. Some said there was too little land anyway, and that the natives could not support themselves on it, even with the most progressive methods of agriculture. But there were many sides to such a question. For if they got more land, and treated it as they treated what they had already, the country would turn into a desert. And where was the land to come from, and who would pay for it? And indeed there was still another argument, for if they got more land, and if by some chance they could make a living from it, who would work on the white men's farms? There was a system whereby a native could live at Ndotsheni, and go to work at his will on the adjoining farms. And there was another system whereby a native could get land from the farmer, and set up his kraal and have his family there, and be given his own piece of land and work it, provided that he and his family gave so much labour each year to the white farmer. But even that was not perfect, for some of them had sons and daughters that left for the towns, and never came back to fulfil their portion of the contract; and some of them abused the land that they had; and some of them stole cattle and sheep for meat; and some of them were idle and worthless, till one had to clear them off the farm, and not be certain if their successors would be any better.

Jarvis turned these old thoughts over in his mind as he climbed to the tops, and when he reached them he sat down on a stone and took off his hat, letting the breeze cool him. This was a view that a man could look at without tiring of it, this great valley of the Umzimkulu. He could look around on the green rich hills that he had inherited from his father, and down on the rich valley where he lived and farmed. It had been his wish that his son, the only child that had been born to them, would have taken it after him. But the young man had entertained other ideas, and had gone in for engineering, and well—good luck to him. He had married a fine girl, and had presented his parents with a pair of fine grandchildren. It had been a heavy blow when he decided against High Place, but his life was his own, and no other man had a right to put his hands on it.

Down in the valley below there was a car going up to the house. He recognized it as the police-car from Ixopo, and it would probably be Binnendyk on his patrol, and a decent fellow for an Afrikaner. Indeed Ixopo was full of Afrikaners now, whereas once there had been none of them. For all the police were Afrikaners, and the post-office clerks, and the men at the railway-station, and the village people got on well with them one way and the other. Indeed, many of them had married English-speaking girls, and that was happening all over the country. His own father had sworn that he would disinherit any child of his who married an Afrikaner, but times had changed. The war had put things back a bit, for some of the Afrikaners had joined the army, and some were for the war but didn't join the army, and some were just for neutrality and if they had any feelings they concealed them, and some were for Germany but it wasn't wise for them to say anything about it.

His wife was coming out of the house to meet the car, and there were two policemen climbing out of it. One looked like the captain himself, van Jaarsveld, one of the most popular men in the village, a great rugby player in his day, and a soldier of the Great War. He supposed they picked their officers carefully for an English-speaking district like Ixopo. They seemed to have come to see him, for his wife was pointing up to the tops. He prepared to go down, but before he left, he looked over the great valley. There was no rain, and nothing that looked as if it would ever come. He called his dog, and set out along the path that would soon drop down steeply amongst the stones. When he reached a little plateau about half-way down to the fields, he found that van Jaarsveld and Binnendyk were already climbing the slope, and saw that they had brought their car down the rough track to the ploughing. They caught sight of him, and he waved to them, and sat down upon a stone to wait for them. Binnendyk dropped behind, and the captain came on above to meet him.

—Well, captain, have you brought some rain for us?

The captain stopped and turned to look over the valley to the mountains beyond.

—I don't see any, Mr. Jarvis, he said.

—Neither do I. What brings you out today? They shook hands, and the captain looked at him.

—Mr. Jarvis.

—Yes.

—I have bad news for you.

—Bad news?

Jarvis sat down, his heart beating loudly. Is it my son? he asked.

—Yes, Mr. Jarvis.

—Is he dead?

—Yes, Mr. Jarvis. The captain paused. He was shot dead at 1:30 P.M. this afternoon in Johannesburg.

Jarvis stood up, his mouth quivering. Shot dead, he asked. By whom?

—It is suspected by a native housebreaker. You know his wife was away!

—Yes, I knew that.

—And he stayed at home for the day, a slight indisposition. I suppose this native thought no one was at home. It appears that your son heard a noise, and came down to investigate. The native shot him dead. There was no sign of any struggle.

—My God!

—I'm sorry, Mr. Jarvis. I'm sorry to have to bring this news to you.

He offered his hand, but Jarvis had sat down again on the stone, and did not see it. My God, he said.

van Jaarsveld stood silent while the older man tried to control himself.

—You didn't tell my wife, captain?

—No, Mr. Jarvis.

Jarvis knitted his brows as he thought of that task that must be performed. She isn't strong, he said. I don't know how she will stand it.

—Mr. Jarvis, I am instructed to offer you every assistance. Binnendyk can drive your car to Pietermaritzburg if you wish. You could catch the fast mail at nine o'clock. You will be in Johannesburg at eleven tomorrow morning. There's a private compartment reserved for you and Mrs. Jarvis.

—That was kind of you.

—I'll do anything you wish, Mr. Jarvis.

—What time is it?

—Half-past three, Mr. Jarvis.

—Two hours ago.

—Yes, Mr. Jarvis.

—Three hours ago he was alive.

—Yes, Mr. Jarvis.

—My God!

—If you are to catch this train, you should leave at six. Or if you wish, you could take an aeroplane. There's one waiting at Pietermaritzburg. But we must let them know by four o'clock. You could be in Johannesburg at midnight.

—Yes, yes. You know, I cannot think.

—Yes, I can understand that.

—Which would be better?

—I think the aeroplane, Mr. Jarvis.

—Well, we'll take it. We must let them know, you say.

—I'll do that as soon as we get to the house. Can I telephone where Mrs. Jarvis won't hear me? I must hurry, you see.

—Yes, yes, you can do that.

—I think we should go.

But Jarvis sat without moving.

—Can you stand up, Mr. Jarvis? I don't want to help you. Your wife's watching us.

—She's wondering, captain. Even at this distance, she knows something is wrong.

—It's quite likely. Something she saw in my face, perhaps, though I tried not to show it.

Jarvis stood up. My God, he said. There's still that to do.

As they walked down the steep path, Binnendyk went ahead of them. Jarvis walked like a dazed man. Out of a cloudless sky these things come.

—Shot dead? he said.

—Yes, Mr. Jarvis.

—Did they catch the native?

—Not yet, Mr. Jarvis.

The tears filled the eyes, the teeth bit the lips. What does that matter? he said. They walked down the hill, they were near the field. Through the misted eyes he saw the plough turn over the clods, then ride high over the iron ground. Leave it, Thomas, he said. He was our only child, captain.

—I know that, Mr. Jarvis.

They climbed into the car, and in a few minutes were at the house.

—James, what's the matter?

—Some trouble, my dear. Come with me to the office. Captain, you want to use the telephone. You know where it is?

—Yes, Mr. Jarvis.

The captain went to the telephone. It was a party-line, and two neighbours were talking.

—Please put down your receivers, said the captain. This is an urgent call from the police. Please put down your receivers.

He rang viciously, and got no answer. There should be a special police call to exchange on these country lines. He would see about it. He rang more viciously. Exchange, he said, Police Pietermaritzburg. It is very urgent.

—You will be connected immediately, said exchange.

He waited impatiently, listening to the queer

inexplicable noises. Your call to Police Pietermaritz-burg, said exchange.

He started to talk to them about the aeroplane. His hand felt for the second earpiece, so that he could use that also, to shut out the sound of the woman, of her crying and sobbing.

19

A YOUNG man met them at the airport.

—Mr. and Mrs. Jarvis?

—Yes.

—I'm John Harrison, Mary's brother. I don't think you remember me. I was only a youngster when you saw me last. Let me carry your things. I've a car here for you.

As they walked to the control building, the young man said, I needn't tell you how grieved we are, Mr. Jarvis. Arthur was the finest man I ever knew.

In the car he spoke to them again. Mary and the children are at my mother's, and we're expecting you both to stay with us.

—How is Mary?

—She's suffering from the shock, Mr. Jarvis, but she's very brave.

—And the children?

—They've taken it very badly, Mr. Jarvis. And that has given Mary something to occupy herself.

They did not speak again. Jarvis held his wife's hand, but they all were silent with their own thoughts, until they drove through the gates of a

suburban house, and came to a stop before a lighted
porch. A young woman came out at the sound of the
car, and embraced Mrs. Jarvis, and they wept together. Then she turned to Jarvis, and they embraced each other. This first meeting over, Mr. and
Mrs. Harrison came out also, and after they had
welcomed one another, and after the proper words
had been spoken, they all went into the house.

Harrison turned to Jarvis. Would you like a
drink? he asked.

—It would be welcome.

—Come to my study, then.

—And now, said Harrison, you must do as you
wish. If there's anything we can do, you've only to
ask us. If you would wish to go to the mortuary at
once, John will go with you. Or you can go tomorrow morning if you wish. The police would like to
see you, but they won't worry you tonight.

—I'll ask my wife, Harrison. You know, we've
hardly spoken of it yet. I'll go to her, don't you
worry to come.

—I'll wait for you here.

He found his wife and his daughter-in-law hand
in hand, tiptoeing out of the room where his grandchildren were sleeping. He spoke to her, and she
wept again and sobbed against him. Now, she said.
He went back to Harrison, and swallowed his drink,
and then he and his wife and their daughter-in-law
went out to the car, where John Harrison was waiting for them.

While they were driving to the Police Laboratories, John Harrison told Jarvis all that he knew

about the crime, how the police were waiting for the house-boy to recover consciousness, and how they had combed the plantations on Parkwold Ridge. And he told him too of the paper that Arthur Jarvis had been writing just before he was killed, on "The Truth About Native Crime."

—I'd like to see it, said Jarvis.

—We'll get it for you tomorrow, Mr. Jarvis.

—My son and I didn't see eye to eye on the native question, John. In fact, he and I got quite heated about it on more than one occasion. But I'd like to see what he wrote.

—My father and I don't see eye to eye on the native question either, Mr. Jarvis. You know, Mr. Jarvis, there was no one in South Africa who thought so deeply about it, and no one who thought so clearly, as Arthur did. And what else is there to think deeply and clearly about in South Africa, be used to say.

So they came to the Laboratories, and John Harrison stayed in the car, while the others went to do the hard thing that had to be done. And they came out silent but for the weeping of the two women, and drove back as silently to the house, where Mary's father opened the door to them.

—Another drink, Jarvis. Or do you want to go to bed?

—Margaret, do you want me to come up with you?

—No, my dear, stay and have your drink.

—Goodnight then, my dear.

—Goodnight, James.

He kissed her, and she clung to him for a

moment. And thank you for all your help, she said. The tears came again into her eyes, and into his too for that matter. He watched her climb the stairs with their daughter-in-law, and when the door closed on them, he and Harrison turned to go to the study.

—It's always worse for the mother, Jarvis.

—Yes.

He pondered over it, and said then, I was very fond of my son, he said. I was never ashamed of having him.

They settled down to their drinks, and Harrison told him that the murder had shocked the people of Parkwold, and how the messages had poured into the house.

—Messages from every conceivable place, every kind of person, he said. By the way, Jarvis, we arranged the funeral provisionally for tomorrow afternoon, after a service in the Parkwold Church. Three o'clock the service will be.

Jarvis nodded. Thank you, he said.

—And we kept all the messages for you. From the Bishop, and the Acting Prime Minister, and the Mayor, and from dozens of others. And from native organizations too, something called the Daughters of Africa, and a whole lot of others that I can't remember. And from coloured people, and Indians, and Jews.

Jarvis felt a sad pride rising in him. He was clever, he said. That came from his mother.

—He was that right enough—you must hear John on it. But people liked him too, all sorts of people. You know he Spoke Afrikaans like an Afrikaner!

—I knew he had learnt it.

—It's a lingo I know nothing about, thank God. But he thought he ought to know it, So he took lessons in it, and went to an Afrikaner farm. He spoke Zulu as you know, but he was talking of learning Sesuto. You know these native M.P.'s they have— well, there was talk of getting him to stand at the next election.

—I didn't know that.

—Yes, he was always speaking here and there. You know the kind of thing. Native Crime, and more Native Schools, and he kicked up a hell of a dust in the papers about the conditions at the non-European Hospital. And you know he was hot about the native compound system in the Mines, and wanted the Chamber to come out one hundred per cent for settled labour—you know, wife and family to come with the man.

Jarvis filled his pipe slowly, and listened to this tale of his son, to this tale of a stranger.

—Hathaway of the Chamber of Mines spoke to me about it, said Harrison. Asked me if I wouldn't warn the lad to pipe down a bit, because his firm did a lot of business with the Mines. So I spoke to him, told him I knew he felt deeply about these things, but asked him to go slow a bit. Told him there was Mary to consider, and the children. I didn't speak on behalf of Mary, you understand? I don't poke my nose into young people's business.

—I understand.

—I've spoken to Mary, he said to me. She and I

agree that it's more important to speak the truth than to make money.

Harrison laughed at that, but cut himself short, remembering the sadness of the occasion. My son John was there, he said, looking at Arthur as though he were God Almighty. So what could I say?

They smoked in silence awhile. I asked him, said Harrison, about his partners. After all their job was to sell machinery to the Mines. I've discussed it with my partners, he said to me, and if there's any trouble, I've told them I'll get out. And what would you do? I asked him. What won't I do? he said. His face was sort of excited. Well, what could I say more?

Jarvis did not answer. For this boy of his had gone journeying in strange waters, further than his parents had known. Or perhaps his mother knew. It would not surprise him if his mother knew. But he himself had never done such journeying, and there was nothing he could say.

—Am I tiring you, Jarvis? Or is there perhaps something else you'd like to talk about? Or go to bed, perhaps?

—Harrison, you're doing me more good by talking.

—Well, that's how it was. He and I didn't talk much about these things. It's not my line of country. I try to treat a native decently, but he's not my food and drink. And to tell you the truth, these crimes put me off. I tell you, Jarvis, we're scared stiff at the moment in Johannesburg.

—Of crime?

—Yes, of native crime. There are too many of these murders and robberies and brutal attacks. I tell you we don't go to bed at night without barricading the house. It was at the Phillipsons, three doors down, that a gang of these roughs broke in; they knocked old Phillipson unconscious, and beat up his wife. It was lucky the girls were out at a dance, or one doesn't know what might have happened. I asked Arthur about that, but he reckoned we were to blame somehow. Can't say I always followed him, but he had a kind of sincerity. You sort of felt that if you had the time you could get some sort of sense out of it.

—There's one thing I don't get the sense of, said Jarvis. Why this should have happened. . . .

—You mean . . . to him, of all people?

—Yes.

—That's one of the first things that we said. Here he was, day in and day out, on a kind of mission. And it was he who was killed.

—Mind you, said Jarvis, coming to a point. Mind you, it's happened before. I mean, that missionaries were killed.

Harrison made no answer, and they smoked their pipes silently. A missionary, thought Jarvis, and thought how strange it was that he had called his son a missionary. For he had never thought much of missionaries. True, the church made a lot of it, and there were special appeals to which he had given, but one did that kind of thing without believing much in missionaries. There was a mission near him, at Ndotsheni. But it was a sad place as he remembered it. A dirty old wood-and-iron church, patched and forlorn, and a dirty old parson, in a barren valley where the grass hardly grew. A dirty old school where he had heard them reciting, parrot-fashion, on the one or two occasions that he had ridden past there, reciting things that could mean little to them.

—Bed, Jarvis? Or another drink?

—Bed, I think. Did you say the police were coming?

—They're coming at nine.

—And I'd like to see the house.

—I thought that you would. They'll take you there.

—Good, then I'll go to bed. Will you say goodnight to your wife for me?

—I'll do that. You know your room? And breakfast? Eight-thirty?

—Eight-thirty. Goodnight, Harrison. And many thanks for your kindnesses.

—No thanks are needed. Nothing is too much trouble. Goodnight, Jarvis, and I hope you and Margaret will get some sleep.

Jarvis walked up the stairs, and went into the room. He walked in quietly, and closed the door, and did not put on the light. The moon was shining through the windows, and he stood there looking out on the world. All that he had heard went quietly through his mind. His wife turned in the bed, and said, James.

—My dear.

—What were you thinking, my dear?

He was silent, searching for an answer. Of it all, he said.

—I thought you would never come.

He went to her quickly, and she caught at his hands. We were talking of the boy, he said. All that he did, and tried to do. All the people that are grieved.

—Tell me, my dear.

And so he told her in low tones all he had heard. She marvelled a little, for her husband was a quiet silent man, not given to much talking. But tonight he told her all that Harrison had told him.

—It makes me proud, she whispered.

—But you always knew he was like that.

—Yes, I knew.

—I knew too that he was a decent man, he said. But you were always nearer to him than I was.

—It's easier for a mother, James.

—I suppose so. But I wish now that I'd known more of him. You see, the things that he did, I've never had much to do with that sort of thing.

—Nor I either, James. His life was quite different from ours.

—It was a good life by all accounts.

He sat, she lay, in silence, with their thoughts and their memories and their grief.

—Although his life was different, he said, you understood it.

—Yes, James.

—I'm sorry I didn't understand it.

Then he said in a whisper, I didn't know it would ever be so important to understand it.

—My dear, my dear. Her arms went about him, and she wept. And he continued to whisper, There's one thing I don't understand, why it should have happened to him.

She lay there thinking of it, the pain was deep, deep and ineluctable. She tightened her arms about him. James, let's try to sleep, she said.

20

JARVIS sat in the chair of his son, and his wife and Mary left him to return to the Harrisons. Books, books, books, more books than he had ever seen in a house! On the table papers, letters and more books. Mr. Jarvis, will you speak at the Parkwold Methodist Guild? Mr. Jarvis, will you speak at the Anglican Young People's Association in Sophiatown? Mr. Jarvis, will you speak in a symposium at the University? No, Mr. Jarvis would be unable to speak at any of these.

Mr. Jarvis, you are invited to the Annual Meeting of the Society of Jews and Christians. Mr. Jarvis, you and your wife are invited to the wedding of Sarajini, eldest daughter of Mr. and Mrs. H. B. Singh. Mr. Jarvis, you and your wife are invited to a Toc H Guest Night in Van Wyk's Valley. No, Mr. Jarvis would be unable to accept these kind invitations.

On the walls between the books there were four pictures, of Christ crucified, and Abraham Lincoln, and the white gabled house of Vergelegen, and a painting of leafless willows by a river in a wintry veld.

He rose from the chair to look at the books. Here were hundreds of books, all about Abraham Lincoln. He had not known that so many books had been written about any one man. One bookcase was full of them. And another was full of books about South Africa, Sarah Gertrude Millin's *Life of Rhodes*, and her book about Smuts, and Engelenburg's *Life of Louis Botha*, and books on South African race problems, and books on South African birds, and the Kruger Park, and innumerable others. Another bookcase was full of Afrikaans books but the titles conveyed nothing to him. And here were books about religion and Soviet Russia, and crime and criminals, and books of poems. He looked for Shakespeare, and here was Shakespeare too.

He went back to the chair, and looked long at the pictures of Christ crucified, and Abraham Lincoln, and Vergelegen, and the willows by the river. Then he drew some pieces of paper towards him.

The first was a letter to his son from the secretary of the Claremont African Boys' Club, Gladiolus Street, Claremont, regretting that Mr. Jarvis had not been able to attend the Annual Meeting of the Club, and informing him he had again been elected as President. And the letter concluded, with quaintness of phrase—

I am compelled by the Annual Meeting to congratulate you with this matter, and to express considerable thanks to you for all the time you have been spending with us, and for the presents you have been giving the Club. How this Club would be arranged without your participation, would be a mystery to many minds amongst us. It is on these accounts that we desire to elect you again to the Presidency.

I am asking an apology for this writing-paper, but our Club writing-paper is lost owing to unforeseen circumstances.

I am,

Your obedient servant,
WASHINGTON LEFIFI.

The other papers were in his son's handwriting. They were obviously part of some larger whole, for the first line was the latter end of a sentence, and the last line was a sentence unfinished. He looked for the rest of it, but finding nothing, settled down to read what he had:—

was permissible. What we did when we came to South Africa was permissible. It was permissible to develop our great resources with the aid of what labour we could find. It was permissible to use unskilled men for unskilled work. But it is not permissible to keep men unskilled for the sake of unskilled work.

It was permissible when we discovered gold to bring labour to the mines. It was permissible to build compounds and to keep women and children away from the towns. It was permissible as an experiment, in the light of what we knew. But in the light of what we know now, with certain exceptions, it is no longer permissible. It is not permissible for us to go on destroying family life when we know that we are destroying it.

It is permissible to develop any resources if the labour is forthcoming. But it is not permissible to develop any resources if they can be developed only at the cost of the labour. It is not permissible to mine any gold, or manufacture any product, or cultivate any land, if such mining and manufacture and cultivation depend for their success on a policy of keeping labour poor. It is not permissible to add to one's possessions if these things can only be done at the cost of other men. Such development has only one true name, and that is exploitation. It might have been permissible in the early days of our country, before we became aware of its cost, in the disintegration of native community life, in the deterioration of native family life, in poverty, slums and crime. But now that the cost is known, it is no longer permissible.

It was permissible to leave native education to those who wanted to develop it. It was permissible to doubt its benefits. But it is no longer permissible in the light of what we know. Partly because it made possible industrial development, and partly because it happened in spite of us, there is now a large urbanized native population. Now society has always, for reasons of self-interest if for no other, educated its children so that they grow up law-abiding, with socialized aims and purposes. There is no other way that it can be done. Yet we continue to leave the education of our native urban society to those few Europeans who feel strongly about it, and to deny opportunities and money for its expansion. That is not permissible. For reasons of self-interest alone, it is dangerous.

It was permissible to allow the destruction of a tribal system that impeded the growth of the country. It was permissible to believe that its destruction was inevitable. But it is not permissible to watch its destruction, and to replace it by nothing, or by so little, that a whole people deteriorates, physically and morally.

The old tribal system was, for all its violence and savagery, for all its superstition and witchcraft, a moral system. Our natives today produce criminals and prostitutes and drunkards, not because it is their nature to do so, but because their simple system of order and tradition and convention has been destroyed. It was destroyed by the impact of our own civilization. Our civilization has therefore an inescapable duty to set up another system of order and tradition and convention.

It is true that we hoped to preserve the tribal system by a policy of segregation. That was permissible. But we never did it thoroughly or honestly. We set aside one-tenth of the land for four-fifths of the people. Thus we made it inevitable, and some say we did it knowingly, that labour would come to the towns. We are caught in the toils of our own selfishness.

No one wishes to make the problem seem smaller than it is. No one wishes to make its solution seem easy. No one wishes to make light of the fears that beset us. But whether we be fearful or no, we shall never, because we are a Christian people, be able to evade the moral issues.

It is time—

And there the manuscript and the page ended. Jarvis, who had become absorbed in the reading, searched again amongst the papers on the table, but he could find nothing to show that anything more than this had been written. He lit his pipe, and pulling the papers toward him, began to read them again.

After he had finished them the second time, he sat smoking his pipe and was lost in thought. Then he got up from his chair and went and stood in front of the Lincoln bookcase, and looked up at the picture of the man who had exercised such an influence over his son. He looked at the hundreds of books, and slid aside the glass panel and took one of them out. Then he returned to his chair, and began to turn over its pages. One of the chapters was headed "The Famous Speech at Gettysburg," apparently a speech that was a failure, but that had since become one of the great speeches of the world. He turned over the preliminary pages till he came to the speech, and read it through carefully. That done, he smoked again, lost in a deep abstraction. After some time he rose and replaced the book in the case, and shut the case. Then he opened the case again, and slipped the book into his pocket, and shut the case. He looked at his watch, knocked out his pipe in the fireplace, put on his hat, took up his stick. He walked slowly down the stairs, and opened the door into the fatal passage. He took off his hat and looked down at the dark stain on the floor. Unasked, unwanted, the picture of the small boy came into his mind, the small boy at High Place, the small boy with the wooden guns. Unseeing he walked along the passage and out of the door through which death had come so suddenly. The policeman saluted him, and he answered him with words that meant nothing, that made no sense at all. He put on his hat, and walked to the gate. Undecided he looked up and down the road. Then with an effort he began to walk. With a sigh the policeman relaxed.

21

THE service in the Parkwold Church was over, and the church had been too small for all who wanted to come. White people, black people, coloured people, Indians—it was the first time that Jarvis and his wife had sat in a church with people who were not white. The Bishop himself had spoken, words that pained and uplifted. And the Bishop too had said that men did not understand this riddle, why a young man so full of promise was cut off in his youth, why a woman was widowed and children were orphaned, why a country was bereft of one who might have served it greatly. And the Bishop's voice rose when he spoke of South Africa, and he spoke in a language of beauty, and Jarvis listened for a while without pain, under the spell of the words. And the Bishop said that here had been a life devoted to South Africa, of intelligence and courage, of love that cast out fear, so that the pride welled up in the heart, pride in the stranger who had been his son.

*　　　*　　　*　　　*　　　*

The funeral was over. The brass doors opened soundlessly, and the coffin slid soundlessly into the furnace that would reduce it to ashes. And people that he did not know shook hands with him, some speaking their sympathy in brief conventional phrases, some speaking simply of his son. The black people—yes, the black people also—it was the first time he had ever shaken hands with black people.

They returned to the house of the Harrisons, for the night that is supposed to be worst of all the nights that must come. For Margaret it would no doubt be so; he would not leave her again to go to bed alone. But for him it was over; he could sit quietly in Harrison's study, and drink his whisky and smoke his pipe, and talk about any matter that Harrison wanted to talk about, even about his son.

—How long will you stay, Jarvis? You're welcome to stay as long as you wish.

—Thank you, Harrison. I think Margaret will go back with Mary and the children, and we'll arrange for the son of one of my neighbours to stay with them. A nice lad, just out of the Army. But I'll stay to wind up Arthur's affairs, at least in the preliminary stages.

—And what did the police say, if I may ask?

—They're still waiting for the boy to recover. They have hopes that he recognized one of them. Otherwise they say it will be very difficult. The whole thing was over so quickly. They hope too that someone may have seen them getting away. They think they were frightened and excited, and wouldn't have walked away normally.

—I hope to God they get them. And string 'em all up. Pardon me, Jarvis.

—I know exactly what you mean.

—We're not safe, Jarvis. I don't even know that stringing 'em up will make us safe. Sometimes I think it's got beyond us.

—I know what you mean. But myself—perhaps it's too soon to think about it.

—I know what *you* mean. I understand—I kind of understand—that side of it isn't the side you feel about the most. I might be the same. I don't really know.

—I don't really know either. But you're right, it's not that side of it that seems important, not yet anyway. But I realize there *is* another side to it.

—We've been agitating for more police, Jarvis. There's going to be a big meeting in Parkwold tomorrow night. The place is alive with indignation. You know, Jarvis, there's hardly a householder in these suburbs who knows who lives in the servants' quarters. I won't have it. I tell my servants that I won't have a stranger near the place, let alone allow him to sleep here. Our girl's husband comes in occasionally from the place where he works, Benoni or Springs or somewhere, and she brings him in decently, and I give permission. But I'll allow no one else. If I didn't look out, I'd have the place full of cousins and uncles and brothers, and most of 'em up to no good.

—Yes, I suppose that happens in Johannesburg.

—And these sanitary lanes that run behind the houses. We've urged them to close the damned things up now that we have proper sewerage. They're dark and dangerous, and these damned loafers use 'em as hide-outs. God knows what's coming to the country, I don't. I'm not a nigger-hater, Jarvis. I try to give 'em a square deal, decent wages, and a clean room, and reasonable time off. Our servants stay with us for years. But the natives as a whole are getting out of hand. They've even started Trade Unions, did you know that?

—I didn't know that.

—Well they have. They're threatening to strike here in the Mines for ten shillings a day. They get about three shillings a shift now, and some of the mines are on the verge of closing down. They live in decent compounds—some of the latest compounds I wouldn't mind living in myself. They get good balanced food, far better than they'd ever get at home, free medical attention, and God knows what. I tell you, Jarvis, if mining costs go up much more there won't be any mines. And where will South Africa be then? And where would the natives be themselves? They'd die by the thousands of starvation.

—Am I intruding? asked John Harrison, coming in to his father's study.

—Sit down, John, said Harrison.

So the young man sat down, and his father, who was growing warm and excited, proceeded to develop his theme.

—And where would the farmers be, Jarvis? Where would you sell your products, and who could afford to buy them? There wouldn't be any subsidies. There wouldn't be any industry either; industry depends on the mines to provide the money that will buy its products. And this Government of ours soaks the mines every year for a cool seventy per cent of the profits. And where would they be if there were no mines? Half the Afrikaners in the country would be out of work. There wouldn't be any civil service, either. Half of them would be out of work, too.

He poured out some more whisky for them both, and then resumed his subject.

—I tell you there wouldn't be any South Africa at all if it weren't for the mines. You could shut the place up, and give it back to the natives. That's what makes me so angry when people criticize the mines. Especially the Afrikaners. They have some fool notion that the mining people are foreign to the country, and are sucking the blood out of it, ready to clear out when the goose stops laying the eggs. I'm telling you that most of the mining shares are held here in the country itself, they're *our* mines. I get sick and tired of all this talk. Republic! Where would we be if we ever got a republic?

—Harrison, I'm going to bed. I don't want Margaret to go to bed alone.

—Old man, I'm sorry. I'm afraid I forgot myself.

—There's nothing to be sorry about. It's done me good to listen to you. I haven't done much talking myself, it's not because I'm not interested. I'm sure you understand.

—I'm sorry, I'm sorry, said Harrison humbly. I quite forgot myself.

—Believe me, said Jarvis, I'm sincere when I say that it's done me good to listen to you.

He looked at the two Harrisons. I'm not a man to sit and talk about death by the hour, he said.

Harrison looked at him uncomfortably. Really, really, you make it easy for me, he said.

—I could have wished that he was here tonight, said Jarvis, that I could have heard him argue with you.

—You would have enjoyed it, Mr. Jarvis, said John Harrison eagerly, responding to this natural invitation to talk about a man not long since dead. I never heard anyone argue about these things as he could.

—I didn't agree with him, said Harrison, his discomfort passing, but I had a great respect for anything that he said.

—He was a good man, Harrison. I'm not sorry that we had him. Goodnight to you.

—Goodnight, Jarvis. Did you sleep last night? Did Margaret sleep?

—We both got some sleep.

—I hope you get some more tonight. Don't forget, the house is at your service.

—Thank you, goodnight. John?

—Yes, Mr. Jarvis.

—Do you know the Boys' Club in Gladiolus Road, Claremont?

—I know it well. It was our Club. Arthur's and mine.

—I should like to see it. Any time that suits.

—I'd be glad to take you, Mr. Jarvis. And Mr. Jarvis—

—Yes, John.

—I just want to tell you that when father says Afrikaners he means Nationalists. Arthur was always telling him that. And father would agree too, but he just doesn't seem able to remember.

Jarvis smiled, first at the boy, then at his father. It's a good point, he said. Goodnight, Harrison. Goodnight, John.

*   *   *   *   *

The next morning Harrison waited for his guest at the foot of the stairs.

—Come in to the study, he said. They went in, and Harrison closed the door behind him.

—The police have just telephoned, Jarvis. The boy recovered consciousness this morning. He says there were three right enough. They had their mouths and noses covered, but he is sure that the one that knocked him out was an old garden-boy of Mary's. Mary had to get rid of him for some trouble or other. He recognized him because of some twitching about the eyes. When he left Mary, he got a job at some textile factory in Doornfontein. Then he left the factory, and no one can say where he went. But they got information about some other native who had been very friendly with him. They're after him now, hoping that he can tell them

where to find the garden-boy. They certainly seem
to be moving.

—They do seem to be.

—And here is a copy of Arthur's manuscript on
native crime. Shall I leave it on the table and you
can read it in peace after breakfast?

—Thank you, leave it there.

—How did you sleep? And Margaret?

—She slept heavily, Harrison. She needed it.

—I'm sure she did. Come to breakfast.

*   *   *   *   *

After breakfast, Jarvis returned to his host's
study, and began to read his son's manuscript. He
turned first to the last page of it, and read with
pain the last unfinished paragraph. This was almost the last thing that his son had done. When
this was done he had been alive. Then at this moment, at this very word that hung in the air, he had
got up and gone down the stairs to his death. If one
could have cried then, don't go down! If one could
have cried, stop, there is danger! But there was no
one to cry. No one knew then what so many knew
now. But these thoughts were unprofitable; it was
not his habit to dwell on what might have been but
what could never be. There was no point in imag-
ining that if one had been there, one could have
prevented a thing that had happened only because
it had not been prevented. It was the pain that did
that, that compelled one to these unprofitable

thoughts. He wanted to understand his son, not to desire what was no more accessible to desire. So he compelled himself to read the last paragraph slowly—with his head, not his heart, so that he could understand it.

The truth is that our Christian civilization is riddled through and through with dilemma. We believe in the brotherhood of man, but we do not want it in South Africa. We believe that God endows men with diverse gifts, and that human life depends for its fullness on their employment and enjoyment, but we are afraid to explore this belief too deeply. We believe in help for the underdog, but we want him to stay under. And we are therefore compelled, in order to preserve our belief that we are Christian, to ascribe to Almighty God, Creator of Heaven and Earth, our own human intentions, and to say that because He created white and black, He gives the Divine Approval to any human action that is designed to keep black men from advancement. We go so far as to credit Almighty God with having created black men to hew wood and draw water for white men. We go so far as to assume that He blesses any action that is designed to prevent black men from the full employment of the gifts He gave them. Alongside of these very arguments we use others totally inconsistent, so that the accusation of repression may be refuted. We say we withhold education because the black child has not the intelligence to profit by it; we withhold opportunity to develop gifts because black people have no gifts; we justify our action by saying that it took us thousands of years to achieve our own advancement, and it would be foolish to suppose that it will take the black man any lesser time, and that therefore there is no need for hurry. We shift our ground again when a black man does achieve something remarkable, and feel deep pity for a man who is condemned to the loneliness of being remarkable, and decide that it is a Christian kindness not to let black men become remarkable. Thus even our God becomes a confused and inconsistent creature, giving gifts and denying them employment. Is it strange then that our civilization is riddled through and through with dilemma? The truth is that our civilization is not Christian; it is a tragic compound of great ideal and fearful practice, of high assurance and desperate anxiety, of loving charity and fearful clutching of possessions. Allow me a minute. . . .

Jarvis sat, deeply moved. Whether because this was his son, whether because this was almost the last act of his son, he could not say. Whether because there was some quality in the words, that too he could not say, for he had given little time in his life to the savouring and judging of words. Whether because there was some quality in the ideas, that too he could not say, for he had given little time to the study of these particular matters. He rose and went up the stairs to his room, and was glad to find his wife not there, for here was a sequence not to be interrupted. He picked up the

Abraham Lincoln and went down to the study again, and there opened the book at the Second In-augural Address of the great president. He read it through, and felt with a sudden lifting of the spirit that here was a secret unfolding, a track picked up again. There was increasing knowledge of a stran-ger. He began to understand why the picture of this man was in the house of his son, and the mul-titude of books.

He picked up the page again, but for his son, not for the words or the ideas. He looked at the words.

Allow me a minute . . .

And nothing more. Those fingers would not write any more. Allow me a minute, I hear a sound in the kitchen. Allow me a minute, while I go to my death. Allow me a thousand minutes, I am not coming back any more.

Jarvis shook it off, and put another match to his pipe, and after he had read the paper through, sat in a reverie, smoking.

—James.

He started. Yes, my dear, he said.

—You shouldn't sit by yourself, she said.

He smiled at her. It's not my nature to brood, he said.

—Then what have you been doing?

—Thinking. Not brooding, thinking. And read-ing. This is what I have been reading.

She took it, looked at it, and held it against her breast.

—Read it, he said quietly, it's worth reading.

So she sat down to read it, and he watching her, knew what she would do. She turned to the last page, to the last words. Allow me a minute, and sat looking at them. She looked at him, she was going to speak, he accepted that. Pain does not go away so quickly.

22

AT the head of the Court is a high seat where the Judge sits. Down below it is a table for officers of the Court, and to the left and to the right of the table are other seats. Some of these seats form a block that is enclosed, and they are for the jury if there is a jury. In front of the table are other seats, arranged in arcs of circles, with curved tables in front of the seats and it is there that the lawyers sit. And behind them is the dock, with a passage leading to some place that is underground, and from this place that is underground will be brought the men that are to be judged. At the back of the Court there are seats rising in tiers, those on the right for Europeans, those on the left for non-Europeans, according to the custom.

You may not smoke in this Court, you may not whisper or speak or laugh. You must dress decently, and if you are a man, you may not wear your hat unless such is your religion. This is in honour of the Judge and in honour of the King whose officer he is; and in honour of the Law behind the Judge, and in honour of the People behind the Law. When the

Judge enters you will stand, and you will not sit till he is seated. When the Judge leaves you will stand, and you will not move till he has left you. This is in honour of the Judge, and of the things behind the Judge.

For to the Judge is entrusted a great duty, to judge and to pronounce sentence, even sentence of death. Because of their high office, Judges are called Honourable, and precede most other men on great occasions. And they are held in great honour by men both white and black. Because the land is a land of fear, a Judge must be without fear, so that justice may be done according to the Law; therefore a Judge must be incorruptible.

The Judge does not make the Law. It is the People that make the Law. Therefore if a Law is unjust, and if the Judge judges according to the Law, that is justice, even if it is not just.

It is the duty of a Judge to do justice, but it is only the People that can be just. Therefore if justice be not just, that is not to be laid at the door of the Judge, but at the door of the People, which means at the door of the White People, for it is the White People that make the Law.

In South Africa men are proud of their Judges, because they believe they are incorruptible. Even the black men have faith in them, though they do not always have faith in the Law. In a land of fear this incorruptibility is like a lamp set upon a stand, giving light to all that are in the house.

*   *   *   *   *

They call for silence in the Court, and the people stand. Even if there were one there greater than the Judge he would stand, for behind the judge are things greater than any man. And the Judge enters with his two assessors, and they sit, and then the people sit also. The Court is begun.

From the place under the ground come the three that are to be judged, and all the people look at them. Some people think that they look like murderers, they even whisper it, though it is dangerous to whisper. Some people think they do not look like murderers, and some think this one looks like a murderer, but that one does not.

A white man stands up and says that these three are accused of the murder of Arthur Trevelyan Jarvis, in his house at Plantation Road, Parkwold, Johannesburg, on Tuesday the eighth day of October, 1946, in the early afternoon. The first is Absalom Kumalo, the second is Matthew Kumalo, the third is Johannes Pafuri. They are called upon to plead guilty or not guilty, and the first says, I plead guilty to killing, but I did not mean to kill. The second says I am not guilty, and the third likewise. Everything is said in English and in Zulu, so that these three may understand. For though Pafuri is not a Zulu, he understands it well, he says.

The lawyer, the white man who is taking the case for God, says that Absalom Kumalo will plead guilty to culpable homicide, but not to murder, for he had no intention to kill. But the prosecutor says there is no charge of culpable homicide; for it is murder, and nothing less than murder, with which he is charged. So Absalom Kumalo pleads, like the two others, not guilty.

Then the prosecutor speaks for a long time, and tells the Court the whole story of the crime. And Absalom Kumalo is still and silent, but the other two look grieved and shocked to think such things are said.

*　　　*　　　*　　　*　　　*

—Then after this plan was made you decided on this day, the eighth day of October?

—That is so.

—Why did you choose this day?

—Because Johannes said that no one would be in the house.

—This same Johannes Pafuri?

—This same Johannes Pafuri who is charged with me now.

—And you chose this time of half-past-one?

—That is so.

—Was it not a bad time to choose? White people come home to eat at this time.

But the accused makes no answer.

—Why did you choose this time?

—It was Johannes who chose this time. He said it was told to him by a voice.

—What voice?

—No, that I do not know.

—An evil voice?

And again there is no answer.

—Then you three went to the back door of the house?

—That is so.

—You and these two who are charged with you?

—I and these very two.

—And then?

—Then we tied the handkerchiefs over our mouths.

—And then?

—Then we went into the kitchen.

—Who was there?

—The servant of the house was there.

—Richard Mpiring?

—No, I do not know his name.

—Is this the man here?

—Yes, that is the man.

—And then? Tell the Court what happened.

—This man was afraid. He saw my revolver. He stood back against the sink where he was working. He said, what do you want? Johannes said, we want money and clothes. This man said, you cannot do such a thing. Johannes said, do you want to die? This man was afraid and did not speak. Johannes said, when I speak, people must tremble. Then he said again, do you want to die? The man said nothing, but he suddenly called out, master, master. Then Johannes struck him over the head with the iron bar that he had behind his back.

—How many times did he strike him?

—Once.

—Did he call out again?

—He made no sound.

—What did you do?

—No, we were silent. Johannes said we must be silent.

—What did you do? Did you listen?

—We listened.

—Did you hear anything?

—We heard nothing.

—Where was your revolver?

—In my hand.

—And then?

—Then a white man came into the passage.

—And then?

—I was frightened. I fired the revolver.

—And then?

The accused looked down at the floor. The white man fell, he said.

—And then?

—Johannes said quickly, we must go. So we all went quickly.

—To the back gate?

—Yes.

—And then over the road into the plantation?

—Yes.

—Did you stay together?

—No, I went alone.

—And when did you see these two again?

—At the house of Baby Mkize.

But the Judge interrupts. You may proceed shortly with your examination, Mr. Prosecutor. But I have one or two questions to ask the first accused.

—As your lordship pleases.

—Why did you carry this revolver?

—It was to frighten the servant of the house.

—But why do you carry any revolver?

The boy is silent.

—You must answer my question.

—They told me to carry it.

—Who told you?

—No, they told me Johannesburg was dangerous.

—Who told you?

The boy is silent.

—You mean you were told by the kind of man who is engaged in this business of breaking in and stealing?

—No, I do not mean that.

—Well, who told you?

—I do not remember. It was said in some place where I was.

—You mean you were all sitting there, and some man said, one needs a revolver in Johannesburg, it is dangerous?

—Yes, I mean that.

—And you knew this revolver was loaded?

—Yes, I knew it.

—If this revolver is to frighten people, why must it be loaded?

But the boy does not answer.

—You were therefore ready to shoot with it?

—No, I would not have shot a decent person. I would have shot only if someone had shot at me.

—Would you have shot at a policeman if he had shot at you in the execution of his duty?

—No, not at a policeman.

The Judge pauses and everything is silent. Then

he says gravely, and this white man you shot, was he not a decent person?

The accused looks down again at the floor. Then he answers in a low voice, I was afraid, I was afraid. I never meant to shoot him.

—Where did you get this revolver?

—I bought it from a man.

—Where?

—In Alexandra.

—Who is this man? What is his name?

—I do not know his name.

—Where does he live?

—I do not know where he lives.

—Could you find him?

—I could try to find him.

—Was this revolver loaded when you bought it?

—It had two bullets in it.

—How many bullets were in it when you went to this house?

—There was one bullet in it.

—What happened to the other?

—I took the revolver into one of the plantations in the hills beyond Alexandra, and I fired it there.

—What did you fire at?

—I fired at a tree.

—Did you hit this tree?

—Yes, I hit it.

—Then you thought, now I can fire this revolver?

—Yes, that is so.

—Who carried the iron bar?

—Johannes carried it.

—Did you know he carried it?

—I knew it.

—You knew it was a dangerous weapon? That it could kill a man?

The boy's voice rises. It was not meant for killing or striking, he said. It was meant only for frightening.

—But you had a revolver for frightening?

—Yes, but Johannes said he would take the bar. It had been blessed, he said.

—It had been blessed?

—That is what he said.

—What did Johannes mean when he said the bar had been blessed?

—I do not know.

—Did he mean by a priest?

—I do not know.

—You did not ask?

—No, I did not ask.

—Your father is a priest?

The boy looks down again at the floor and in a low voice he answers, yes.

—Would he bless such a bar?

—No.

—You did not say to Johannes, you must not take this bar?

—No.

—You did not say to him, how can such a thing be blessed?

—No.

—Proceed, Mr. Prosecutor.

*　　　*　　　*　　　*　　　*

—And if these two say there was no murder discussed at the house of Baby Mkize, they are lying?

—They are lying.

—And if they say that you made up this story after meeting them at the house of Mkize, they are lying?

—They are lying.

—And if Baby Mkize says that no murder was discussed in her presence, she is lying?

—She is lying. She was afraid, and said we must leave her house and never return to it.

—Did you leave together?

—No, I left first.

—And where did you go?

—I went into a plantation.

—And what did you do there?

—I buried the revolver.

—Is this the revolver before the Court?

The revolver is handed up to the accused and he examines it. This is the revolver, he says.

—How was it found?

—No, I told the Police where to find it.

—And what did you do next?

—I prayed there.

The Prosecutor seems taken aback for a moment, but the Judge says, and what did you pray there?

—I prayed for forgiveness.

—And what else did you pray?

—No, there was nothing else that I wished to pray.

*   *   *   *   *

—And on the second day you walked again to Johannesburg?

—Yes.

—And you again walked amongst the people who were boycotting the buses?

—Yes.

—Were they still talking about the murder?

—They were still talking. Some said they heard it would soon be discovered.

—And then?

—I was afraid.

—So what did you do?

—That night I went to Germiston.

—But what did you do that day? Did you hide again?

—No, I bought a shirt, and then I walked about with the parcel.

—Why did you do that?

—No, I thought they would think I was a messenger.

—Was there anything else that you did?

—There was nothing else.

—Then you went to Germiston? To what place?

—To the house of Joseph Bhengu, at 12 Maseru Street, in the Location.

—And then?

—While I was there the Police came.

—What happened?

—They asked me if I was Absalom Kumalo. And I agreed, and I was afraid, and I had meant to go that day to confess to the Police, and now I could see I had delayed foolishly.

—Did they arrest you?

—No, they asked if I could tell them where to find Johannes. I said no, I did not know, but it was not Johannes who had killed the white man, it was I myself. But it was Johannes who had struck down the servant of the house. And I told them that Matthew was there also. And I told them I would show them where I had hidden the revolver. And I told them that I had meant that day to confess, but had delayed foolishly, because I was afraid.

—You then made a statement before Andries Coetzee, Esquire, Additional Magistrate at Johannesburg?

—I do not know his name.

—Is this the statement?

The statement is handed up to the boy. He looks at it and says, Yes, that is the statement.

—And every word is true?

—Every word is true.

—There is no lie in it?

—There is no lie in it, for I said to myself, I shall not lie any more, all the rest of my days, nor do anything more that is evil.

—In fact you repented?

—Yes, I repented.

—Because you were in trouble?

—Yes, because I was in trouble.

—Did you have any other reason for repenting?

—No, I had no other reason.

*   *   *   *   *

The people stand when the Court is adjourned, and while the Judge and his assessors leave the Court. Then they pass out through the doors at the back of the tiers of seats, the Europeans through their door, and the non-Europeans through their door, according to the custom.

Kumalo and Msimangu, Gertrude and Mrs. Lithebe, come out together, and they hear people saying, there is the father of the white man who was killed. And Kumalo looks and sees that it is true, there is the father of the man who was murdered, the man who has the farm on the tops above Ndot-sheni, the man he has seen riding past the church. And Kumalo trembles, and does not look at him any more. For how does one look at such a man?

23

THERE is little attention being paid to the trial of those accused of the murder of Arthur Jarvis of Parkwold. For gold has been discovered, more gold, rich gold. There is a little place called Odendaalsrust in the province of the Orange Free State. Yesterday it was quite unknown, today it is one of the famous places of the world.

This gold is as rich as any gold that has ever been discovered in South Africa, as rich as anything in Johannesburg. Men are prophesying that a new Johannesburg will rise there, a great city of tall buildings and busy streets. Men that were gloomy because the gold in Johannesburg could not last forever, are jubilant and excited. A new lease of life, they say, South Africa is to have a new lease of life.

There is excitement in Johannesburg. At the Stock Exchange men go mad, they shout and scream and throw their hats in the air, for the shares that they had bought in hope, the shares that they had bought in mines that did not exist, these shares are climbing in price to heights that are beyond expectation.

There was nothing there but the flat rolling veld of the Orange Free State, nothing but sheep and cattle and native herd-boys. There was nothing but grass and bushes, and here and there a field of maize. There was nothing there that looked like a mine, except the drilling machines, and the patient engineers probing the mysteries of the earth; nobody to watch them but a passing native, a herd-boy, an old Afrikaans-speaking farmer that would ride by on his horse, looking at them with contempt or fear or hope, according to his nature.

Look at the wonder-share of Tweede Vlei. For it was twenty shillings, and then forty shillings, and then sixty shillings, and then—believe it or not—eighty shillings. And many a man wept because he sold at twelve o'clock instead of two o'clock, or because he bought at two o'clock instead of twelve o'clock. And the man that sold will feel worse to-morrow morning, when the shares go to a hundred shillings.

Oh, but it is wonderful, South Africa is wonderful. We shall hold up our heads the higher when we go abroad, and people say, ah, but you are rich in South Africa.

Odendaalsrust, what a name of magic. Yet some of them are already saying at the Stock Exchange, for their Afrikaans is nothing to wonder at, that there must be a simpler name. What could be easier than Smuts or Smutsville? What could be easier than Hofmeyr—no—but there is a place called Hofmeyr already and apart from that—well—perhaps it is not quite the name after all.

That is the worst of these mines, their names are unpronounceable. What a pity that a great industry, controlled by such brains, advanced by such enterprise, should be hampered by such unpronounceable names; Blyvooruitzicht, and Welgedacht, and Langlaagte, and now this Odendaalsrust. But let us say these things into our beards, let us say them in our clubs, let us say them in private, for most of us are members of the United Party, that stands for co-operation and fellowship and brotherly love and mutual understanding. But it would save a devil of a lot of money, if Afrikaners could only see that bilingualism was a devil of a waste of it.

*   *   *   *   *

Gold, gold, gold. The country is going to be rich again. Shares are up from twenty shillings to a hundred shillings, think of it, thank God for it. There are people, it is true, who are not very thankful. But it must be admitted that they do not hold many shares, indeed it must be admitted that some hold no shares at all. Some of these people are speaking in public, and indeed it is interesting and exasperating to some, to note at this point that very often people without shares have quite a trick of words, as though Destiny or Nature or the Life Force or whoever controls these things, gives some sort of compensation. Not in any kindly way, you understand, but not ironically either, just impersonally. But this is a fanciful idea, and in fact it might have been better not to have mentioned it. Now these people, with this trick of words but no financial standing to talk of, speak mostly to small organizations like Left Clubs and Church Guilds and societies that promote love and brotherhood. And they write too, but mostly for small publications like *New Society* and *Mankind is Marching;* and for that extraordinary *Cross at the Crossroads,* an obscure eight-page pamphlet brought out weekly by that extraordinary Father Beresford, who looks as though he hasn't eaten for weeks. But he speaks beautiful English, the kind they speak at Oxford, I mean, not the kind they speak at Rhodes or Stellenbosch, and that makes him acceptable, for he never brushes his hair or has his trousers pressed. He looks for all the world like a converted tiger, and has burning eyes; and in fact he burns bright in the forests of the night, writing his extraordinary paper. He is a missionary and believes in God, intensely I mean, but it takes all kinds to make a world.

Well, some of these people are saying it would be nice if these shares could have stayed at twenty shillings, and the other eighty shillings had been used, for example, to erect great anti-erosion works to save the soil of the country. It would have been nice to have subsidized boys' clubs and girls' clubs, and social centres, and to have had more hospitals. It would have been nice to have paid more to the miners.

Well anyone can see that this thinking is muddled, because the price of shares has really nothing to do with the question of wages at all, for this is a matter determined solely by mining costs and the price of gold. And by the way, it is said too that there are actually some big men in the mines who hold no shares at all, and this is fine to think of, because it must really be a temptation.

In any case, we musn't be too gloomy, as we might be disposed to be when we think that this eighty shillings has gone into something that isn't any different from what it was before the eighty shillings went into it. Let us look at it in another way. When shares rise from twenty shillings to a hundred shillings, someone makes eighty shillings. Not necessarily one man, because that would be too good to be true, and entitle such a man to be known as a financial wizard, and as a figure behind the Government. It's more likely that several men will share this eighty shillings, because they get nervous and sell out while the share has a lot of kick in it. It's true of course that these men don't actually work for this money, I mean, actually sweat and callous their hands. But a man must get something for his courage and foresight, and there's mental strain too, to be taken into consideration. Now these men will spend the eighty shillings, and make more work for other people, so that the country will be richer for the eighty shillings. And many of them give generously to the boys' clubs and girls' clubs, and the social centres, and the hospitals. It is wrong to say, as they do in remote places like Bloemfontein and Grahamstown and Beaufort West, that Johannesburg thinks only of money. We have as many good husbands and fathers, I think, as any town or city, and some of our big men make great collections of works of art, which means work for artists, and saves art from dying out; and some have great ranches in the North, where they shoot game and feel at one with Nature.

Now when there is more work for other people, these people will start spending part of this eighty shillings. Not all of it, of course, for the men who sell at a hundred shillings must keep some to buy back the shares when they haven't got quite so much kick in them. But the farmers will be able to produce more food, and the manufacturers will be able to make more articles, and the Civil Service will be able to offer more posts, though why we should want more Civil Servants is another question that we can hardly deal with here. And the natives need not starve in these reserves. The men can come to the mines and bigger and better compounds can be built for them, and still more vitamins be put in their food. But we shall have to be careful about that, because some fellow has discovered that labour can be over-vitaminized. This is an example of the Law of Diminishing Returns.

And perhaps a great city will grow up, a second Johannesburg, with a second Parktown and a second Houghton, a second Parkwold and a second Kensington, a second Jeppe and a second Vrededorp, a second Pimville and a second Shanty Town, a great city that will be the pride of any Odendaalsrust. But isn't that name impossible?

* * * * *

But there are some who say that it must not be so. All the welfare workers and this Father Beresford and the other Kafferboeties say it must not be so, though it must be admitted that most of them haven't one share-certificate to rub against another. And they take heart too, for Sir Ernest Oppenheimer, one of the great men of the mines, has also said that it need not be so. For here is a chance, he says, to try out the experiment of settled mine labour, in villages, not compounds, where a man can live with his wife and children. And there is talk too that the Government will set up something like the Tennessee Valley Authority, to control the development of the Free State mining areas.

They want to hear your voice again, Sir Ernest Oppenheimer. Some of them applaud you, and some of them say thank God for you, in their hearts, even at their bedsides. For mines are for men, not for money. And money is not something to go mad about, and throw your hat into the air for. Money is for food and clothes and comfort, and a visit to the pictures. Money is to make happy the lives of children. Money is for security, and for dreams, and for hopes, and for purposes. Money is for buying the fruits of the earth, of the land where you were born.

*   *   *   *   *

No second Johannesburg is needed upon the earth. One is enough.

24

JARVIS thought he would go to the house again. It was foolish to go through the kitchen, past the stain on the floor, up the stairs that led to the bedroom. But that was the way he went. He went not to the bedroom but to the study that was so full of books. And he went round the books again, past the case full of Abraham Lincoln, and the case full of South Africa, and the case full of Afrikaans, and the case full of religion and sociology and crime and criminals, and the case full of poetry and novels and Shakespeare. He looked at the pictures of the Christ crucified, and Abraham Lincoln, and Vergelegen, and the willows in the winter. He sat down at the table, where lay the invitations to do this and that, and the invitations to come to this and that, and the paper on what was permissible and what was not permissible in South Africa.

He opened the drawers of his son's table, and here were accounts, and here were papers and envelopes, and here were pens and pencils, and here were old cheques stamped and returned by the bank. And here in a deep drawer were typewritten articles, each neatly pinned together, and placed one on top of the other. Here was an article on "The Need for Social Centres," and one on "Birds of a Parkwold Garden," and another on "India and South Africa." And here was one called "Private Essay on the Evolution of a South African," and this he took out to read:

It is hard to be born a South African. One can be born an Afrikaner, or an English-speaking South African, or a coloured man, or a Zulu. One can ride, as I rode when I was a boy, over green hills and into great valleys. One can see, as I saw when I was a boy, the reserves of the Bantu people and see nothing of what was happening there at all. One can hear, as I heard when I was a boy, that there are more Afrikaners than English-speaking people in South Africa, and yet know nothing, see nothing, of them at all. One can read, as I read when I was a boy, the brochures about lovely South Africa, that land of sun and beauty sheltered from the storms of the world, and feel pride in it and love for it, and yet know nothing about it at all. It is only as one grows up that one learns that there are other things here than sun and gold and oranges. It is only then that one learns of the hates and fears of our country. It is only then that one's love grows deep and passionate, as a man may love a woman who is true, false, cold, loving, cruel and afraid.

I was born on a farm, brought up by honourable parents, given all that a child could need or desire. They were upright and kind and law-abiding; they taught me my prayers and took me regularly to church; they had no trouble with servants and my father was never short of labour. From them I learned all that a child should learn of honour and charity and generosity. But of South Africa I learned nothing at all.

Shocked and hurt, Jarvis put down the papers. For a moment he felt something almost like anger, but he wiped his eyes with his fingers and shook it from him. But he was trembling and could read no further. He stood up and put on his hat, and went down the stairs, and as far as the stain on the floor. The policeman was ready to salute him, but he turned again, and went up the stairs, and sat down again at the table. He took up the papers and read them through to the end. Perhaps he was some judge of words after all, for the closing paragraphs moved him. Perhaps he was some judge of ideas after all:

Therefore I shall devote myself, my time, my energy, my talents, to the service of South Africa. I shall no longer ask myself if this or that is expedient, but only if it is right. I shall do this, not because I am noble or unselfish, but because life slips away, and because I need for the rest of my journey a star that will not play false to me, a compass that will not lie. I shall do this, not because I am a negrophile and a hater of my own, but because I cannot find it in me to do anything else. I am lost when I balance this against that, I am lost when I ask if this is safe, I am lost when I ask if men, white men or black men, Englishmen or Afrikaners, Gentiles or Jews, will approve. Therefore I shall try to do what is right, and to speak what is true.

I do this not because I am courageous and honest, but because it is the only way to end the conflict of my deepest soul. I do it because I am no longer able to aspire to the highest with one part of myself, and to deny it with another. I do not wish to live like that, I would rather die than live like that. I understand better those who have died for their convictions, and have not thought it was wonderful or brave or noble to die. They died rather than live, that was all.

Yet it would not be honest to pretend that it is solely an inverted selfishness that moves me. I am moved by something that is not my own, that moves me to do what is right, at whatever cost it may be. In this I am fortunate that I have married a wife who thinks as I do, who has tried to conquer her own fears and hates. Aspiration is thus made easy. My children are too young to understand. It would be grievous if they grew up to hate me or fear me, or to think of me as a betrayer of those things that I call our possessions. It would be a source of unending joy if they grew up to think as we do. It would be exciting, exhilarating, a matter for thanksgiving. But it cannot be bargained for. It must be given or withheld, and whether the one or the other, it must not alter the course that is right.

Jarvis sat a long time smoking, he did not read any more. He put the papers back in the drawer and closed it. He sat there till his pipe was finished. When it was done he put on his hat and came down the stairs. At the foot of the stairs he turned and walked towards the front door. He was not afraid of the passage and the stain on the floor; he was not going that way any more, that was all.

The front door was self-locking and he let himself out. He looked up at the sky from the farmer's habit, but these skies of a strange country told him nothing. He walked down the path and out of the gate. The policeman at the back door heard the door lock, and shook his head with understanding. He cannot face it any more, he said to himself, the old chap cannot face it any more.

25

ONE of the favourite nieces of Margaret Jarvis, Barbara Smith by name, had married a man from Springs, and both Jarvis and his wife, on a day when the Court was not holding the case, went to spend a day with them. He had thought it would be a good thing for his wife, who had taken the death of their son even more hardly than he had feared. The two women talked of the people of Ixopo and Lufafa and Highflats and Umzimkulu, and he left them and walked in the garden, for he was a man of the soil. After a while they called to him to say they were going into the town, and asked if he wished to go with them. But he said that he would stay at the house, and read the newspaper while they were away, and this he did.

The newspaper was full of the new gold that was being found at Odendaalsrust, and of the great excitement that still prevailed on the share-market. Someone with authority was warning people against buying at higher and still higher prices, and saying that there was no proof that these shares were worth what they were fetching, and that they might come down after a while and cause much loss of money and much suffering. There was some crime too; most of the assaults reported were by natives against Europeans, but there was nothing of the terrible nature that made some people afraid to open their newspapers.

While he was reading there was a knock at the kitchen door, and he went out to find a native parson standing on the paved stone at the foot of the three stone steps that led up to the kitchen. The parson was old, and his black clothes were green with age, and his collar was brown with age or dirt. He took off his hat, showing the whiteness of his head, and he looked startled and afraid and he was trembling.

—Good morning, umfundisi, said Jarvis in Zulu, of which he was a master.

The parson answered in a trembling voice, Umnumzana, which means Sir, and to Jarvis' surprise, he sat down on the lowest step, as though he were ill or starving. Jarvis knew this was not rudeness, for the old man was humble and well-mannered, so he came down the steps, saying, Are you ill, umfundisi? But the old man did not answer. He continued to tremble, and he looked down on the ground, so that Jarvis could not see his face, and could not have seen it unless he had lifted the chin with his hand, which he did not do, for such a thing is not lightly done.

—Are you ill, umfundisi?

—I shall recover, umnumzana.

—Do you wish water? Or is it food? Are you hungry?

—No, umnumzana, I shall recover.

Jarvis stood on the paved stone below the lowest step, but the old man was not quick to recover. He continued to tremble, and to look at the ground. It is not easy for a white man to be kept waiting, but Jarvis waited, for the old man was obviously ill and weak. The old man made an effort to rise, using his stick, but the stick slipped on the paved stone, and fell clattering on the stone. Jarvis picked it up and restored it to him, but the old man put it down as a hindrance, and he put down his hat also, and tried to lift himself up by pressing his hands on the steps. But his first effort failed, and he sat down again, and continued to tremble. Jarvis would have helped him, but such a thing is not so lightly done as picking up a stick; then the old man pressed his hands again on the steps, and lifted himself up. Then he lifted his face also and looked at Jarvis, and Jarvis saw that his face was full of a suffering that was of neither illness nor hunger. And Jarvis stooped, and picked up the hat and stick, and he held the hat carefully for it was old and dirty, and he restored them to the parson.

—I thank you, umnumzana.

—Are you sure you are not ill, umfundisi?

—I am recovered, umnumzana.

—And what are you seeking, umfundisi?

The old parson put his hat and his stick down again on the step, and with trembling hands pulled out a wallet from the inside pocket of the old green coat, and the papers fell out on the ground, because his hands would not be still.

—I am sorry, umnumzana.

He stooped to pick up the papers, and because he was old he had to kneel, and the papers were old and dirty, and some that he had picked up fell out of his hands while he was picking up others, and the wallet fell too, and the hands were trembling and shaking. Jarvis was torn between compassion and irritation, and he stood and watched uncomfortably.

—I am sorry to detain you, umnumzana.

—It is no matter, umfundisi.

At last the papers were collected, and all were restored to the wallet except one, and this one he held out to Jarvis, and on it were the name and address of this place where they were.

—This is the place, umfundisi.

—I was asked to come here, umnumzana. There is a man named Sibeko of Ndotsheni—

—Ndotsheni, I know it. I come from Ndotsheni.

—And this man had a daughter, umnumzana, who worked for a white man uSmith in Ixopo—

—Yes, yes.

—And when the daughter of uSmith married, she married the white man whose name is on the paper.

—That is so.

—And they came to live here in Springs, and the daughter of Sibeko came here also to work for them. Now Sibeko has not heard of her for these twelve months, and he asked—I am asked—to inquire about this girl.

Jarvis turned and went into the house, and returned with the boy who was working there. You may inquire from him, he said, and he turned again and went into the house. But when he was there it came suddenly to him that this was the old parson of Ndotsheni himself. So he came out again.

—Did you find what you wanted, umfundisi?

—This boy does not know her, umnumzana. When he came she had gone already.

—The mistress of the house is out, the daughter of uSmith. But she will soon be returning, and you may wait for her if you wish.

Jarvis dismissed the boy, and waited till he was gone.

—I know you, umfundisi, he said.

The suffering in the old man's face smote him, so that he said, sit down, umfundisi. Then the old man would be able to look at the ground, and he would not need to look at Jarvis, and Jarvis would not need to look at him, for it was uncomfortable to look at him. So the old man sat down and Jarvis said to him, not looking at him, there is something between you and me, but I do not know what it is.

—Umnumzana.

—You are in fear of me, but I do not know what it is. You need not be in fear of me.

—It is true, umnumzana. You do not know what it is.

—I do not know but I desire to know.

—I doubt if I could tell it, umnumzana.

—You must tell it, umfundisi. Is it heavy?

—It is very heavy, umnumzana. It is the heaviest thing of all my years.

He lifted his face, and there was in it suffering

that Jarvis had not seen before. Tell me, he said, it will lighten you.

—I am afraid, umnumzana.

—I see you are afraid, umfundisi. It is that which I do not understand. But I tell you, you need not be afraid. I shall not be angry. There will be no anger in me against you.

—Then, said the old man, this thing that is the heaviest thing of all my years, is the heaviest thing of all your years also.

Jarvis looked at him, at first bewildered, but then something came to him. You can only mean one thing, he said, you can only mean one thing. But I still do not understand.

—It was my son that killed your son, said the old man.

So they were silent. Jarvis left him and walked out into the trees of the garden. He stood at the wall and looked out over the veld, out to the great white dumps of the mines, like hills under the sun. When he turned to come back, he saw that the old man had risen, his hat in one hand, his stick in the other, his head bowed, his eyes on the ground. He went back to him.

—I have heard you, he said. I understand what I did not understand. There is no anger in me.

—Umnumzana.

—The mistress of the house is back, the daughter of uSmith. Do you wish to see her? Are you recovered?

—It was that that I came to do, umnumzana.

—I understand. And you were shocked when you

saw me. You had no thought that I would be here. How did you know me?

—I have seen you riding past Ndotsheni, past the church where I work.

Jarvis listened to the sounds in the house. Then he spoke very quietly. Perhaps you saw the boy also, he said. He too used to ride past Ndotsheni. On a red horse with a white face. And he carried wooden guns, here in his belt, as small boys do.

The old man's face was working. He continued to look on the ground, and Jarvis could see that tears fell on it. He himself was moved and unmanned, and he would have brought the thing to an end, but he could find no quick voice for it.

—I remember, umnumzana. There was a brightness in him.

—Yes, yes, said Jarvis, there was a brightness in him.

—Umnumzana, it is a hard word to say. But my heart holds a deep sorrow for you, and for the inkosikazi, and for the young inkosikazi, and for the children.

—Yes, yes, said Jarvis. Yes, yes, he said fiercely. I shall call the mistress of the house.

He went in and brought her out with him. This old man, he said in English, has come to inquire about the daughter of a native named Sibeko, who used to work for you in Ixopo. They have heard nothing of her for months.

—I had to send her away, said Smith's daughter. She was good when she started, and I promised her father to look after her. But she went to the bad and

started to brew liquor in her room. She was arrested
and sent to jail for a month, and after that of course
I could not take her back again.

—You do not know where she is? asked Jarvis.

—I'm sure I do not know, said Smith's daughter
in English. And I do not care.

—She does not know, said Jarvis in Zulu. But he
did not add that Smith's daughter did not care.

—I thank you, said the old man in Zulu. Stay
well, umnumzana. And he bowed to Smith's
daughter and she nodded her acknowledgment.

He put on his hat and started to walk down the
path to the back gate, according to the custom.
Smith's daughter went into the house, and Jarvis
followed the old man slowly, as though he were not
following him. The old man opened the gate and
went out through it and closed it behind him. As he
turned to close it he saw that Jarvis had followed
him, and he bowed to him.

—Go well, umfundisi, said Jarvis.

—Stay well, umnumzana. The old man raised his
hat and put it back again on his head. Then he
started to walk slowly down the road to the station,
Jarvis watching him until he was out of sight. As he
turned to come back, he saw that his wife was coming to join him, and he saw with a pang that she too
walked as if she were old.

He walked to join her, and she put her arm in his.

—Why are you so disturbed, James? she asked.
Why were you so disturbed when you came into the
house?

—Something that came out of the past, he said. You know how it comes suddenly.

She was satisfied, and said, I know.

She held his arm more closely. Barbara wants us for lunch, she said.

26

THE great bull voice is speaking there in the square. There are many policemen there, both white and black; it gives one no doubt a sense of power to see them there, and to be speaking to so many people, for the great bull voice growls and rises and falls.

There are those who can be moved by the sound of the voice alone. There are those who remember the first day they heard it as if it were today, who remember their excitement, and the queer sensations of their bodies as though electricity were passing through them. For the voice has magic in it, and it has threatening in it, and it is as though Africa itself were in it. A lion growls in it, and thunder echoes in it over black mountains.

Dubula and Tomlinson listen to it, with contempt, and with envy. For here is a voice to move thousands, with no brain behind it to tell it what to say, with no courage to say it if it knew.

The policemen hear it, and one says to the other, this man is dangerous. And the other says, it is not my job to think about such things.

We do not ask for what cannot be given, says John Kumalo. We ask only for our share of what is produced by our labour. New gold has been found, and South Africa is rich again. We ask only for our share of it. This gold will stay in the bowels of the earth if we do not dig it out. I do not say it is our gold, I say only that we should get our share in it. It is the gold of the whole people, the white, and the black, and the coloured, and the Indian. But who will get the most of this gold?

And here the great voice growls in the bull throat. A wave of excitement passes through the crowd. The policemen stand more alert, except those who have heard this before. For they know that this Kumalo goes so far and no further. What if this voice should say words that it speaks already in private, should rise and not fall again, should rise and rise and rise, and the people rise with it, should madden them with thoughts of rebellion and dominion, with thoughts of power and possession? Should paint for them pictures of Africa awakening from sleep, of Africa resurgent, of Africa dark and savage? It would not be hard to do, it does not need a brain to think such words. But the man is afraid, and the deep thundering prowl dies down, and the people shiver and come to themselves.

Is it wrong to ask more money? John Kumalo asks. We get little enough. It is only our share that we ask, enough to keep our wives and our families from starvation. For we do not get enough. The

Lansdown Commission said that we do not get enough. The Smit Commission said that we do not get enough.

And here the voice growls again, and the people stir.

We know that we do not get enough, Kumalo says. We ask only for those things that laboring men fight for in every country in the world, the right to sell our labour for what it is worth, the right to bring up our families as decent men should.

They say that higher wages will cause the mines to close down. Then what is it worth, this mining industry? And why should it be kept alive, if it is only our poverty that keeps it alive? They say it makes the country rich, but what do we see of these riches? Is it we that must be kept poor so that others may stay rich?

The crowd stirs as though a great wind were blowing through it. Here is the moment, John Kumalo, for the great voice to reach even to the gates of Heaven. Here is the moment for words of passion, for wild indiscriminate words that can waken and madden and unleash. But he knows. He knows the great power that he has, the power of which he is afraid. And the voice dies away, as thunder dies away over mountains, and echoes and re-echoes more and more faintly.

—I tell you, the man is dangerous, said the one policeman.

—I believe you now that I have heard him, said the other. Why don't they put the bastard inside?

—Why don't they shoot him? asked the first.

—Or shoot him, agreed the other.

—The Government is playing with fire, said the first.

—I believe you, said the second.

All we ask is justice, says Kumalo. We are not asking here for equality and the franchise and the removal of the colour-bar. We are asking only for more money from the richest industry in the world. This industry is powerless without our labour. Let us cease to work and this industry will die. And I say, it is better to cease to work than to work for such wages.

The native policemen are smart and alert. They stand at their posts like soldiers. Who knows what they think of this talk, who knows if they think at all? The meeting is quiet and orderly. So long as it stays quiet and orderly, there is nothing to be done. But at the first sign of disorder, John Kumalo will be brought down and put in the van, and taken to some other place. And what will happen to the carpenter's shop, that brings in eight, ten, twelve pounds a week? What will happen to the talks in the carpenter's shop, where men come from every part of the country to listen to him?

There are some men who long for martyrdom, there are those who know that to go to prison would bring greatness to them, these are those who would go to prison not caring if it brought greatness or not. But John Kumalo is not one of them. There is no applause in prison.

I shall not keep you any longer, says John Kumalo. It is getting late, and there is another speaker, and many of you will be in trouble with the police if you do not get home. It does not matter to me, but it matters to those of you who must carry a pass. And we do not wish to trouble the police. I tell you we have labour to sell, and it is a man's freedom to sell his labour for what it is worth. It is for that freedom that this war has just been fought. It is for that freedom that many of our own African soldiers have been fighting.

The voice growls again, something is coming.

Not only here, he says, but in all Africa, in all the great continent where we Africans live.

The people growl also. The one meaning of this is safe, but the other meaning is dangerous. And John Kumalo speaks the one meaning, and means the other meaning.

Therefore let us sell our labour for what it is worth, he says. And if an industry cannot buy our labour, let that industry die. But let us not sell our labour cheap to keep any industry alive.

John Kumalo sits down, and the people applaud him, a great wave of shouting and clapping. They are simple people, and they do not know that this is one of the country's greatest orators, with one thing lacking. They have heard only the great bull voice, they have been lifted up, and let fall again, but by a man who can lift up again after he has let fall.

—Now you have heard him, said Msimangu.

Stephen Kumalo nodded his head. I have never heard its like, he said. Even I—his brother—he played with me as though I were a child.

—Power, said Msimangu, power. Why God should give such power is not for us to understand. If this man were a preacher, why, the whole world would follow him.

—I have never heard its like, said Kumalo.

—Perhaps we should thank God he is corrupt, said Msimangu solemnly. For if he were not corrupt, he could plunge this country into bloodshed. He is corrupted by his possessions, and he fears their loss, and the loss of the power he already has. We shall never understand it. Shall we go, or shall we listen to this man Tomlinson?

—I could listen to him.

—Then let us go nearer. He is difficult to hear.

*   *   *   *   *

—Shall we go, Mr. Jarvis?

—Yes, John, let's go.

—What did you think of it, Mr. Jarvis?

—I don't care for that sort of thing, said Jarvis briefly.

—I don't quite mean that. I mean, it's happening, isn't it?

Jarvis grunted. I don't care for it, John. Let's go on to your Club.

—He's too old to face it, thought John Harrison to himself, just like my father.

He climbed into the car and started up the engine.

—But we have to face it, he reflected soberly.

*   *   *   *   *

The captain saluted the high officer.

—The report, sir.

—How did it go, captain?

—No trouble, sir. But this man Kumalo is dangerous. He works the crowd up to a point, and then he pulls back. But I could imagine what he would be like if we weren't there.

—Well, we shall have to be there, that's all. It's strange, the reports always say that; he goes so far and no further. What do you mean, he's dangerous?

—It's the voice, sir. I've never heard anything like it. It's like the grand stop of an organ. You can see the whole crowd swaying. I felt it myself. It's almost as though he sees what's happening, and pulls himself in.

—Yellow, said the high officer briefly. I've heard

that about the voice too. I must go to hear it myself one day.

—Will there be a strike, sir?

—Wish to God I knew. It may be a nasty business. As though we hadn't enough to do. It's time you went home.

—Goodnight, sir.

—Goodnight, Harry. Harry!

—Sir.

—I hear there may be a promotion for you.

—Thank you, sir.

—That puts you in line for my job one day. Good salary, high rank, prestige. And all the worry in the world. Like sitting on the top of a volcano. God knows if it's worth it. Goodnight, Harry.

—Goodnight, sir.

The high officer sighed, and pulled the papers toward him. Lines of worry puckered his brow.

—Good pay, high rank, prestige, he said. Then he settled down to work.

*   *   *   *   *

It will be a serious matter if there is a strike. For there are three hundred thousand black miners here on the Witwatersrand. They come from the Transkei, from Basutoland and Zululand and Bechuanaland and Sekukuniland, and from countries outside South Africa. They are simple people, illiterate, tribal people, an easy tool in the hand. And when they strike they go mad; they imprison mine officials in their offices, and throw bottles and stones, and set places on fire. It is true they are in compounds in a hundred mines, and that makes control of them easier. But they can do great damage, and endanger human life, and bring the great industry of South Africa to a standstill, the industry on which South Africa was built up, and on which it depends.

There are worrying rumours about, that the strike will not be limited to the mines, but will spread to every kind of industry, to the railways and the ships. There are even rumours that every black man, every black woman, will stop working; that every school, every church, will close. They will stand idle and sullen about the streets, in every city and town and village, on every road and every farm, eight millions of them. But such a thing is fantastic. They are not organized for it, they would suffer untold hardships, they would die of starvation. Yet the thought of so fantastic a thing is terrifying, and white people realize how dependent they are on the labour of the black people.

The times are anxious, there can be no doubt about that. Strange things are happening in the world, and the world has never let South Africa alone.

$$* \quad * \quad * \quad * \quad *$$

The strike has come and gone. It never went beyond the mines. The worst trouble was at the

Driefontein, where the police were called in to drive the black miners into the mine. There was fighting, and three of the black miners were killed. But all is quiet, they report, all is quiet.

The annual Synod of the Diocese of Johannesburg cannot be supposed to know too much about the mines. The days seem over when Synods confined themselves to religion, and one of the clergymen made a speech about the matter. He urged that it was time to recognise the African Mine Workers' Union, and prophesied a bloodbath if it were not. It is supposed that he meant that the Union should be treated as a responsible body, competent to negotiate with its employers about conditions of work and pay. But a man called a spokesman has pointed out that the African Miners are simple souls, hardly qualified in the art of negotiation, and an easy tool for unscrupulous agitators. And in any event, everyone knows that rising costs would threaten the very existence of the mines, and the very existence of South Africa.

There are many sides to this difficult problem. And people persist in discussing soil-erosion, and tribal decay, and lack of schools, and crime, as though they were all parts of the matter. If you think long enough about it, you will be brought to consider republics, and bilingualism, and immigration, and Palestine, and God knows what. So in a way it is best not to think about it at all.

In the meantime the strike is over, with a

remarkable low loss of life. All is quiet, they report, all is quiet.

*   *   *   *   *

In the deserted harbour there is yet water that laps against the quays. In the dark and silent forest there is a leaf that falls. Behind the polished panelling the white ant eats away the wood. Nothing is ever quiet, except for fools.

27

MRS. Lithebe and Gertrude entered the house, and Mrs. Lithebe shut the door behind them.

—I have done my best to understand you, my daughter. But I do not succeed in it.

—I did no wrong.

—I did not say you did wrong. But you do not understand this house, you do not understand the people that live in it.

Gertrude stood sullenly. I do not understand it, she said.

—Then why do you speak with such people, my daughter?

—I did not know they were not decent people.

—Do you not hear the way they speak, the way they laugh? Do you not hear them laugh idly and carelessly?

—I did not know it was wrong.

—I did not say it was wrong. It is idle and careless, the way they speak and laugh. Are you not trying to be a good woman?

—I am trying.

—Then such people will not help you.

—I hear you.

—I do not like to reproach you. But your brother the umfundisi has surely suffered enough.

—He has suffered.

—Then do not make him suffer further, my daughter.

—I shall be glad to leave this place, Gertrude said. The tears came into her eyes. I do not know what to do in this place.

—It is not this place only, said Mrs. Lithebe. Even in Ndotsheni you will find those who are ready to laugh and speak carelessly.

—It is the place, said Gertrude. I have known nothing but trouble in this Johannesburg. I shall be glad to be gone.

—It will not be long before you go, for the case will finish tomorrow. But I am afraid for you, and for the umfundisi also.

—There is no need to be afraid.

—I am glad to hear it, my daughter. I am not afraid for the child, she is willing and obedient. She desires to please the umfundisi. And indeed it should be so, for she receives from him what her own father denied her.

—She can also talk carelessly.

—I am not blind, my child. But she learns otherwise, and she learns quickly. Let us finish with the matter. Someone is coming.

There was a knock at the door, and a great stout woman stood there, breathing heavily from her walk to the house. There is a bad thing in the paper, she said, I have brought it to show you. She put the paper down on the table, and showed the other women the headlines. ANOTHER MURDER TRAGEDY IN CITY. EUROPEAN HOUSE-HOLDER SHOT DEAD BY NATIVE HOUSE-BREAKER.

They were shocked. These were the headlines that men feared in these days. Householders feared them, and their wives feared them. All those who worked for South Africa feared them. All law-abiding black men feared them. Some people were urging the newspapers to drop the word native from their headlines, others found it hard to know what the hiding of the painful truth would do.

—It is a hard thing that this should happen at this moment, said the stout woman, just when the case is to finish.

For she knew all about the case, and had gone each time with Mrs. Lithebe to the trial.

—That is a true thing that you say, said Mrs. Lithebe.

She heard the click of the gate, and threw the paper under a chair. It was Kumalo and the girl. The girl was holding his arm, for he was frail in these days. She guided him to his room, and they were hardly gone before the gate clicked again, and Msimangu entered. His eyes fell on the paper at once, and he picked it up from under the chair.

—Has he seen it? he asked.

—No, umfundisi, said the stout woman. Is it not a hard thing that this should happen at this moment?

—This judge is a great judge, said Msimangu. But

it is a hard thing, as you say. He likes to read the paper. What shall we do?

—There is no paper here but the one that she has brought, said Mrs. Lithebe. But when he goes to eat at the Mission House he will see it.

—That is why I came, said Msimangu. Mother, could we not eat here tonight?

—That is a small thing to ask. There is food enough, though it is simple.

—Indeed, mother, you are always our helper.

—For what else are we born? she said.

—And after the meal we can go straight to the meeting, said Msimangu. Tomorrow will be easy, he does not read the paper on the days we go to the case. And after that it will not matter.

So they hid the newspaper. They all ate at Mrs. Lithebe's, and after the meal they went to the meeting at the church, where a black woman spoke to them about her call to become a nun and to renounce the world, and how God had taken from her that desire which is in the nature of women.

After the meeting, when Msimangu had left, and Kumalo had gone to his room, and while the girl was making up the bed in the place where they ate and lived, Gertrude followed Mrs. Lithebe to her room.

—May I speak to you, mother?

—That is nothing to ask, my child.

She shut the door, and waited for Gertude to speak.

—I was listening to the black sister, mother, and it came to me that perhaps I should become a nun.

Mrs. Lithebe clapped her hands, she was happy, and then solemn.

—I clap my hands not because you should do it, she said, but because you should think of it. But there is the boy.

Gertrude's eyes filled with tears.

—Perhaps the wife of my brother would care better for him, she said. I am a weak woman, you know it. I laugh and speak carelessly. Perhaps it would help me to become a nun.

—You mean, the desire?

Gertrude hung her head. It is that I mean, she said.

Mrs. Lithebe took Gertrude's hands in hers.

—It would be a great thing, she said. But they say it is not to be done lightly or quickly. Did she not say so?

—She said so, mother.

—Let us keep it unspoken except between us. I shall pray for you, and you shall pray also. And after a time we shall speak again. Do you think that is wise?

—That is very wise, mother.

—Then sleep well, my daughter. I do not know if this will happen. But if it happens, it will comfort the old man.

—Sleep well, mother.

Gertrude closed the door of Mrs. Lithebe's room, and on the way to her own, moved by sudden impulse, she dropped on the floor by the bed of the girl.

—I have a feeling to become a nun, she said.

The girl sat up in her blankets.

—Au! she said, that is a hard thing.

—It is a hard thing, said Gertrude, I am not yet decided. But if it should be so, would you care for the boy?

—Indeed, the girl answered, and her face was eager. Indeed I should care for him.

—As though he were your own?

—Indeed so. As though he were my own.

—And you will not talk carelessly before him?

The girl was solemn. I do not talk carelessly any more, she said.

—I too shall not talk carelessly any more, said Gertrude. Remember, it is not yet decided.

—I shall remember.

—And you must not speak of it yet. My brother would be grieved if we talked of it and decided otherwise.

—I understand you.

—Sleep well, small onc.

—Sleep well.

28

THE people stand when the great Judge comes into the Court, they stand more solemnly today, for this is the day of the judgement. The Judge sits, and then his two assessors, and then the people; and the three accused are brought from the place under the Court.

I have given long thought and consideration to this case, says the Judge, and so have my assessors. We have listened carefully to all the evidence that has been brought forward, and have discussed it and tested it piece by piece.

And the interpreter interprets into Zulu what the Judge has said:

The accused Absalom Kumalo has not sought to deny his guilt. The defence has chosen to put the accused in the witness-box, where he has told straightforwardly and simply the story of how he shot the late Arthur Jarvis in his house at Parkwold. He has maintained further that it was not his intention to kill or even to shoot, that the weapon was brought to intimidate the servant Richard Mpiring, that he supposed the murdered man to have been elsewhere. With this evidence we must later deal, but part of it is of the gravest importance in determining the guilt of the second and third accused. The first accused states that the plan was put forward by the third accused Johannes Pafuri, and that Pafuri struck the blow that rendered unconscious the servant Mpiring. In this he is supported by Mpiring himself, who says that he recognized Pafuri by the twitching of the eyes above the mask. It is further true that he picked out Pafuri from among ten men similarly disguised, more than one of whom suffered from a tic similar to that suffered by Pafuri. But the defence has pointed out that these tics were similar and not identical, that it was difficult to find even a few men of similar build with any tic at all, and that Pafuri was well-known to Mpiring. The defence has argued that the identification would have been valid only if all ten men had been of similar build and had suffered from identical tics. We cannot accept this argument in its entirety, because it would seem to lead to the conclusion that identification is only valid when all the subjects are identical. But the partial validity of the argument is clear; a marked characteristic like a tic can lead as easily to wrong identification as to correct identification, especially when the lower half of the face is concealed. It must be accepted that identification depends on the recognition of a pattern, of a whole, and that it becomes uncertain when the pattern is partially concealed. In fact it becomes dangerous, because it would obviously be possible to conceal the unlike features, and to reveal only the like. Two people with similar scars, shall we say, are more easily confused one with the other when the area surrounding the scar is revealed, and the rest concealed. It would appear therefore that Mpiring's identification of his assailant is not of itself sufficient proof that Pafuri was that man.

It must further be borne in mind that, although the first accused, Absalom Kumalo, stated that Pafuri was present, and that he had assaulted Mpiring, he made this statement only after the Police had questioned him as to the whereabouts of Pafuri. Did it then first occur to him to implicate Pafuri? Or was there a pre-existing connection between Pafuri and the murder? Counsel for the first accused has argued that Absalom Kumalo had been in a continuous state of fear for some days, and that once he had been arrested, no matter what name or names had been submitted to him, he would have confessed what was so heavily burdening his mind, and that it was this state of mind that led to the confession, and not the mention of Pafuri's name. Indeed his own account of his fearful state lends colour to that supposition. But one cannot exclude the possibility that he seized upon Pafuri's name, and said that Pafuri was one of the three, not wishing to be alone on so grave a charge. Why however should he not give the names of his real confederates, for there seems no reason to doubt Mpiring's evidence that three men came into the kitchen? He has given a straightforward account of his own actions. Why should he then implicate two innocent men and conceal the names of two guilty men?

One must also bear in mind the strange coincidence that what is argued to be a wrong identification led to the apprehension of an associate who immediately confessed.

There is a further difficulty in this perplexing case. Neither of the other accused, nor the woman Baby Mkize, denies that all four were present at 79 Twenty-third Avenue, Alexandra, on the night following the murder. Was this again a chance meeting that caused the first accused to name both the second and third accused as his confederates? Or was it indeed the kind of meeting that he claims it to be? Was the murder discussed at this meeting? The woman Baby Mkize is a most unsatisfactory witness, and while the prosecution, and the Counsel for the defence of the first accused, demonstrated this most clearly, neither was able to produce that conclusive proof that the murder had been discussed. This woman at first lied to the Police, telling them that she had not seen the first accused for a year. She was a confused, contradictory, and frightened witness, but was this fear and its resulting confusion caused by mere presence in a Court, or by knowledge of other crimes to which she had been a party, or by the guilty knowledge that the murder was in fact discussed? That does not seem to us to have been clearly established.

The prosecution has made much of the previous association of the three accused, and indeed has made out so strong a case that further investigation is called for into the nature of that association. But previous association, even of a criminal nature, is not in itself a proof of association in the grave crime of which these three persons stand accused.

After long and thoughtful consideration, my assessors and I have come to the conclusion that the guilt of the second and third accused is not established, and they will be accordingly discharged. But I have no doubt that their previous criminal association will be exhaustively investigated.

There is a sigh in the Court. One act of this drama is over. The accused Absalom Kumalo makes no sign. He does not even look at the two who are now free. But Pafuri looks about as though he would say, this is right, this is just, what has been done.

There remains the case against the first accused. His confession has been thoroughly investigated, and where it could be tested, it has been found to be true. There seems no reason to suppose that an innocent person is confessing the commission of a crime that he did not in fact commit. His learned Counsel pleads that he should not suffer the extreme penalty, argues that he is shocked and overwhelmed and stricken by his act, commends him for his truthful and straightforward confession, draws attention to his youth and to the disastrous effect of a great and wicked city on the character of a simple tribal boy. He has dealt profoundly with the disaster that has overwhelmed our native tribal society, and has argued cogently the case of our own complicity in this disaster. But even if it be true that we have, out of fear and selfishness and thoughtlessness, wrought a destruction that we have done little to repair, even if it be true that we should be ashamed of it and do something more courageous and forthright than we are doing, there is nevertheless a law, and it is one of the most monumental achievements of this defective society that it has made a law, and has set judges to administer it, and has freed those judges from any obligation whatsoever but to administer the law. But a Judge may not trifle with the Law because the society is defective. If the law is the law of a society that some feel to be unjust, it is the law and the society that must be changed. In the meantime there is an existing law that must be administered, and it is the sacred duty of a Judge to administer it. And the fact that he is left free to administer it must be counted as righteousness in a society that may in other respects not be righteous. I am not suggesting of course that the learned Counsel for the defence for a moment contemplated that the law should not be administered. I am only pointing out that a Judge cannot, must not, dare not allow the existing defects of society to influence him to do anything but administer the law.

Under the law a man is held responsible for his deeds, except under certain circumstances which no one has suggested here to obtain. It is not for a judge otherwise to decide in how far human beings are in truth responsible; under the law they are fully responsible. Nor is it for a judge to show mercy. A higher authority, in this case the Governor-General-in-Council, may be merciful, but that is a matter for that authority. What are the facts of this case? This young man goes to a house with the intention to break in and steal. He takes with him a loaded revolver. He maintains that this was for the purpose of intimidation. Why then must it be loaded? He maintains that it was not his intention to kill. Yet one of his accomplices cruelly struck down the native servant, and one must suppose that the servant might easily have been killed. He states himself that the weapon was an iron bar, and there is surely no more cruel, no more dangerous way to do such a deed. In this plan he concurred, and when the Court questioned him, he said that he had made no protest against the taking of this murderous and dangerous weapon. It is true that the victim was a black man, and there is a school of thought which would regard such an offence as less serious when the victim is black. But no Court of Justice could countenance such a view.

The most important point to consider here is the accused's repeated assertion that he had no intention to kill, that the coming of the white man was unexpected, and that he fired the revolver out of panic and fear. If the Court could accept this as truth, then the Court must find that the accused did not commit murder.

What again are the facts of the case? How can one suppose otherwise than that here were three murderous and dangerous young men? It is true that they did not go to the house with the express intention of killing a man. But it is true that they took with them weapons the use of which might well result in the death of any man who interfered with the carrying out of their unlawful purpose.

The law on this point has been stated by a great South African judge. "An intention to kill," he says, "is an essential element in murder; but its existence may be inferred from the relevant circumstances. And the question is whether on the facts here proved an inference of that nature was rightly drawn. Such an intent is not confined to cases where there is a definite purpose to kill; it is also present in cases where the object is to inflict grievous bodily harm, calculated to cause death regardless of whether death results or not."

Are we to suppose that in this small room, where in this short and tragic space of time an innocent black man is cruelly struck down and an innocent white man is shot dead, that there was no intention to inflict grievous bodily harm of this kind should the terrible need for it arise? I cannot bring myself to entertain such a supposition.

They are silent in the Court. And the Judge too is silent. There is no sound there. No one coughs or moves or sighs. The Judge speaks:

This Court finds you guilty, Absalom Kumalo, of the murder of Arthur Trevelyan Jarvis at his residence in Parkwold, on the afternoon of the eighth day of October, 1946. And this Court finds you,

Matthew Kumalo, and Johannes Pafuri, not guilty, and you are accordingly discharged.

So these two go down the stairs into the place that is under the ground, and leave the other alone. He looks at them going, perhaps he is thinking, now it is I alone.

The Judge speaks again. On what grounds, he asks, can this Court make any recommendation to mercy? I have given this long and serious thought, and I cannot find any extenuating circumstances. This is a young man, but he has reached the age of manhood. He goes to a house with two companions, and they take with them two dangerous weapons, either of which can encompass the death of a man. These two weapons are used, one with serious, the other with fatal results. This Court has a solemn duty to protect society against the murderous attacks of dangerous men, whether they be old or young, and to show clearly that it will punish fitly such offenders. Therefore I can make no recommendation to mercy.

The Judge speaks to the boy.

—Have you anything to say, he asks, before I pronounce sentence?

—I have only this to say, that I killed this man, but I did not mean to kill him, only I was afraid.

They are silent in the Court, but for all that a white man calls out in a loud voice for silence. Kumalo puts his face in his hands, he has heard what it means. Jarvis sits stern and erect. The young white man looks before him and frowns fiercely. The girl sits like the child she is, her eyes are fixed on the Judge, not on her lover.

I sentence you, Absalom Kumalo, to be returned to custody, and to be hanged by the neck until you are dead. And may the Lord have mercy upon your soul.

The Judge rises, and the people rise. But not all is silent. The guilty one falls to the floor, crying and sobbing. And there is a woman wailing, and an old man crying, *Tixo, Tixo*. No one calls for silence, though the Judge is not quite gone. For who can stop the heart from breaking?

*   *   *   *   *

They come out of the Court, the white on one side, the black on the other, according to the custom. But the young white man breaks the custom, and he and Msimangu help the old and broken man, one on each side of him. It is not often that such a custom is broken. It is only when there is a deep experience that such a custom is broken. The young man's brow is set, and he looks fiercely before him. That is partly because it is a deep experience, and partly because of the custom that is being broken. For such a thing is not lightly done.

29

THEY passed again through the great gate in the grim high wall, Father Vincent and Kumalo, Gertrude and the girl and Msimangu. The boy was brought to them, and for a moment some great hope showed in his eyes, and he stood there trembling and shaking. But Kumalo said to him gently, we are come for the marriage, and the hope died out.

—My son, here is your wife that is to be.

The boy and the girl greeted each other like strangers, each giving hands without life, not to be shaken, but to be held loosely, so that the hands fell apart easily. They did not kiss after the European fashion, but stood looking at each other without words, bound in a great constraint. But at last she asked, Are you in health? and he answered, I am greatly. And he asked, are you in health? and she answered, I am greatly also. But beyond that there was nothing spoken between them.

Father Vincent left them, and they all stood in the same constraint. Msimangu saw that Gertrude would soon break out into wailing and moaning, and he turned his back on the others and said to her gravely and privately, heavy things have happened, but this is a marriage, and it were better to go at once than to wail or moan in this place. When she did not answer he said sternly and coldly, do you understand me? And she said resentfully, I understand you. He left her and went to a window in the great grim wall, and she stood sullenly silent, but he knew she would not do what it was in her mind to have done.

And Kumalo said desperately to his son, are you in health? And the boy answered, I am greatly. Are you in health, my father! So Kumalo said, I am greatly. He longed for other things to say, but he could not find them. And indeed it was a mercy for them all, when a white man came to take them to the prison chapel.

Father Vincent was waiting there in his vestments, and he read to them from his book. Then he asked the boy if he took this woman, and he asked the girl if she took this man. And when they had answered as it is laid down in that book, for better for worse, for richer for poorer, in sickness and in health, till death did them part, he married them. Then he preached a few words to them, that they were to remain faithful, and to bring up what children there might be in the fear of God. So were they married and signed their names in the book.

After it was done, the two priests and the wife and Gertrude left father and son, and Kumalo said to him, I am glad you are married.

—I also am glad, my father.

—I shall care for your child, my son, even as if it were my own.

But when he realized what it was he had said, his mouth quivered and he would indeed have done that which he was determined not to do, had not the boy said out of his own suffering, when does my father return to Ndotsheni?

—Tomorrow, my son.

—Tomorrow?

—Yes, tomorrow.

—And you will tell my mother that I remember her.

Yes, indeed I shall tell her. Yes, indeed, I shall take her that message. Why yes indeed. But he did not speak those words, he only nodded his head.

—And my father.

—Yes, my son.

—I have money in a Post Office Book. Nearly four pounds is there. It is for the child. They will give it to my father at the office. I have arranged for it.

Yes, indeed I shall get it. Yes, indeed, even as you have arranged. Why yes indeed.

—And my father.

—Yes, my son.

—If the child is a son, I should like his name to be Peter.

And Kumalo said in a strangled voice, Peter.

—Yes, I should like it to be Peter.

—And if it is a daughter?

—No, if it is a daughter, I have not thought of any name. And my father.

—Yes, my son.

—I have a parcel at Germiston, at the home of Joseph Bhengu, at Number 12, Maseru Street. I should be glad if it could be sold for my son.

—Yes, I hear you.

—There are other things that Pafuri had. But I think he will deny that they are mine.

—Pafuri? This same Pafuri?

—Yes, my father.

—It is better to forget them.

—It is as my father sees.

—And these things at Germiston, my son. I do not know how I could get them, for we leave tomorrow.

—Then it does not matter.

But because Kumalo could see that it did matter, he said, I shall speak to the Reverend Msimangu.

—That would be better.

—And this Pafuri, said Kumalo bitterly. And your cousin. I find it hard to forgive them.

The boy shrugged his shoulders hopelessly.

—They lied, my father. They were there, even as I said.

— Indeed they were there. But they are not here now.

—They are here, my father. There is another case against them.

—I did not mean that, my son. I mean they are not . . . they are not. . . .

But he could not bring himself to say what he meant.

— They are here, said the boy not understanding.

Here in this very place. Indeed, my father, it is I who must go.

—Go?

—Yes. I must go . . . to . . .

Kumalo whispered, to Pretoria?

At those dread words the boy fell on the floor, he was crouched in the way that some of the Indians pray, and he began to sob, with great tearing sounds that convulsed him. For a boy is afraid of death. The old man, moved to it by that deep compassion which was there within him, knelt by his son, and ran his hand over his head.

—Be of courage, my son.

—I am afraid, he cried. I am afraid.

—Be of courage, my son.

The boy reared up on his haunches. He hid nothing, his face was distorted by his cries. Au! au! I am afraid of the hanging, he sobbed, I am afraid of the hanging.

Still kneeling, the father took his son's hands, and they were not lifeless any more, but clung to his, seeking some comfort, some assurance. And the old man held them more strongly, and said again, be of good courage, my son.

The white warder, hearing these cries, came in and said, but not with unkindness, old man, you must go now.

—I am going, sir. I am going, sir. But give us a little time longer.

So the warder said, well, only a little time longer, and he withdrew.

—My son, dry your tears.

So the boy took the cloth that was offered him and dried his tears. He kneeled on his knees, and though the sobbing was ended, the eyes were far-seeing and troubled.

—My son, I must go now. Stay well, my son. I shall care for your wife and your child.

—It is good, he says. Yes, he says it is good, but his thoughts are not on any wife or child. Where his thoughts are there is no wife or child, where his eyes are there is no marriage.

—My son, I must go now.

He stood up, but the boy caught his father by the knees, and cried out to him, you must not leave me, you must not leave me. He broke out again into the terrible sobbing, and cried, No, no, you must not leave me.

The white warder came in again and said sternly, old man, you must go now. And Kumalo would have gone, but the boy held him by the knees, crying out and sobbing. The warder tried to pull his arms away, but he could not, and he called another man to help him. Together they pulled the boy away, and Kumalo said desperately to him, stay well, my son, but the boy did not hear him.

And so they parted.

Heavy with grief Kumalo left him, and went out to the gate in the wall where the others were waiting. And the girl came to him, and said shyly, but with a smile, umfundisi.

—Yes, my child.

—I am now your daughter.

He forced himself to smile at her. It is true, he

said. And she was eager to talk of it, but when she looked at him she could see that his thoughts were not of such matters. So she did not speak of it further.

*   *   *   *   *

After he had returned from the prison, Kumalo walked up the hill that led to the street where his brother had the carpenter's shop. For a wonder there was no one in the shop except the big bull man, who greeted him with a certain constraint.

—I am come to say farewell to you, my brother.

—Well, well, you are returning to Ndotsheni. You have been a long time away, my brother, and your wife will be glad to see you. When are you leaving?

—We leave tomorrow by the train that goes at nine o'clock.

—So Gertude is going with you. And her child. You are doing a good thing, my brother. Johannesburg is not a place for a woman alone. But we must drink some tea.

He stood up to go and call to the woman at the back of the house, but Kumalo said, I do not wish for any tea, my brother.

—You must do as you wish, my brother, said John Kumalo. It is my custom to offer tea to my visitors.

He sat down and made much show of lighting a big bull pipe, holding it between his teeth, and searching amongst some papers for matches, but not looking at his brother.

—It is a good thing you are doing, my brother, he

said with the pipe between his teeth. Johannesburg is not a place for a woman alone. And the child will be better in the country.

—I am taking another child also, said Kumalo. The wife of my son. And she is with child.

—Well, well, I have heard of it, said John Kumalo, giving attention to the match above his pipe. That is another good thing you are doing.

His pipe was lit, and he thumbed the tobacco down giving it much attention. But at last there was nothing left to do, and he looked at his brother through the smoke.

—Not one, but more than one person has said to me, these are good things that your brother is doing. Well, well, you must give my remembrances to your wife, and to our other friends. You will get to Pietermaritzburg early in the morning, and you will catch the train to Donnybrook. And that evening you will be at Ndotsheni. Well, well, it is a long journey.

—My brother, there is a matter that must be spoken between us.

—It is as you wish, my brother.

—I have considered it very deeply. I have not come here to reproach you.

And John Kumalo said quickly—as though he had been expecting it:

—Reproach me? why should you reproach me? There is a case and a judge. That is not for you or me or any other person.

The veins stood out on the bull neck, but Kumalo was quick to speak.

—I do not say that I should reproach you. As you

say there is a case and a judge. There is also a great judge, but of Him you and I do not speak. But there is quite another matter that must be spoken.

—Well, well, I understand. What is this matter?

—One thing is to greet you before I go. But I could not greet you and say nothing. You have seen how it is with my son. He left his home and he was eaten up. Therefore I thought that this must be spoken, what of your own son? He also has left his home.

—I am thinking about this matter, said John Kumalo. When this trouble is finished, I shall bring him back here.

—Are you determined?

—I am determined. I promise you that. He laughed his bull laugh. I cannot leave all the good deeds to you, my brother. The fatted calf will be killed here.

—That is a story to remember.

—Well, well, it is a story to remember. I do not throw away good teaching because—well—you understand me.

—And there is one last thing, said Kumalo.

—You are my older brother. Speak what you wish.

—Your politics, my brother. Where are they taking you?

The bull veins stood out again on the bull throat. My politics, my brother, are my own. I do not speak to you about your religion.

—You said, speak what you wish.

—Well, well, I did say it. Well—yes—I am listening.

—Where are they taking you?

—I know what I am fighting for. You will pardon me—he laughed his great laugh—the Reverend Msimangu is not here, so you will pardon me if I talk English.

—Speak what you will.

—You have read history, my brother. You know that history teaches that the men who do the work cannot be kept down for ever. If they will stand together, who will stand against them? More and more our people understand that. If they so decide, there will be no more work done in South Africa.

—You mean if they strike?

—Yes, I mean that.

—But this last strike was not successful.

John Kumalo stood on his feet, and his voice growled in his throat.

—Look what they did to us, he said. They forced us into the mines as though we were slaves. Have we no right to keep back our labour?

—Do you hate the white man, my brother?

John Kumalo looked at him with suspicion. I hate no man, he said. I hate only injustice.

—But I have heard some of the things you have said.

—What things?

—I have heard that some of them are dangerous things. I have heard that they are watching you, that they will arrest you when they think it is time. It is this matter that I must bring to you, because you are my brother.

Have no doubt it is fear in the eyes. The big man

looks like a boy that is caught. I do not know what these things are, he says.

—I hear it is some of the things that are said in this shop, said Kumalo.

—In this shop? Who would know what is said in this shop?

For all his prayers for the power to forgive, Kumalo desired to hurt his brother. Do you know every man who comes to this shop? he asked. Could a man not be sent to this shop to deceive you?

The big bull man wiped the sweat from his brow. He was wondering, Kumalo knew, if such a thing might not be. And for all the prayers, the desire to hurt was stronger, so strong that he was tempted to lie, yielded, and lied. I have heard, he said, that a man might have been sent to this shop to deceive you. As a friend.

— You heard that?

And Kumalo, ashamed, had to say, I heard it.

—What a friend, said the big bull man. What a friend.

And Kumalo cried at him out of his suffering, my son had two such friends.

The big man looked at him. Your son? he said. Then the meaning of it came to him, and anger overwhelmed him. Out of my shop, he roared, out of my shop.

He kicked over the table in front of him, and came at Kumalo, so that the old man had to step out of the door into the street, and the door shut against him, and he could hear the key turned and the bolt shot home in his brother's anger.

Out there in the street, he was humiliated and ashamed. Humiliated because the people passing looked in astonishment, ashamed because he did not come for this purpose at all. He had come to tell his brother that power corrupts, that a man who fights for justice must himself be cleansed and purified, that love is greater than force. And none of these things had he done. God have mercy on me, Christ have mercy on me. He turned to the door, but it was locked and bolted. Brother had shut out brother, from the same womb had they come.

The people were watching, so he walked away in his distress.

*   *   *   *   *

—I cannot thank you enough, said Jarvis.

—We would have done more if we could, Jarvis.

John Harrison drove up, and Jarvis and Harrison stood for a moment outside the car.

—Our love to Margaret, and to Mary and the children, Jarvis. We'll come down and see you one of these days.

—You'll be welcome, Harrison, very welcome.

—One thing I wanted to say, Jarvis, said Harrison, dropping his voice. About the sentence. It can't bring the dead back, but it was right, absolutely right. It couldn't have been any other way so far as I'm concerned. If it had been any other way, I'd have felt there was no justice in the world. I'm only sorry the other two got off. The Crown made a mess of the case. They should have hammered at that woman Mkize.

—Yes, I felt that way too. Well, goodbye to you, and thank you again.

—I'm glad to do it.

At the station Jarvis gave John Harrison an envelope.

—Open it when I'm gone, he said.

So when the train had gone, young Harrison opened it: For your club, it said. Do all the things you and Arthur wanted to do. If you like to call it the "Arthur Jarvis Club," I'll be pleased. But that is not a condition.

Young Harrison turned it over to look at the cheque underneath. He looked at the train as though he might have run after it. One thousand pounds, he said. Helen of Troy, one thousand pounds!

*   *   *   *   *

They had a party at Mrs. Lithebe's at which Msimangu was the host. It was not a gay party, that was hardly to be thought of. But the food was plentiful, and there was some sad pleasure in it. Msimangu presided after the European fashion, and made a speech commending the virtues of his brother priest, and the motherly care that Mrs. Lithebe had given to all under her roof. Kumalo made a speech too, but it was stumbling and uncertain, for the lie and the quarrel were uppermost in his mind. But he thanked Msimangu and Mrs. Lithebe for all their kindnesses. Mrs. Lithebe would not speak, but giggled like a girl, and said that people were born to do such kindness. But her friend the stout woman spoke for her, a long speech that seemed as if it would never end, about the goodness of both priests, and the goodness of Mrs. Lithebe; and she spoke plainly about the duty of Gertrude and the girl to lead good lives, and to repay all the kindnesses shown to them. And that led her on to talk about Johannesburg, and the evils of that great city, and the sinfulness of the people in Sophiatown and Claremont and Alexandra and Pimville. Indeed Msimangu was compelled to rise and say to her, Mother, we must rise early in the morning, otherwise we could listen to you for ever, so that happy and smiling she sat down. Then Msimangu told them that he had news for them, news that had been private until now, and that this was the first place where it would be told. He was retiring into a community, and would forswear the world and all possessions, and this was the first time that a black man had done such a thing in South Africa. There was clapping of hands, and all gave thanks for it. And Gertrude sat listening with enjoyment to the speeches at this great dinner, her small son asleep against her breast. And the girl listened also, with eager and smiling face, for in all her years she had never seen anything the like of this.

Then Msimangu said, We must all rise early to catch the train, my friends, and it is time we went to our beds, for the man with the taxi will be here at seven.

So they closed with a hymn and prayers, and the stout woman went off with yet more thanks to Mrs. Lithebe for her kindness to these people. Kumalo went with his friend to the gate, and Msimangu said, I am forsaking the world and all possessions, but I have saved a little money. I have no father or mother to depend on me, and I have the permission of the Church to give this to you, my friend, to help you with all the money you have spent in Johannesburg, and all the new duties you have taken up. This book is in your name.

He put the book into Kumalo's hand, and Kumalo knew by the feeling of it that it was a Post Office Book. And Kumalo put his hands with the book on the top of the gate, and he put his head on his hands, and he wept bitterly. And Msimangu said to him, do not spoil my pleasure, for I have never had a pleasure like this one. Which words of his made the old man break from weeping into sobbing, so that Msimangu said, there is a man coming, be silent, my brother.

They were silent till the man passed, and then Kumalo said, in all my days I have known no one as you are. And Msimangu said sharply, I am a weak and sinful man, but God put His hands on me, that is all. And as for the boy, he said, it is the Governor-General-in-Council who must decide if there will be mercy. As soon as Father Vincent hears, he will let you know.

—And if they decide against him?

—If they decide against him, said Msimangu soberly, one of us will go to Pretoria on that day, and let you know—when it is finished. And now I must go, my friend. We must be up early in the morning. But of you too I ask a kindness.

—Ask all that I have, my friend.

—I ask that you will pray for me in this new thing I am about to do.

—I shall pray for you, morning and evening, all the days that are left.

—Goodnight, brother.

—Goodnight, Msimangu, friend of friends. And may God watch over you always.

—And you also.

Kumalo watched him go down the street and turn into the Mission House. Then he went into the room and lit his candle and opened the book. There was thirty-three pounds four shillings and fivepence in the book. He fell on his knees and groaned and repented of the lie and the quarrel. He would have gone there and then to his brother, even as it is commanded, but the hour was late. But he would write his brother a letter. He thanked God for all the kindnesses of men, and was comforted and uplifted. And these things done, he prayed for his son. Tomorrow they would all go home, all except his son. And he would stay in the place where they would put him, in the great prison in Pretoria, in the barred and solitary cell; and mercy failing, would stay there till he was hanged. Aye, but the hand that had murdered had once pressed the mother's breast into the thirsting mouth, had stolen into the father's hand when they went out into the dark. Aye, but the murderer afraid of death had once been a child afraid of the night.

In the morning he rose early, it was yet dark. He lit his candle, and suddenly remembering, went on his knees and prayed his prayer for Msimangu. He opened the door quietly, and shook the girl gently. It is time for us to rise, he said. She was eager at once, she started up from the blankets. I shall not be long, she said. He smiled at the eagerness. Ndotsheni, he said, tomorrow it is Ndotsheni. He opened Gertrude's door, and held up his candle. But Gertrude was gone. The little boy was there, the red dress and the white turban were there. But Gertrude was gone.

BOOK
III

30

THE engine steams and whistles over the veld of the Transvaal. The white flat hills of the mines drop behind, and the country rolls away as far as the eye can see. They sit all together, Kumalo, and the little boy on his knees, and the girl with her worldly possessions in one of those paper carriers that you find in the shops. The little boy has asked for his mother, but Kumalo tells him she has gone away, and he does not ask any more.

At Volksrust the steam engine leaves them, and they change it for one that has the cage, taking power from the metal ropes stretched overhead. Then they wind down the escarpment, into the hills of Natal, and Kumalo tells the girl this is Natal. And she is eager and excited, never having seen it before.

Darkness falls, and they thunder through the night, over battlefields of long ago. They pass without seeing them the hills of Mooi River, Rosetta, Balgowan. As the sun rises they wind down the greatest hills of all, to Pietermaritzburg, the lovely city.

Here they enter another train, and the train runs along the valley of the Umsindusi, past the black slums, past Edendale, past Elandskop, and down into the great valley of the Umkomaas, where the tribes live, and the soil is sick almost beyond healing. And the people tell Kumalo that the rains will not fall; they cannot plough or plant, and there will be hunger in this valley.

At Donnybrook they enter still another train, the small toy train that runs to Ixopo through the green rolling hills of Eastwolds and Lufafa. And at Ixopo they alight, and people greet him and say, au! but you have been a long time away.

There they enter the last train, that runs beside the lovely road that goes into the hills. Many people know him, and he is afraid of their questions. They talk like children, these people, and it is nothing to ask, who is this person, who is this girl, who is this child, where do they come from, where do they go. They will ask how is your sister, how is your son, so he takes his sacred book and reads in it, and they turn to another who has taste for conversation.

The sun is setting over the great valley of the Umzimkulu, behind the mountains of East Griqualand. His wife is there, and the friend to help the umfundisi with his bags. He goes to his wife quickly, and embraces her in the European fashion. He is glad to be home.

She looks her question, and he says to her, our son is to die, perhaps there may be mercy, but let us not talk of it now.

—I understand you, she says.

—And Gertrude. All was ready for her to come. There we were all in the same house. But when I went to wake her, she was gone. Let us not talk of it now.

She bows her head.

—And this is the small boy, and this is our new daughter.

Kumalo's wife lifts the small boy and kisses him after the European fashion. You are my child, she says. She puts him down and goes to the girl who stands there humbly with her paper bag. She takes her in her arms after the European fashion, and says to her, you are my daughter. And the girl bursts suddenly into weeping, so that the woman must say to her, Hush, hush, do not cry. She says to her further, our home is simple and quiet, there are no great things there. The girl looks up through her tears and says, mother, that is all that I desire.

Something deep is touched here, something that is good and deep. Although it comes with tears, it is like a comfort in such desolation.

Kumalo shakes hands with his friend, and they all set out on the narrow path that leads into the setting sun, into the valley of Ndotsheni. But here a man calls, umfundisi, you are back, it is a good thing that you have returned. And here a woman says to another, look, it is the umfundisi that has returned. One woman dressed in European fashion throws her apron over her head, and runs to the hut, calling and crying more like a child than a woman, it is the umfundisi that has returned. She brings her children to the door and they peep out behind her dresses to see the umfundisi that has returned.

A child comes into the path and she stands before Kumalo so that he must stop. We are glad that the umfundisi is here again, she says.

—But you have had an umfundisi here, he says, speaking of the young man that the Bishop had sent to take his place.

—We did not understand him, she says. It is only our umfundisi that we understand. We are glad that he is back.

The path is dropping now, from the green hills where the mist feeds the grass and the bracken. It runs between the stones, and one must walk carefully for it is steep. A woman with child must walk carefully, so Kumalo's wife goes before the girl, and tells her, here is a stone, be careful that you do not slip. Night is falling, and the hills of East Griqualand are blue and dark against the sky.

The path is dropping into the red land of Ndotsheni. It is a wasted land, a land of old men and women and children, but it is home. The maize hardly grows to the height or a man, but it is home.

—It is dry here, umfundisi. We cry for rain.

—I have heard it, my friend.

—Our mealies are nearly finished, umfundisi. It is known to *Tixo* alone what we shall eat.

The path grows more level, it goes by the little stream that runs by the church. Kumalo stops to listen to it, but there is nothing to hear.

—The stream does not run, my friend.

—It has been dry for a month, umfundisi.

—Where do you get water, then?

—The women must go to the river, umfundisi, that comes from the place of uJarvis.

At the sound of the name of Jarvis, Kumalo feels fear and pain, but he makes himself say, how is uJarvis?

—He returned yesterday, umfundisi. I do not know how he is. But the inkosikazi returned some weeks ago, and they say she is sick and thin. I work there now, umfundisi.

Kumalo is silent, and cannot speak. But his friend says to him, it is known here, he says.

—Ah, it is known.

—It is known, umfundisi.

They do not speak again, and the path levels out, running past the huts, and the red empty fields. There is calling here, and in the dusk one voice calls to another in some far distant place. If you are a Zulu you can hear what they say, but if you are not, even if you know the language, you would find it hard to know what is being called. Some white men call it magic, but it is no magic, only an art perfected. It is Africa, the beloved country.

—They call that you are returned, umfundisi.

—I hear it, my friend.

—They are satisfied, umfundisi.

Indeed they are satisfied. They come from the huts along the road, they come running down from the hills in the dark. The boys are calling and crying, with the queer tremulous call that is known in this country.

—Umfundisi, you have returned.

—Umfundisi, we give thanks for your return.

—Umfundisi, you have been too long away.

A child calls to him, there is a new teacher at the school. A second child says to her, foolish one, it is a long time since she came. A boy salutes as he has learned in the school, and cries umfundisi. He waits for no response, but turns away and gives the queer tremulous call, to no person at all, but to the air. He turns away and makes the first slow steps of a dance, for no person at all, but for himself.

There is a lamp outside the church, the lamp they light for the services. There are women of the church sitting on the red earth under the lamp; they are dressed in white dresses, each with a green cloth about her neck. They rise when the party approaches, and one breaks into a hymn, with a high note that cannot be sustained; but others come in underneath it, and support and sustain it, and some men come in too, with the deep notes and the true. Kumalo takes off his hat and he and his wife and his friend join in also, while the girl stands and watches in wonder. It is a hymn of thanksgiving, and man remembers God in it, and prostrates himself and gives thanks for the Everlasting Mercy. And it echoes in the bare red hills and over the bare red fields of the broken tribe. And it is sung in love and humility and gratitude, and the humble simple people pour their lives into the song.

And Kumalo must pray. He prays, *Tixo*, we give thanks to Thee for Thy unending mercy. We give thanks to Thee for this safe return. We give thanks

to Thee for the love of our friends and our families.
We give thanks to Thee for all Thy mercies.

Tixo, give us rain, we beseech Thee—

And here they say Amen, so many of them that he
must wait till they are finished.

Tixo, give us rain, we beseech Thee, that we may
plough and sow our seed. And if there is no rain,
protect us against hunger and starvation, we pray
Thee.

And here they say Amen, so that he must wait
again till they are finished. His heart is warmed that
they have so welcomed him, so warmed that he casts
out his fear, and prays that which is deep within him.

Tixo, let this small boy be welcome in Ndotsheni,
let him grow tall in this place. And his mother—

His voice stops as though he cannot say it, but he
humbles himself, and lowers his voice.

And his mother—forgive her her trespasses.

A woman moans, and Kumalo knows her, she is
one of the great gossips of this place. So he adds
quickly—

Forgive us all, for we all have trespasses. And
Tixo, let this girl be welcome in Ndotsheni, and de-
liver her child safely in this place.

He pauses, then says gently—

Let her find what she seeks, and have what she desires.

And this is the hardest that must be prayed, but he humbles himself.

And *Tixo*, my son—

They do not moan, they are silent. Even the woman who gossips does not moan. His voice drops to a whisper—

Forgive him his trespasses.

It is done, it is out, the hard thing that was so feared. He knows it is not he, it is these people who have done it. Kneel, he says. So they kneel on the bare red earth, and he raises his hand, and his voice also, and strength comes into the old and broken man, for is he not a priest?

The Lord bless you and keep you, and make His face to shine upon you, and give you peace, now and for ever. And the grace of our Lord Jesus Christ, and the love of God, and the fellowship of the Holy Spirit, be with you and abide with you, and with all those that are dear to you, now and forever more. Amen.

They rise, and the new teacher says, can we not sing *Nkosi Sikelel' iAfrika*, God Save Africa? And the old teacher says, they do not know it here, it has not come here yet. The new teacher says, we have it in Pietermaritzburg, it is known there. Could we not have it here? The old teacher says, we are not in Pietermaritzburg here. We have much to do in our school. For she is cold with this new teacher, and she is ashamed too, because she does not know *Nkosi Sikelel' iAfrika*, God save Africa.

*   *   *   *   *

Yes, God save Africa, the beloved country. God save us from the deep depths of our sins. God save us from the fear that is afraid of justice. God save us from the fear that is afraid of men. God save us all.

Call oh small boy, with the long tremulous cry that echoes over the hills. Dance oh small boy, with the first slow steps of the dance that is for yourself. Call and dance, Innocence, call and dance while you may. For this is a prelude, it is only a beginning. Strange things will be woven into it, by men you have never heard of, in places you have never seen. It is life you are going into, you are not afraid because you do not know. Call and dance, call and dance. Now, while you may.

*   *   *   *   *

The people have all gone now, and Kumalo turns to his friend.

—There are things I must tell you. Some day I shall tell you others, but some I must tell you now. My sister Gertrude was to come with us. We were all together, all ready in the house. But when I went to wake her, she was gone.

—Au! umfundisi.

—And my son, he is condemned to be hanged. He may be given mercy. They will let me know as soon as they hear.

—Au! umfundisi.

—You may tell your friends. And they will tell their friends. It is not a thing that can be hidden. Therefore you may tell them.

—I shall tell them, umfundisi.

—I do not know if I should stay here, my friend.

—Why, umfundisi?

—What, said Kumalo bitterly. With a sister who has left her child, and a son who has killed a man? Who am I to stay here?

—Umfundisi, it must be what you desire. But I tell you that there is not one man or woman that would desire it. There is not one man or woman here that has not grieved for you, that is not satisfied that you are returned. Why, could you not see? Could it not touch you?

—I have seen and it has touched me. It is something, after all that has been suffered. My friend, I do not desire to go. This is my home here. I have lived so long here, I could not desire to leave it.

—That is good, umfundisi. And I for my part have no desire to live without you. For I was in darkness—

—You touch me, my friend,

—Umfundisi, did you find out about Sibeko's daughter? You remember?

—Yes, I remember, And she too is gone. Where, there is not one that knows. They do not know, they said.

Some bitterness came suddenly into him and he added, they said also, they do not care.

—Au! umfundisi.

—I am sorry, my friend.

—This world is full of trouble, umfundisi.

—Who knows it better?

—Yet you believe?

Kumalo looked at him under the light of the lamp. I believe, he said, but I have learned that it is a secret. Pain and suffering, they are a secret. Kindness and love, they are a secret. But I have learned that kindness and love can pay for pain and suffering. There is my wife, and you, my friend, and these people who welcomed me, and the child who is so eager to be with us here in Ndotsheni—so in my suffering I can believe.

—I have never thought that a Christian would be free of suffering, umfundisi. For our Lord suffered. And I come to believe that he suffered, not to save us from suffering, but to teach us how to bear suffering. For he knew that there is no life without suffering.

Kumalo looked at his friend with joy. You are a preacher, he said.

His friend held out his rough calloused hands. Do I look like a preacher? he asked.

Kumalo laughed. I look at your heart, not your hands, he said. Thank you for your help, my friend.

—It is yours whenever you ask, umfundisi. Stay well.

—Go well, my friend. But what road are you going?

The man sighed. I go past Sibeko's, he said. I promised him as soon as I knew.

Kumalo walked soberly to the little house. Then he turned suddenly and called after his friend.

—I must explain to you, he said. It was the daughter of uSmith who said, she did not know, she did not care. She said it in English. And when uJarvis said it to me in Zulu, he said, she does not know. But uJarvis did not tell me that she said, she did not care. He kept it for himself.

—I understand you, umfundisi.

—Go well, my friend.

—Stay well, umfundisi.

Kumalo turned again and entered the house, and his wife and the girl were eating.

—Where is the boy? he asked.

—Sleeping, Stephen. You have been a long time talking.

—Yes, there were many things to say.

—Did you put out the lamp?

—Let it burn a little longer.

—Has the church so much money, then?

He smiled at her. This is a special night, he said.

Her brow contracted with pain, he knew what she was thinking.

—I shall put it out, he said.

—Let it burn a little longer. Put it out when you have had your food.

—That will be right, he said soberly. Let it burn for what has happened here, let it be put out for what has happened otherwise.

He put his hand on the girl's head. Have you eaten, my child?

She looked up at him, smiling. I am satisfied, she said.

—To bed then, my child.

—Yes, father.

She got up from her chair. Sleep well, father, she said. Sleep well, mother.

—I shall take you to your room, my child.

When she came back, Kumalo was looking at the Post Office Book. He gave it to her and said, there is money there, more than you and I have ever had.

She opened it and cried out when she saw how much there was. Is it ours? she asked.

—It is ours, he said. It is a gift, from the best man of all my days.

—You will buy new clothes, she said. New black clothes, and new collars, and a new hat.

—And you will buy new clothes, also, he said. And a stove. Sit down, and I shall tell you about Msimangu, he said, and about other matters.

She sat down trembling. I am listening, she said.

31

KUMALO began to pray regularly in his church for the restoration of Ndotsheni. But he knew that was not enough. Somewhere down here upon the earth men must come together, think something, do something. And looking round the hills of his country he could find only two men, the chief and the headmaster. Now the chief was a great stout man in riding breeches, and he wore a fur cap such as they wear in cold countries, and he rode about with counsellors, though what they counselled him to, it was hard to understand. The headmaster was a small smiling man in great round spectacles, and his office was filled with notices in blue and red and green. For reasons of diplomacy Kumalo decided first to go to the chief.

The morning was already hot beyond endurance, but the skies were cloudless and held no sign of rain. There had never been such a drought in this country. The oldest men of the tribe could not remember such a time as this, when the leaves fell from the trees till they stood as though it were winter, and the small tough-footed boys ran from shade to shade because of the heat of the ground. If one walked on the grass, it crackled underfoot as it did after a fire, and in the whole valley there was not one stream that was running. Even on the tops the grass was yellow, and neither below nor above was there any ploughing. The sun poured down out of the pitiless sky, and the cattle moved thin and listless over the veld to the dried-up streams, to pluck the cropped grass from the edge of the beds.

Kumalo climbed the hill to the place of the chief and was told to wait. This was no strange thing, for if he wished a chief could tell a man to wait simply because he was a chief. If he wished he could tell a man to wait while he idly picked his teeth, or stared out day-dreaming over a valley. But Kumalo was glad of the chance to rest. He took off his coat and sat in the shade of a hut, and pondered over the ways of a chief. For who would be chief over this desolation? It was a thing the white man had done, knocked these chiefs down, and put them up again, to hold the pieces together. But the white men had taken most of the pieces away. And some chiefs sat with arrogant and blood-shot eyes, rulers of pitiful kingdoms that had no meaning at all. They were not all like that; there were some who had tried to help their people, and who had sent their sons to schools. And the Government had tried to help them too. But they were feeding an old man with milk, and pretending that he would one day grow into a boy.

Kumalo came to himself with a start and realized how far he had travelled since that journey to Johannesburg. The great city had opened his eyes to something that had begun and must now be continued. For there in Johannesburg things were happening that had nothing to do with any chief. But he got to his feet, for they had summoned him to the presence of the ruler of the tribe.

He made his greetings, and put as deep a respect into them as he could find, for he knew that a chief had a sharp ear for such things.

—And what is it you want, umfundisi?

—Inkosi, I have been to Johannesburg.

—Yes, that is known to me.

—Many of our people are there, inkosi.

—Yes.

—And I have thought, inkosi, that we should try to keep some of them in this valley.

—Ho! And how would we do it?

—By caring for our land before it is too late. By teaching them in the school how to care for the land. Then some at least would stay in Ndotsheni.

Then the chief was silent and alone with his thoughts, and it is not the custom to interrupt a chief who is thus occupied with his thoughts. But Kumalo could see that he did not know what to say. He commenced to speak more than once, but whether he checked himself, or whether he could not see to the end of the words that he had in his mind, Kumalo could not say. Indeed a man is always so when another brings heavy matters to him, matters that he himself has many times considered, finding no answers to them.

But at last he spoke, and he said, I have thought many times over these heavy matters.

—Yes, inkosi.

—And I have thought on what must be done.

—Yes, inkosi.

—Therefore I am pleased to find that you too have thought about them.

And with that there was more silence, and Kumalo could see that the chief was struggling with his words.

—You know, umfundisi, that we have been teaching these things for many years in the schools. The white inspector and I have many times spoken about these things.

—I know that, inkosi.

—The inspector will be coming again soon, and we shall take these things yet further.

The chief ended his words in a tone of hope and encouragement, and he spoke as though between them they had brought the matter to a successful end. Kumalo knew that the interview would now be quickly finished, and although it was not altogether proper to do so, he summoned up courage and said in a way that meant he had other words to follow, Inkosi?

—Yes.

—It is true, inkosi, that they have been teaching these things for many years. Yet it is sad to look upon the place where they are teaching it. There is neither grass nor water there. And when the rain comes, the maize will not reach to the height of a man. The cattle are dying there, and there is no milk. Malusi's child is dead, Kuluse's child is dying. And what others must die, *Tixo* alone knows.

And Kumalo knew he had said a hard and bitter thing, and had destroyed the hope and encouragement, so that the matter was no longer at a successful end. Indeed the chief might have been angered, not because these things were not true, but because Kumalo had prevented him from bringing the matter to an end.

—It is dry, umfundisi. You must not forget that it is dry.

—I do not forget it, said Kumalo respectfully. But dry or not, for many years it has been the same.

So the chief was silent again and had no word to say. He too was no doubt thinking that he could have brought this to an end with anger, but it was not easy to do that with a priest.

At last he spoke, but it was with reluctance. I shall see the magistrate, he said.

Then he added heavily, For I too have seen these things that you see.

He sat for a while lost in his thoughts, then he said with difficulty, for such a thing is not easy to say, I have spoken to the magistrate before.

He sat frowning and perplexed. Kumalo knew that nothing more would come, and he made small movements so that the chief would know that he was ready to be dismissed. And while he was waiting he looked at the counsellors who stood behind the chief, and he saw too that they were frowning and perplexed, and that for this matter there was no counsel that they could give at all. For the counsellors of a broken tribe have counsel for many things, but none for the matter of a broken tribe.

The chief rose wearily to his feet, and he offered his hand to the priest. I shall go to see the magistrate, he said. Go well, umfundisi.

—Stay well, inkosi.

Kumalo walked down the hill, and did not stop till he reached the church. There he prayed for the chief, and for the restoration of Ndotsheni. The wood-and-iron building was like an oven, and his spirit was depressed, his hope flagging in the lifeless heat. So he prayed briefly, Into Thy hands, oh God, I commend Ndotsheni. Then he went out again into the heat to seek the headmaster of the school.

Yet there he was not more successful. The headmaster was polite and obliging behind the great spectacles, and showed him things that he called schemes of work, and drawings of flowers and seeds, and different kinds of soil in tubes. The headmaster explained that the school was trying to relate the life of the child to the life of the community, and showed him circulars from the Department in Pietermaritzburg, all about these matters. He took Kumalo out into the blazing sun, and showed him the school gardens, but this was an academic lecture, for there was no water, and everything was dead. Yet perhaps not so academic, for everything in the valley was dead too; even children were dying.

Kumalo asked the headmaster how some of these children could be kept in Ndotsheni. And the headmaster shook his head, and talked about economic causes, and said that the school was a place of little power. So Kumalo walked back again to his church, and sat there dispirited and depressed. Where was the great vision that he had seen at Ezenzeleni, the vision born of such great suffering? Of how a priest could make of his parish a real place of life for his people, and preparation for his children? Was he old then and finished? Or was his vision a delusion, and these things beyond all helping? No power but the power of God could bring about such a miracle, and he prayed again briefly, Into Thy hands, oh God, I commend Ndotsheni.

He went into the house, and there in the great heat he struggled with the church accounts, until he heard the sounds of a horse, and he heard it stop outside the church. He rose from his chair, and went out to see who might be riding in this merciless sun. And for a moment he caught his breath in astonishment, for it was a small white boy on a red horse, a small white boy as like to another who had ridden here as any could be.

The small boy smiled at Kumalo and raised his cap and said, Good morning. And Kumalo felt a strange pride that it should be so, and a strange humility that it should be so, and an astonishment that the small boy should not know the custom.

—Good morning, inkosana, he said. It is a hot day for riding.

—I don't find it hot. Is this your church?

—Yes, this is my church.

—I go to a church school, St. Mark's. It's the best school in Johannesburg. We've a chapel there.

—St. Mark's, said Kumalo excited. This church is St. Mark's. But your chapel—it is no doubt better than this?

—Well—yes—it *is* better, said the small boy smiling. But it's in the town, you know. Is that your house?

—Yes, this is my house.

—Could I see inside it? I've never been inside a parson's house, I mean a native parson's house.

—You are welcome to see inside it, inkosana.

The small boy slipped off his horse and made it fast to the poles, that were there for the horses of those that came to the church. He dusted his feet on the frayed mat outside Kumalo's door, and taking off his cap, entered the house.

—This is a nice house, he said. I didn't expect it would be so nice.

—Not all our houses are such, said Kumalo gently. But a priest must keep his house nice. You have seen some of our other houses, perhaps?

—Oh yes, I have. On my grandfather's farm. They're not so nice as this. Is that your work there?

—Yes, inkosana.

—It looks like Arithmetic.

—It *is* Arithmetic. They are the accounts of the Church.

—I didn't know that churches had accounts. I thought only shops had those.

And Kumalo laughed at him. And having laughed once, he laughed again, so that the small boy said to him, Why are you laughing? But the small boy was laughing also, he took no offence.

—I am just laughing, inkosana.

—Inkosana? That's little inkosi, isn't it?

—It is little inkosi. Little master, it means.

—Yes, I know. And what are you called? What do I call you?

—Umfundisi.

—I see. Imfundisi.

—No. Umfundisi.

—Umfundisi. What does it mean?

—It means parson.

—May I sit down, umfundisi? the small boy pronounced the word slowly. Is that right? he said.

Kumalo swallowed the laughter. That is right, he said. Would you like a drink of water? You are hot.

—I would like a drink of milk, said the boy. Ice-cold, from the fridge, he said.

—Inkosana, there is no fridge in Ndotsheni.

—Just ordinary milk then, umfundisi.

—Inkosana, there is no milk in Ndotsheni.

The small boy flushed. I would like water, umfundisi, he said.

Kumalo brought him the water, and while he was drinking, asked him, How long are you staying here, inkosana?

—Not very long now, umfundisi.

—He went on drinking his water, then he said, These are not our real holidays now. We are here for special reasons.

And Kumalo stood watching him, and said in his heart, O child bereaved, I know your reasons.

—Water is amanzi, umfundisi.

And because Kumalo did not answer him, he said, umfundisi.

And again, umfundisi.

—My child.

—Water is amanzi, umfundisi.

Kumalo shook himself out of his reverie. He smiled at the small eager face. and he said, That is right, inkosana.

—And horse is ihashi.

—That is right also.

—And house is ikaya.

—Right also.

—And money is imali.

—Right also.

—And boy is umfana.

—Right also.

—And cow is inkomo.

Kumalo laughed outright. Wait, wait, he said, I am out of breath. And he pretended to puff and gasp, and sat down on the chair, and wiped his brow.

—You will soon talk Zulu, he said.

—Zulu is easy. What's the time, umfundisi?

—Twelve o'clock, inkosana.

—Jeepers creepers, it's time I was off. Thank you for the water, umfundisi.

The small boy went to his horse. Help me up, he cried. Kumalo helped him up, and the small boy said, I'll come and see you again, umfundisi. I'll talk more Zulu to you.

Kumalo laughed. You will be welcome, he said.

—Umfundisi?

—Inkosana?

—Why is there is no milk in Ndotsheni? Is it because the people are poor?

—Yes, inkosana.

—And what do the children do?

Kumalo looked at him. They die, my child, he said. Some of them are dying now.

—Who is dying now?

—The small child of Kuluse.

—Didn't the doctor come?

—Yes, he came.

—And what did he say?

—He said the child must have milk, inkosana.

—And what did the parents say?

—They said, Doctor, we have heard what you say.

And the small boy said in a small voice, I see. He raised his cap and said solemnly, Goodbye, umfundisi. He set off solemnly too, but there were spectators along the way, and it was not long before he was galloping wildly along the hot dirt road.

*   *   *   *   *

The night brought coolness and respite. While they were having their meal, Kumalo and his wife, the girl and the small boy, there was a sound of wheels, and a knock at the door, and there was the friend who had carried the bags.

—Umfundisi. Mother.

—My friend. Will you eat?

—No indeed. I am on my way home. I have a message for you.

—For me?

—Yes, from uJarvis. Was the small white boy here today?

Kumalo had a dull sense of fear, realizing for the first time what had been done.

—He was here, he said.

—We were working in the trees, said the man, when this small boy came riding up. I do not understand English, umfundisi, but they were talking about Kuluse's child. And come and look what I have brought you.

There outside the door was the milk, in the shining cans in the cart.

—This milk is for small children only, for those who are not yet at school, said the man importantly. And it is to be given by you only. And these sacks must be put over the cans, and small boys must bring water to pour over the sacks. And each morning I shall take back the cans. This will be done till the grass comes and we have milk again.

The man lifted the cans from the cart and said, Where shall I put them, umfundisi? But Kumalo was dumb and stupid, and his wife said, We shall put them in the room that the umfundisi has in the church. So they put them there, and when they came back the man said, You would surely have a message for uJarvis, umfundisi? And Kumalo stuttered and stammered, and at last pointed his hand up at the sky. And the man said, *Tixo* will bless him, and Kumalo nodded.

The man said, I have worked only a week there, but the day he says to me, die, I shall die.

He climbed into the cart and took up the reins. He was excited and full of conversation. When I come home in this, he said, my wife will think they have made me a magistrate. They all laughed, and Kumalo came out of his dumbness and laughed also, first at the thought that this humble man might be a magistrate and second at the thought that a magistrate should drive in such a car. And he laughed again that a grown man should play in such fashion, and he laughed again that Kuluse's child might live, and he laughed again at the thought of the stern silent man at High Place. He turned into the house sore with laughing, and his wife watched him with wondering eyes.

32

A CHILD brought the four letters from the store to the school, and the headmaster sent them over to the house of the umfundisi. They were all letters from Johannesburg, one was from the boy Absalom to his wife, and another to his parents; they were both on His Majesty's Service, from the great prison in Pretoria. The third was from Msimangu himself, and the fourth from Mr. Carmichael. This one Kumalo opened fearfully, because it was from the lawyer who took the case for God, and would be about the mercy. And there the lawyer told him, in gentle and compassionate words, that there would be no mercy, and that his son would be hanged on the fifteenth day of that month. So he read no more but sat there an hour, two hours maybe. Indeed he neither saw sight nor heard sound till his wife said to him, It has come, then, Stephen.

And when he nodded, she said, Give it to me, Stephen. With shaking hands he gave it to her, and she read it also, and sat looking before her, with lost and terrible eyes, for this was the child of her womb, of her breasts. Yet she did not sit as long as he had done, for she stood up and said, It is not good to sit idle. Finish your letters, and go to see Kuluse's child, and the girl Elizabeth that is ill. And I shall do my work about the house.

—There is another letter, he said.

—From him? she said.

—From him.

He gave it to her, and she sat down again and opened it carefully and read it. The pain was in her eyes and her face and her hands, but he did not see it, for he stared before him on the floor, only his eyes were not looking at the floor but at no place at all, and his face was sunken, in the same mould of suffering from which it had escaped since his return to this valley.

—Stephen, she said sharply.

He looked at her.

—Read it, finish it, she said. Then let us go to our work.

He took the letter and read it, it was short and simple, and except for the first line, it was in Zulu, as is often the custom:

MY DEAR FATHER AND MOTHER:

I am hoping you are all in health even as I am. They told me this morning there will be no mercy for the thing that I have done. So I shall not see you or Ndotsheni again.

This is a good place. I am locked in, and no one may come and talk to me. But I may smoke and read and write letters, and the white men do not speak badly to me.

There is a priest who comes to see me, a black priest from Pretoria. He is preparing me, and speaks well to me.

There is no more news here, so I close my letter. I think of you all at Ndotsheni, and if I were back there I should not leave it again.

Your son,
ABSALOM.

Is the child born? If it is a boy, I should like his name to be Peter. Have you heard of the case of Matthew and Johannes? I have been to the court to give evidence in this case, but they did not let me see it finish. My father, did you get the money in my Post Office Book?

—Stephen, shall we go and work now?

—Yes, he said, that would be better. But I have not read Msimangu's letter. And here is a letter for our daughter.

—I shall take it. Read your letter first then. And tell me, will you go to Kuluse's?

—I shall go there.

—And would it tire you too greatly to go up to the store?

He looked out of the windows.

—Look, he said, look at the clouds.

She came and stood by him, and saw the great heavy clouds that were gathering on the other side of the Umzimkulu valley.

—It will rain, he said. Why do you want me to go to the store? It is something you need badly?

—It is nothing I need, Stephen. But I thought you might go to the store and ask the white man, when these letters come on His Majesty's Service from the Central Prison to hold them privately till we come. For our shame is enough.

—Yes, yes, he said. I shall do that for a certainty.

—Read your letter then.

He opened Msimangu's letter, and read about all the happenings of Johannesburg and was astonished to find within himself a faint nostalgia for that great bewildering city. When he had finished he went out to look at the clouds, for it was exciting to see them after weeks of pitiless sun. Indeed one or two of them were already sailing overhead, and they cast great shadows over the valley, moving slowly and surely till they reached the slopes to the tops, and then they passed up these slopes with sudden swift-ness and were gone. It was close and sultry, and soon there would be thunder from across the Umzimkulu, for on this day the drought would break, with no doubt at all.

While he stood there he saw a motor car coming down the road from Carisbrooke into the valley. It was a sight seldom seen, and the car went slowly be-cause the road was not meant for cars, but only for carts and wagons and oxen. Then he saw that not far from the church there was a white man sitting still upon a horse. He seemed to be waiting for the car, and with something of a shock he realized that it was Jarvis. A white man climbed out of the car, and he saw with further surprise that it was the magis-trate, and the foolish jest of the night before came back to him at once. Jarvis got down from his horse, and he shook hands with the magistrate, and with other white men that were climbing out of the car, bringing out with them sticks and flags. Then lo! from the other direction came riding the stout chief, in the fur cap and the riding breeches, surrounded by his counsellors. The chief saluted the magistrate, and the magistrate the chief, and there were other salutes also. Then they all stayed and talked together, so that it was clear that they had met together for some purpose. There was pointing of hands, to places distant and to places at hand. Then one of the counsellors began to cut down a small tree with straight clean branches. These branches he cut into lengths, and sharpened the ends, so that Kumalo stood more and more mystified. The white men brought out more sticks and flags from the car, and one of them set up a box on three legs, as though he would take photographs. Jarvis took some of the sticks and flags, and so did the magistrate, after he had taken off his coat because of the heat. They pointed to the clouds also, and Kumalo heard Jarvis say, It looks like it at last.

Now the chief was not to be outdone by the white men, so he too got down from his horse and took some of the sticks, but Kumalo could see that he did not fully understand what was being done. Jarvis, who seemed to be in charge of these matters, planted one of the sticks in the ground, and the chief gave a stick to one of his counsellors, and said something to him. So the counsellor also planted the stick in the ground, but the white man with the box on the three legs called out, Not there, not there, take that stick away. The counsellor was in two minds, and he looked hesitantly at the chief, who said angrily, Not there, not there, take it away. Then the chief, embarrassed and knowing still less what was to be done, got back on his horse and sat there, leaving the white men to plant the sticks.

So an hour passed, while there was quite an array of sticks and flags, and Kumalo looked on as mystified as ever. Jarvis and the magistrate stood together, and they kept on pointing at the hills, then turned and pointed down the valley. Then they talked to the chief, and the counsellors stood by, listening with grave attention to the conversation. Kumalo heard Jarvis say to the magistrate, That's too long. The magistrate shrugged his shoulders, saying, That's the way these things are done. Then Jarvis said, I'll go to Pretoria. Would you mind? The magistrate said, I don't mind at all. It may be the way to get it. Then Jarvis said, I don't want to lose your company, but if you want to get home dry, you'd better be starting. This'll be no ordinary storm.

But Jarvis did not start himself. He said goodbye to the magistrate, and began to walk across the bare fields, measuring the distance with his strides. Kumalo heard the magistrate say to one of the white men, They say he's going queer. From what I've heard, he soon won't have any money left.

Then the magistrate said to the chief, You will see that not one of these sticks is touched or removed. He saluted the chief, and he and the other white men climbed into the car and drove away up the hill. The chief said to his counsellors, You will give orders that not one of these sticks is to be touched or removed. The counsellors then rode away, each to some part of the valley, and the chief rode past the church, returning Kumalo's greeting, but not stopping to tell him anything about this matter of the sticks.

Indeed it was true what Jarvis had said, that this would be no ordinary storm. For it was now dark and threatening over the valley. There were no more shadows sailing over the fields, for all was shadow. On the other side of the Umzimkulu the thunder was rolling without pause, and now and then the lightning would strike down among the far-off hills. But it was this for which all men were waiting, the rain at last. Women were hurrying along the paths, and with a sudden babel of sound the children poured out of the school, and the headmaster and his teachers were urging them, Hurry, hurry, do not loiter along the road.

It was something to see, a storm like this. A great bank of black and heavy cloud was moving over the Umzimkulu, and Kumalo stood for a long time and watched it. Out of it the thunder came, and lightning shot out of it to the earth below. Wind sprang up in the valley of Ndotsheni, and the dust whirled over the fields and along the roads. It was very dark and soon the hills beyond the Umzimkulu were shut off by the rain. He saw Jarvis hurrying back to his horse, which stood restlessly against the fence. With a few practised movements he stripped it of saddle and bridle, and saying a word to it, left it loose.

Then he walked quickly in the direction of Kumalo, and called out to him, umfundisi.

—Umnumzana.

—May I put these things in your porch, umfundisi, and stay in your church?

—Indeed, I shall come with you, umnumzana.

So they went into the church, and none too soon, for the thunder boomed out overhead, and they could hear the rain rushing across the fields. In a moment it was drumming on the iron roof, with a deafening noise that made all conversation impossible. Kumalo lit a lamp in the church, and Jarvis sat down on one of the benches, and remained there without moving.

But it was not long before the rain found the holes in the old rusted roof, and Jarvis had to move to avoid it.

Kumalo, nervous and wishing to make an apology, shouted at him, the roof leaks, and Jarvis shouted back at him, I have seen it.

And again the rain came down through the roof on the new place where Jarvis was sitting, so that he had to move again. He stood up and moved about in the semi-darkness, testing the benches with his hand, but it was hard to find a place to sit, for where there was a dry place on a bench, there was rain coming down on the floor, and where there was a dry place on the floor, there was rain coming down on the bench.

—The roof leaks in many places, Kumalo shouted, and Jarvis shouted in reply, I have seen that also.

At last Jarvis found a place where the rain did not fall too badly, and Kumalo found himself a place also, and they sat there together in silence. But outside it was not silent, with the cracking of the thunder, and the deafening downpour on the roof.

It was a long time that they sat there, and it was not until they heard the rushing of the streams, of dead rivers come to life, that they knew that the storm was abating. Indeed the thunder sounded further away and there was a dull light in the church, and the rain made less noise on the roof.

It was nearly over when Jarvis rose and came and stood in the aisle near Kumalo. Without looking at the old man he said, Is there mercy?

Kumalo took the letter from his wallet with trembling hands; his hands trembled partly because of the sorrow, and partly because he was always so with this man. Jarvis took the letter and held it away from him so that the dull light fell on it. Then he put it back again in the envelope, and returned it to Kumalo.

—I do not understand these matters, he said, but otherwise I understand completely.

—I hear you, umnumzana.

Jarvis was silent for a while, looking towards the altar and the cross on the altar.

—When it comes to this fifteenth day, he said, I shall remember. Stay well, umfundisi.

But Kumalo did not say go well. He did not offer to carry the saddle and the bridle, nor did he think to thank Jarvis for the milk. And least of all did he think to ask about the matter of the sticks. And when he rose and went out, Jarvis was gone. It was still raining, but lightly, and the valley was full of sound, of streams and rivers, all red with the blood of the earth.

*   *   *   *   *

That evening they all came out in the pale red light of sunset, and they examined the sticks, but no one understood their purpose. The small boys pretended to pull the sticks out, seizing them near the earth, and turning the whites of their eyes up to heaven in their mock efforts. The small girls looked on, half with enjoyment, half with apprehension. This game went well till the young son of Dazuma pulled one out in error, and stood shocked at what he had done. Then there was silence, and the small boys looked in fear at their elders, and the small girls went to their mothers, some weeping, some giggling with apprehension, some saying, We told you, we told you. The young offender was taken off by his mother, who shook him and said, You have shamed me, you have shamed me. And the grown men that there were in the valley searched round the place, and one said, There is the hole. So they put it in carefully, and one got down on his knees and patted the ground round the stick, so that the place would look as though the stick had never been removed. But one said, Make it rough, for the ground is wet, and it will look as though it has been patted. So they made it rough, and put grass and pebbles over it, and indeed no one could have said that it had been patted.

Then the cart with the milk arrived, and the mothers of the small children, or some messenger that they had sent, went to the church for their portions.

—What is all this with the sticks? Kumalo asked his friend.

—Umfundisi, I do not know. But tomorrow I shall try to discover.

33

THE sticks stood for days in the places where the men had put them, but no one came again to the valley. It was rumored that a dam was to be built here, but no one knew how it would be filled, because the small stream that ran past the church was sometimes dry, and was never a great stream at any time. Kumalo's friend told him that Jarvis had gone away to Pretoria, and his business was surely the business of the sticks, which was the business of the dam.

So the days passed. Kumalo prayed regularly for the restoration of Ndotsheni, and the sun rose and set regularly over the earth.

Kuluse's child was recovered, and Kumalo went about his pastoral duties. The school went on with its work, and they were no doubt learning there about seeds and plants, and the right kind of grass for pastures, and the right kind of stuff to put into the soil, and the right kind of food to give to cattle. More and more he found himself waiting for news of Jarvis's return, so that the people might know what plans were afoot; and more and more he found himself thinking that it was Jarvis and Jarvis alone that could perform the great miracle.

The girl was happy in her new home, for she had a dependent and affectionate nature. The small boy played with the other small boys, and had asked after his mother not more than once or twice; with time he would forget her. About Absalom no one asked, and if they talked about it in their huts, they let it make no difference in their respect for the old umfundisi.

One day the small white boy came galloping up, and when Kumalo came out to greet him, he raised his cap as before, and Kumalo found himself warm with pleasure to see his small visitor again.

—I've come to talk Zulu again, said the boy. He slid down from his horse, and put the reins round the post. He walked over to the house with the assurance of a man, and dusted his feet and took off his cap before entering the house. He sat down at the table and looked round with a pleasure inside him, so that a man felt it was something bright that had come into the house.

—Are the accounts finished, umfundisi?

—Yes, they are finished, inkosana.

—Were they right?

Kumalo laughed, he could not help himself.

—Yes, they were right, he said. But not very good.

—Not very good, eh? Are you ready for the Zulu?

Kumalo laughed again, and sat down in his chair at the other side of the table, and said, Yes, I am ready for the Zulu. When is your grandfather returning?

—I don't know, said the small boy. I want him to come back. I like him, he said.

Kumalo could have laughed again at this, but he thought perhaps it was not a thing to laugh at. But the small boy laughed himself, so Kumalo laughed also. It was easy to laugh with this small boy, there seemed to be laughter inside him.

—When are you going back to Johannesburg, inkosana?

—When my grandfather comes back.

And Kumalo said to him in Zulu, When you go, something bright will go out of Ndotsheni.

—What are you saying, umfundisi?

But when Kumalo would have translated, the small boy cried out, No, don't tell me. Say it again in Zulu. So Kumalo said it again.

—That means when you are gone, said the small boy, and say the rest again.

—Something bright will go out of Ndotsheni, said Kumalo in Zulu.

—Something about Ndotsheni. But it's too hard for me. Say it in English, umfundisi.

—Something bright will go out of Ndotsheni, said Kumalo in English.

—Yes, I see. When I go, something bright will go out of Ndotsheni.

The small boy laughed with pleasure. I hear you, he said in Zulu.

And Kumalo clapped his hands in astonishment, and said, Au! Au! You speak Zulu, so that the small boy laughed with still greater pleasure, and Kumalo clapped his hands again, and made many exclamations. The door opened and his wife came in, and he said to the small boy, this is my wife, and he said to his wife in Zulu, this is the son of the man. The small boy stood up and made a bow to Kumalo's wife, and she stood and looked at him with fear and sorrow. But he said to her, You have a nice house here, and he laughed. She said to her husband in Zulu, I am overcome, I do not know what to say. And the small boy said in Zulu, I hear you, so that she took a step backwards in fear. But Kumalo said to her swiftly, He does not understand you, those are only words that he knows, and for the small boy he clapped his hands again in astonishment and said, Au! Au! But you speak Zulu. And the woman went backwards to the door, and opened it and shut it and was gone.

—Are you ready for the Zulu, umfundisi?

—Indeed I am ready.

—Tree is umuti, umfundisi.

—That is right, inkosana.

—But medicine is also umuti, umfundisi.

And the small boy said this with an air of triumph, and a kind of mock bewilderment, so that they both laughed together.

—You see, inkosana, said Kumalo seriously, our medicines come mostly from trees. That is why the word is the same.

—I see, said the small boy, pleased with this explanation. And box is ibokisi.

—That is right, inkosana. You see, we had no boxes, and so our word is from your word.

—I see. And motor-bike is isitututu.

—That is right. That is from the sound that the motorbike makes, so, isi-tu-tu-tu. But inkosana, let us make a sentence. For you are giving me all the words that you know, and so you will not learn anything that is new. Now how do you say, I see a horse?

So the lesson went on, till Kumalo said to his pupil, It is nearly twelve o'clock, and perhaps it is time you must go.

—Yes, I must go, but I'll come back for some more Zulu.

—You must come back, inkosana. Soon you will be speaking better than many Zulus. You will be able to speak in the dark, and people will not know it is not a Zulu.

The small boy was pleased, and when they went out he said, Help me up, umfundisi. So Kumalo helped him up, and the small boy lifted his cap, and went galloping up the road. There was a car going up the road, and the small boy stopped his horse and cried, my grandfather is back. Then he struck at the horse and set out in a wild attempt to catch up with the car.

There was a young man standing outside the church, a young pleasant-faced man of some twenty-five years, and his bags were on the ground. He took off his hat and said in English, You are the umfundisi?

—I am.

—And I am the new agricultural demonstrator. I have my papers here, umfundisi.

—Come into the house, said Kumalo, excited.

They went into the house, and the young man took out his papers and showed them to Kumalo. These papers were from parsons and school-inspectors and the like, and said that the bearer, Napoleon Letsitsi, was a young man of sober habits and good conduct, and another paper said that he had passed out of a school in the Transkei as an agricultural demonstrator.

—I see, said Kumalo. But you must tell me why you are here. Who sent you to me?

—Why, the white man who brought me.

—uJarvis, was that the name?

—I do not know the name, umfundisi, but it is the white man who has just gone.

—Yes, that is uJarvis. Now tell me all.

—I am come here to teach farming, umfundisi.

—To us, in Ndotsheni?

—Yes, umfundisi.

Kumalo's face lighted up, and he sat there with his eyes shining. You are an angel from God, he said. He stood up and walked about the room, hitting one hand against the other, which the young man watched in amazement. Kumalo saw him and laughed at him, and said again, You are an angel from God. He sat down again and said to the young demonstrator, Where did the white man find you?

—He came to my home in Krugersdorp. I was teaching there at a school. He asked me if I would do a great work, and he told me about this place Ndotsheni. So I felt I would come here.

—And what about your teaching?

—I am not really a teacher, so they did not pay me

well. And the white man said they would pay me ten pounds a month here, so I came. But I did not come only for the money. It was a small work there in the school.

Kumalo felt a pang of jealousy, for he had never earned ten pounds a month in all his sixty years. But he put it from him.

—The white man asked if I could speak Zulu, and I said no, but I could speak Xosa as well as I spoke my own language, for my mother was a Xosa. And he said that would do for Xosa and Zulu are almost the same.

Kumalo's wife opened the door again, and said, It is time for food. Kumalo said in Zulu, My wife, this is Mr. Letsitsi, who has come to teach our people farming. And he said to Letsitsi, You will eat with us.

They went to eat, and Letsitsi was introduced to the girl and the small boy. After Kumalo had asked a blessing, they sat down, and Kumalo said in Zulu, When did you arrive in Pietermaritzburg?

—This morning, umfundisi. And then we came with the motor-car to this place.

—And what did you think of the white man?

—He is very silent, umfundisi. He did not speak much to me.

—That is his nature.

—We stopped there on the road, overlooking a valley. And he said, What could you do in such a valley? Those were the first words we spoke on the journey.

—And did you tell him?

—I told him, umfundisi.

—And what did he say?

—He said nothing, umfundisi. He made a noise in his throat, that was all.

—And then?

—He did not speak till we got here. He said to me, Go to the umfundisi, and ask him to find lodgings for you. Tell him I am sorry I cannot come, but I am anxious to get to my home.

Kumalo looked at his wife, and she at him.

—Our rooms are small, and this is a parson's house, said Kumalo, but you may stay here if you wish.

—My people are also of the church, umfundisi. I should be glad to stay here.

—And what will you do in this valley?

The young demonstrator laughed. I must look at it first, he said.

—But what would you have done in that other valley?

So the young man told them all he would have done in the other valley, how the people must stop burning the dung and must put it back into the land, how they must gather the weeds together and treat them and not leave them to wither away in the sun, how they must stop ploughing up and down the hills, how they must plant trees for fuel, trees that grow quickly like wattles, in some place where they could not plough at all, on the steep sides of streams so that the water did not rush away in the storms. But these were hard things to do, because the people must learn that it is harmful for each man to wrest a living from his own little piece of ground. Some must give up their ground for trees, and some for pastures. And hardest of all would be the custom of lobola, by which a man pays for his wife in cattle, for people kept too many cattle for this purpose, and counted all their wealth in cattle, so that the grass had no chance to recover.

—And is there to be a dam? asked Kumalo.

—Yes, there is to be a dam, said the young man, so that the cattle always have water to drink. And the water from the dam can be let out through a gate, and can water this land and that, and can water the pastures that are planted.

—But where is the water to come from?

—It will come by a pipe from a river, said the young demonstrator. That is what the white man said.

—That will be his river, said Kumalo. And can all these things you have been saying, can they all be done in Ndotsheni?

—I must first see the valley, said the demonstrator laughing.

—But you came down through it, said Kumalo eagerly.

—Yes, I saw it. But I must see it slowly. Yet I think all these things can be done.

They all sat round the table, their faces excited and eager, for this young man could paint a picture before your eyes. And Kumalo looked round at them and said, I told this young man he was an angel from God. He got up in his excitement and walked round the room. Are you impatient to begin? he said.

The young man laughed with embarrassment. I am impatient, he said.

—What is your first step that you take?

—I must first go to the chief, umfundisi.

—Yes, that is the first thing you must do.

Then outside he heard the sounds of a horse, and he got up and went out, wondering if it could be the small boy again, and back so quickly. And indeed it was, but the boy did not climb down, he talked to Kumalo from his horse. He talked excitedly and earnestly, as though it were a serious matter.

—That was a close shave, he said.

—A shave, asked Kumalo. A close shave?

—That's slang, said the small boy. But he did not laugh, he was too serious. It means a narrow escape, he said. You see, if my grandfather hadn't come back so early, I couldn't have come to say goodbye.

—You are going then, inkosana?

But the boy did not answer his question. He saw that Kumalo was puzzled, and he was anxious to explain.

—You see, if my grandfather had come back later, then perhaps it would have been too late for me to ride down here again. But because he came early, there was time.

—That means you are going tomorrow, inkosana.

—Yes, tomorrow. On the narrow gauge train, you know, the small train.

—Au! inkosana.

—But I'm coming back for the holidays. Then we'll learn some more Zulu.

—That will be a pleasure, said Kumalo simply.

—Goodbye then, umfundisi.

—Goodbye, inkosana.

Then he said in Zulu, Go well, inkosana. The small boy thought for a moment, and frowned in concentration. Then he said in Zulu, Stay well, umfundisi. So Kumalo said, Au! Au! in astonishment, and the small boy laughed and raised his cap, and was gone in a great cloud of dust. He galloped up the road, but stopped and turned round and saluted, before he set out on his way. And Kumalo stood there, and the young demonstrator came and stood by him, both watching the small boy.

—And that, said Kumalo earnestly to the demonstrator, is a small angel from God.

They turned to walk back to the house, and Kumalo said, So you think many things can be done?

—There are many things that can be done, umfundisi.

—Truly?

—Umfundisi, said the young man, and his face was eager, there is no reason why this valley should not be what it was before. But it will not happen quickly. Not in a day.

—If God wills, said Kumalo humbly, before I die. For I have lived my life in destruction.

34

EVERYTHING was ready for the confirmation. The women of the church were there, in their white dresses, each with the green cloth about her neck. Those men that were not away, and who belonged to this church, were there in their Sunday clothes, which means their working clothes, patched and cleaned and brushed. The children for the confirmation were there, the girls in their white dresses and caps, the boys in their school-going clothes, patched and cleaned and brushed. Women were busy in the house, helping the wife of the umfundisi, for after the confirmation there would be a simple meal, of tea boiled till the leaves had no more tea left in them, and of heavy homely cakes made of the meal of the maize. It was simple food, but it was to be eaten together.

And over the great valley the storm clouds were gathering again in the heavy oppressive heat, so that one did not know whether to be glad or sorry. The great dark shadows sailed over the red earth, and up the bare red hills to the tops. The people looked at the sky, and at the road by which the Bishop would come, and did not know whether to be glad or sorry. For it was certain that before this sun had set, the lightning would strike amongst the hills, and the thunder would echo amongst them.

Kumalo looked at the sky anxiously, and at the road by which the Bishop would come; and while he was looking he was surprised to see his friend driving along the road, with the cart that brought the milk. For the milk never came so early.

—You are early, my friend.

—I am early, umfundisi, said his friend gravely. We work no more today. The inkosikazi is dead.

—Au! Au! said Kumalo, it cannot be.

—It is so, umfundisi. When the sun stood so— and he pointed above his head—it was then that she died.

—Au! Au! It is a sorrow.

—It is a sorrow, umfundisi.

—And the umnumzana?

—He goes about silent. You know how he is. But this time the silence is heavier. Umfundisi, I shall go and wash myself, then I can come to the confirmation.

—Go then, my friend.

Kumalo went into the house, and he told his wife, The inkosikazi is dead. And she said, Au! Au! and the women also. Some of them wept, and they spoke of the goodness of the woman that was dead. Kumalo went to his table, and sat down there, thinking what he should do. When this confirmation was over he would go up to the house at High Place, and tell Jarvis of their grief here in the valley.

But there came a picture to him of the house of be-reavement, of all the cars of the white people that would be there, of the black-clothed farmers that would stand about in little groups, talking gravely and quietly, for he had seen such a thing before. And he knew that he could not go, for this was not according to the custom. He would stand there by himself, and unless Jarvis himself came out, no one would ask why he was there, no one would know that he had brought a message. He sighed, and took out some paper from the drawer. He decided it must be written in English, for although most white men of these parts spoke Zulu, there were few who could read or write it. So he wrote then. And he wrote many things, and tore them up and put them aside, but at last it was finished.

UMNUMZANA:

We are grieved here at this church to hear that the mother has passed away, and we understand it and suffer with tears. We are certain also that she knew of the things you have done for us, and did something in it. We shall pray in this church for the rest of her soul, and for you also in your suffering.

Your faithful servant,
REV. S. KUMALO.

When it was finished, he sat wondering if he should send it. For suppose this woman had died of a heart that was broken, because her son had been killed. Then was he, the father of the man who had killed him, to send such a letter? Had he not heard that she was sick and thin? He groaned as he wrestled with this difficult matter, but as he sat there uncertain, he thought of the gift of the milk, and of the young demonstrator that had come to teach farming, and above all, he remembered the voice of Jarvis saying, even as if he were speaking now in this room, Is there mercy? And he knew then that this was a man who put his feet upon a road, and that no man would turn him from it. So he sealed the letter, and went out and called a boy to him and said, My child, will you take a letter for me? And the boy said, I shall do it, umfundisi. Go to Kuluse, said Kumalo, and ask him for his horse, and take this letter to the house of uJarvis. Do not trouble the umnumzana, but give this letter to any person that you see about the place. And my child, go quietly and respectfully, and do not call to any person there, and do not laugh or talk idly, for the inkosikazi is dead. Do you understand?

—I understand completely, umfundisi.

—Go then, my child. I am sorry you cannot be here to see the confirmation.

—It does not matter, umfundisi.

Then Kumalo went to tell the people that the inkosikazi was dead. And they fell silent, and if there had been any calling or laughter or talking idly, there was no more. They stood there talking quietly and soberly till the Bishop came.

It was dark in the church for the confirmation, so that they had to light the lamps. The great heavy clouds swept over the valley, and the lightning flashed over the red desolate hills, where the earth had torn away like flesh. The thunder roared over the valleys of old men and old women, of mothers and children. The men are away, the young men and the girls are away, the soil cannot keep them any more. And some of the children are there in the church being confirmed, and after a while they too will go away, for the soil cannot keep them any more.

It was dark there in the church, and the rain came down through the roof. The pools formed on the floor, and the people moved here and there, to get away from the rain. Some of the white dresses were wet, and a girl shivered there with the cold, because this occasion was solemn for her, and she did not dare to move out of the rain. And the voice of the Bishop said, Defend, oh Lord, this Thy child with Thy heavenly grace, that he may continue Thine for ever, and daily increase in Thy Holy Spirit more and more, till he come unto Thy everlasting Kingdom. And this he said to each child that came, and confirmed them all.

After the confirmation they crowded into the house, for the simple food that was to be taken. Kumalo had to ask those who were not that day confirmed, or who were not parents of those confirmed, to stay in the church, for it was still raining heavily, though the lightning and the thunder had passed. Yet the house was full to overflowing; the people were in the kitchen, and in the room where Kumalo did his accounts, and in the room where they ate, and in the room where they slept, even in the room of the young demonstrator.

At last the rain was over, and the Bishop and Kumalo were left alone in the room where Kumalo did his accounts. The Bishop lit his pipe and said to Kumalo, Mr. Kumalo, I should like to talk to you. And Kumalo sat down fearfully, afraid of what would be said.

—I was sorry to hear of all your troubles, my friend.

—They have been heavy, my lord.

—I did not like to worry you, Mr. Kumalo, after all you had suffered. And I thought I had better wait till this confirmation.

—Yes, my lord.

—I speak to you out of my regard for you, my friend. You must be sure of that.

—Yes, my lord.

—Then I think, Mr. Kumalo, that you should go away from Ndotsheni.

Yes, that is what would be said, it is said now. Yes, that is what I have feared. Yet take me away, and I die. I am too old to begin any more. I am old, I am frail. Yet I have tried to be a father to this people. Could you not have been here, O Bishop, the day when I came back to Ndotsheni? Would you not have seen that these people love me, although I am old? Would you not have heard a child say We are glad the umfundisi is back; this other man, we did not understand him? Would you take me away just when new things are beginning, when there is milk for the children, and the young demonstrator has come, and the sticks for the dam are planted in the ground? The tears fill the eyes, and the eyes shut,

and the tears are forced out, and they fall on the new
black suit, made for this confirmation with the
money of the beloved Msimangu. The old head is
bowed, and the old man sits there like a child, with
not a word to be spoken.

—Mr. Kumalo, says the Bishop gently, and then
again, more loudly, Mr. Kumalo.

—Sir. My lord.

—I am sorry to distress you. I am sorry to distress
you. But would it not be better if you went away?

—It is what you say, my lord.

The Bishop sits forward in his chair, and rests his
elbows upon his knees. Mr. Kumalo, is it not true
that the father of the murdered man is your
neighbour here in Ndotsheni? Mr. Jarvis?

—It is true, my lord.

—Then for that reason alone I think you
should go.

Is that a reason why I should go? Why, does he
not ride here to see me, and did not the small boy
come into my house? Did he not send the milk for
the children, and did he not get this young demonstrator to teach the people farming? And does not
my heart grieve for him, now that the inkosikazi is
dead? But how does one say these things to a
Bishop, to a great man in the country? They are
things that cannot be said.

—Do you understand me, Mr. Kumalo?

—I understand you, my lord.

—I would send you to Pietermaritzburg, to your
old friend Ntombela. You could help him there, and
it would take a load off your shoulders. He can

worry about buildings and schools and money, and you can give your mind to the work of a priest. That is the plan I have in my mind.

—I understand you, my lord.

—If you stay here, Mr. Kumalo, there will be many loads on your shoulders. There is not only the fact that Mr. Jarvis is your neighbour, but sooner or later you must rebuild your church, and that will cost a great deal of money and anxiety. You saw for yourself today in what condition it is.

—Yes, my lord.

—And I understand you have brought back to live with you the wife of your son, and that she is expecting a child. Is is fair to them to stay here, Mr. Kumalo? Would it not be better to go to some place where these things are not known?

—I understand you, my lord.

There was a knock at the door, and it was the boy standing there, the boy who took the message. Kumalo took the letter, and it was addressed to the Rev. S. Kumalo, Ndotsheni. He thanked the boy and closed the door, then went and sat down in his chair, ready to listen to the Bishop.

—Read your letter, Mr. Kumalo.

So Kumalo opened the letter, and read it.

UMFUNDISI:

I thank you for your message of sympathy, and for the promise of the prayers of your church. You are right, my wife knew of the things that are being done, and had the greatest part in it. These things we did in memory of our beloved son. It was one of her last wishes that a new church should be built at Ndotsheni, and I shall come to discuss it with you.

Yours truly,
JAMES JARVIS.

You should know that my wife was suffering before we went to Johannesburg.

*   *   *   *   *

Kumalo stood up, and he said in a voice that astonished the Bishop, this is from God, he said. It was a voice in which there was relief from anxiety, and laughter, and weeping, and he said again, looking round the walls of the room, This is from God.

—May I see your letter from God, said the Bishop dryly.

So Kumalo gave it to him eagerly, and stood impatiently while the Bishop read it. And when the Bishop had finished, he said gravely, That was a foolish jest.

He read it again, and blew his nose, and sat with the letter in his hand.

—What are the things that are being done? he asked.

So Kurnalo told him about the milk, and the new dam that was to be built, and the young demonstrator. And the Bishop blew his nose several times, and said to Kumalo, This is an extraordinary thing. It is one of the most extraordinary things that I have ever heard.

And Kumalo explained the words, You should know that my wife was suffering before we went to Johannesburg. He explained how these words were written out of understanding and compassion. And he told the Bishop of the words, Is there mercy? and of the small boy who visited him, the small boy with the laughter inside him.

The Bishop said, Let us go into the church and pray, if there is a dry place to pray in your church. Then I must go, for I have still a long journey. But let me first say goodbye to your wife, and your daughter-in-law. Tell me, what of the other matter, of your daughter-in-law, and the child she is expecting?

—We have prayed openly before the people, my lord. What more could be done than that?

—It was the way it was done in olden days, said the Bishop. In the olden days when men had faith. But I should not say that, after what I have heard today.

The Bishop said farewell to the people of the house, and he and Kumalo went to the church. At the church door he spoke to Kumalo and said gravely, I see it is not God's will that you should leave Ndotsheni.

*　　*　　*　　*　　*

After the Bishop had gone, Kumalo stood outside the church in the gathering dark. The rain had stopped, but the sky was black with promise. It was cool, and the breeze blew gently from the great river, and the soul of the man was uplifted. And while he stood there looking out over the great valley, there was a voice that cried out of heaven, Comfort ye, comfort ye, my people, these things will I do unto you, and not forsake you.

Only it did not happen as men deem such things to happen, it happened otherwise. It happened in that fashion that men call illusion, or the imaginings of people overwrought, or an intimation of the divine.

*   *   *   *   *

When he went into the house, he found his wife and the girl, and some other women of the church, and his friend who carried the bags, busy making a wreath. They had a cypress branch, for there was a solitary cypress near the hut of his friend, the only cypress that grew in the whole valley of Ndotsheni, and how it grew there no man could remember. This branch they had made into a ring, and tied it so that it could not spring apart. Into it they had put the flowers of the veld, such as grew in the bareness of the valley.

—I do not like it, umfundisi. What is wrong with it? It does not look like a white person's wreath.

—They use white flowers, said the new teacher. I have often seen that they use white flowers there in Pietermaritzburg.

—Umfundisi, said the friend excitedly, I know where there are white flowers, arum lilies.

—They use arum lilies, said the new teacher, also excited.

—But they are far away. They grow near the railway line, on the far side of Carisbrooke, by a little stream that I know.

—That is far away, said Kumalo.

—I shall go there, said the man. It is not too far to go for such a thing as this. Can you lend me a lantern, umfundisi?

—Surely, my friend.

—And there must be a white ribbon, said the teacher.

—I have one at my house, said one of the women. I shall go and fetch it.

—And you, Stephen, will you write a card for us? Have you such a card?

—The edges of it should be black, said the teacher.

—Yes, I can find a card, said Kumalo, and I shall put black edges on it with the ink.

He went to his room where he did the accounts, and he found such a card, and printed on it:

With sympathy from the
people of St. Mark's Church,
Ndotsheni

He was busy with the edges, careful not to spoil the card with the ink, when his wife called him to come to his food.

35

THERE is ploughing in Ndotsheni, and indeed on all the farms around it. But the ploughing goes slowly, because the young demonstrator, and behind him the chief, tell the men they must no longer go up and down. They throw up walls of earth, and plough round the hills, so that the fields look no longer as they used to look in the old days of ploughing. Women and boys collect the dung, but it looks so little on the land that the chief has ordered a kraal to be built, where the cattle can stay and the dung be easily collected; but that is a hard thing, because there will be nothing to eat in the kraal. The young demonstrator shakes his head over the dung, but next year he says it will be better. The wattle seed is boiled, and no one has heard of such a thing before in this valley, but those that have worked for the white farmers say it is right, and so they boil it. For this seed one or two desolate places have been chosen, but the young demonstrator shakes his head over them, there is so little food in the soil. And the demonstrator has told the people they can throw away the maize they have kept for planting, because it is inferior and he has better seed from uJarvis. But they do not throw it away, they keep it for eating.

But all this was not done by magic. There have been meetings, and much silence, and much sullenness. It was only the fear of the chief that made anything come out of these meetings. No one was more dissatisfied than those who had to give up their fields. Kuluse's brother was silent for days because the dam was to eat up his land, and he was dissatisfied with the poor piece of land they gave him. Indeed the umfundisi had to persuade him, and it was hard to refuse the umfundisi, because it was through him that had come the milk that had saved his brother's child.

The chief had hinted that there were still harder things he would ask, and indeed the young demonstrator was dissatisfied that they had not been asked at once. But it would be hard to get these people to agree to everything at once. Even this year he hoped, said the young demonstrator, that the people would see something with their eyes, though he shook his head sadly over the poverty-stricken soil.

There was talk that the Government would give a bull to the chief, and the young demonstrator explained to Kumalo that they would get rid of the cows that gave the smallest yield, but he did not talk thus in the meeting, for that was one of the hard things for a people who counted their wealth in cattle, even these miserable cattle.

But the greatest wonder of all is the great machine, that was fighting in the war, they said, and pushes the earth of Kuluse's brother's land over to the line of the sticks, and leaves it there, growing ever higher and higher. And even Kuluse's brother, watching it sullenly, breaks out into unwilling laughter, but remembers again and is sullen. But there is some satisfaction for him, for next year, when the dam is full, Zuma and his brother must both give up their land that lies below the dam, for white man's grass is to be planted there, to be watered from the dam, to be cut and thrown into the kraal where the cattle will be kept. And both Zuma and his brother laughed at him, because he was sullen about the dam; so in some measure he is satisfied.

Indeed, there is something new in this valley, some spirit and some life, and much to talk about in the huts. Although nothing has come yet, something is here already.

*   *   *   *   *

—There was another Napoleon, said Kumalo, who was also a man who did many things. So many things did he do that many books were written about him.

The young demonstrator laughed, but he cast his eyes on the ground, and rubbed his one boot against the other.

—You can be proud, said Kumalo. For there is a new life in this valley. I have been here for many years, but I have never seen ploughing with such spirit.

—There is a new thing happening here, he said. It

is not only these rains, though they too refresh the spirit. There is hope here, such as I have never seen before.

—You must not expect too much, said the young man anxiously. I do not expect much this year. The maize will be a little higher, and the harvest a little bigger, but the soil is poor indeed.

—But next year there will be the kraal.

—Yes, said the young man eagerly. We will save much dung in the kraal. They say to me, umfundisi, that even if the winter is cold, they will not burn the dung.

—How long will it be before the trees are ready?

—Many years, said the demonstrator gloomily. Tell me, umfundisi, he said anxiously, do you think they will bear the winter for seven years?

—Have courage, young man. Both the chief and I are working for you.

—I am impatient for the dam, said the demonstrator. When the dam is made, there will be water for the pastures. I tell you, umfundisi, he said excitedly, there will be milk in this valley. It will not be necessary to take the white man's milk.

Kumalo looked at him. Where would we be without the white man's milk? he asked. Where would we be without all that this white man has done for us? Where would you be also? Would you be working for him here?

—It is true I am paid by him, said the young man stubbornly. I am not ungrateful.

—Then you should not speak so, said Kumalo coldly.

There fell a constraint between them, until the young demonstrator said quietly, umfundisi, I work here with all my heart, is it not so?

—That is true indeed.

—I work so because I work for my country and my people. You must see that, umfundisi. I could not work so for any master.

—If you had no master, you would not be here at all.

—I understand you, said the young man. This man is a good man, and I respect him. But it is not the way it should be done, that is all.

—And what way should it be done?

—Not this way, said the young man doggedly.

—What way then?

—Umfundisi, it was the white man who gave us so little land, it was the white man who took us away from the land to go to work. And we were ignorant also. It is all these things together that have made this valley desolate. Therefore, what this good white man does is only a repayment.

—I do not like this talk.

—I understand you, umfundisi, I understand you completely. But let me ask one thing of you.

—Ask it then.

—If this valley were restored, as you are always asking in your prayers, do you think it would hold all the people of this tribe if they all returned?

—I do not know indeed.

—But I know, umfundisi. We can restore this valley for those who are here, but when the children grow up, there will again be too many. Some will have to go still.

And Kumalo was silent, having no answer. He sighed. You are too clever for me, he said.

—I am sorry, umfundisi.

—You need not be sorry. I see you have a love for truth.

—I was taught that, umfundisi. It was a white man who taught me. There is not even good farming, he said, without the truth.

—This man was wise.

—It was he also who taught me that we do not work for men, that we work for the land and the people. We do not even work for money, he said.

Kumalo was touched, and he said to the young man, Are there many who think as you do?

—I do not know, umfundisi. I do not know if there are many. But there are some.

He grew excited. We work for Africa, he said, not for this man or that man. Not for a white man or a black man, but for Africa.

—Why do you not say South Africa?

—We would if we could, said the young man soberly.

He reflected for a moment. We speak as we sing, he said, for we sing *Nkosi Sikelel' iAfrika*.

—It is getting dark, said Kumalo, and it is time for us to wash.

—You must not misunderstand me, umfundisi, said the young man earnestly. I am not a man for politics. I am not a man to make trouble in your valley. I desire to restore it, that is all.

—May God give you your desire, said Kumalo with equal earnestness. My son, one word.

—Yes, umfundisi.

—I cannot stop you from thinking your thoughts. It is good that a young man has such deep thoughts. But hate no man, and desire power over no man. For I have a friend who taught me that power corrupts.

—I hate no man, umfundisi. I desire power over none.

—That is well. For there is enough hating in our land already.

The young man went into the house to wash, and Kumalo stood for a moment in the dark, where the stars were coming out over the valley that was to be restored. And that for him was enough, for his life was nearly finished. He was too old for new and disturbing thoughts and they hurt him also, for they struck at many things. Yes, they struck at the grave silent man at High Place, who after such deep hurt, had shown such deep compassion. He was too old for new and disturbing thoughts. A white man's dog, that is what they called him and his kind. Well, that was the way his life had been lived, that was the way he would die.

He turned and followed the young man into the house.

36

THIS was the fourteenth day. Kumalo said to his wife, I am going up into the mountain. And she said, I understand you. For twice before he had done it, once when the small boy Absalom was sick unto death, and once when he had thought of giving up the ministry to run a native store at Donnybrook for a white man named Baxter, for more money than the church could ever pay. And there was a third time, but that was without her knowledge, for she was away, and he had been sorely tempted to commit adultery with one of the teachers at Ndotsheni, who was weak and lonely.

—Would you come with me, he said, for I do not like to leave you alone.

She was touched and she said, I cannot come, for the girl is near her time, and who knows when it will be. But you must certainly go.

She made him a bottle of tea, of the kind that is made by boiling the leaves, and she wrapped up a few heavy cakes of maize. He took his coat and his stick and walked up the path that went to the place of the chief. But at the first fork you go to the side of the hand that you eat with, and you climb another hill to other huts that lie beneath the mountain itself. There you turn and walk under the mountain to the east, as though you were going to the far valley of Empayeni, which is another valley where the fields are red and bare, a valley of old men and women, and mothers and children. But when you reach the end of the level path, where it begins to fall to this other valley, you strike upwards into the mountain itself. This mountain is called Emoyeni, which means, in the winds, and it stands high above Carisbrooke and the tops, and higher still above the valleys of Ndotsheni and Empayeni. Indeed it is a rampart of the great valley itself, the valley of the Umzimkulu, and from it you look down on one of the fairest scenes of Africa.

Now it was almost dark, and he was alone in the dusk; which was well, for one did not go publicly on a journey of this nature. But even as he started to climb the path that ran through the great stones, a man on a horse was there, and a voice said to him, It is you, umfundisi?

—It is I, umnumzana.

—Then we are well met, umfundisi. For here in my pocket I have a letter for the people of your church. He paused for a moment, and then he said, The flowers were of great beauty, umfundisi.

—I thank you, umnumzana.

—And the church, umfundisi. Do you desire a new church?

Kumalo could only smile and shake his head,

there were no words in him. And though he shook his head as if it were No, Jarvis understood him.

—The plans will shortly come to you, and you must say if they are what you desire.

—I shall send them to the Bishop, umnumzana.

—You will know what to do. But I am anxious to do it quickly, for I shall be leaving this place.

Kumalo stood shocked at the frightening and desolating words. And although it was dark, Jarvis understood him, for he said swiftly, I shall be often here. You know I have a work in Ndotsheni. Tell me, how is the young man?

—He works night and day. There is no quietness in him.

The white man laughed softly. That is good, he said. Then he said gravely, I am alone in my house, so I am going to Johannesburg to live with my daughter and her children. You know the small boy?

—Indeed, umnumzana, I know him.

—Is he like him?

—He is like him, umnumzana.

And then Kumalo said, Indeed, I have never seen such a child as he is.

Jarvis turned on his horse, and in the dark the grave silent man was eager. What do you mean? he asked.

—Umnumzana, there is a brightness inside him.

—Yes, yes, that is true. The other was even so.

And then he said, like a man with hunger, do you remember?

And because this man was hungry, Kumalo, though he did not well remember, said, I remember.

They stayed there in silence till Jarvis said, um-fundisi, I must go. But he did not go. Instead he said, Where are you going at this hour?

Kumalo was embarrassed, and the words fell about on his tongue, but he answered, I am going into the mountain.

Because Jarvis made no answer he sought for words to explain it, but before he had spoken a word, the other had already spoken. I understand you, he said, I understand completely.

And because he spoke with compassion, the old man wept, and Jarvis sat embarrassed on his horse. Indeed he might have come down from it, but such a thing is not lightly done. But he stretched his hand over the darkening valley, and he said, One thing is about to be finished, but here is something that is only begun. And while I live it will continue. Um-fundisi, go well.

—Umnumzana!

—Yes.

—Do not go before I have thanked you. For the young man, and the milk. And now for the church.

—I have seen a man, said Jarvis with a kind of grim gaiety, who was in darkness till you found him. If that is what you do, I give it willingly.

Perhaps it was something deep that was here, or perhaps the darkness gives courage, but Kumalo said truly, of all the white men that I have ever known—

—I am no saintly man, said Jarvis fiercely.

—Of that I cannot speak, but God put His hands on you.

And Jarvis said, That may be, that may be. He turned suddenly to Kumalo. Go well, umfundisi. Throughout this night, stay well.

And Kumalo cried after him, Go well, go well.

Indeed there were other things, deep things, that he could have cried, but such a thing is not lightly done. He waited till the sounds of the horse had died away, then started to climb heavily, holding onto the greatest stones, for he was young no longer. He was tired and panting when he reached the summit, and he sat down on a stone to rest, looking out over the great valley, to the mountains of Ingeli and East Griqualand, dark against the sky. Then recovered, he walked a short distance and found the place that he had used before on these occasions. It was an angle in the rock, sheltered from the winds, with a place for a man to sit on, his legs at ease over the edge. The first of these occasions he remembered clearly, perhaps because it was the first, perhaps because he had come to pray for the child that no prayer could save any more. The child could not write then, but here were three letters from him now, and in all of them he said, If I could come back to Ndotsheni, I would not leave it any more. And in a day or two they would receive the last he would ever write. His heart went out in a great compassion for the boy that must die, who promised now, when there was no more mercy, to sin no more. If he had got to him sooner, perhaps. He knitted his brows at the memory of that terrible and useless questioning, the terrible and useless answering, it is as my father wishes, it is as my father says. What would it have helped if he had said, My father, I do not know?

He turned aside from such fruitless remembering, and set himself to the order of his vigil. He confessed his sins, remembering them as well as he could since the last time he had been in this mountain. There were some he remembered easily, the lie in the train, the lie to his brother, when John had barred the door against him and shut him out in the street; his loss of faith in Johannesburg, and his desire to hurt the girl, the sinning and innocent child. All this he did as fully as he could, and prayed for absolution.

Then he turned to thanksgiving, and remembered, with profound awareness, that he had great cause for thanksgiving, and that for many things. He took them one by one, giving thanks for each, and praying for each person that he remembered. There was above all the beloved Msimangu and his generous gift. There was the young man from the reformatory saying with angry brows, I am sorry, umfundisi, that I spoke such angry words. There was Mrs. Lithebe, who said so often, Why else were we born? And Father Vincent, holding both his hands and saying. Anything, anything, you have only to ask, I shall do anything. And the lawyer that took the case for God, and had written to say there was no mercy in such kind and gentle words.

Then there was the return to Ndotsheni, with his wife and his friend to meet him. And the woman who threw her apron over her head. And the women waiting at the church. And the great joy of the return, so that pain was forgotten.

He pondered long over this, for might not another man, returning to another valley, have found none of these things? Why was it given to one man to have his pain transmuted into gladness? Why was it given to one man to have such an awareness of God? And might not another, having no such awareness, live with pain that never ended? Why was there a compulsion upon him to pray for the restoration of Ndotsheni, and why was there a white man there on the tops, to do in this valley what no other could have done? And why of all men, the father of the man who had been murdered by his son? And might not another feel also a compulsion, and pray night and day without ceasing, for the restoration of some other valley that would never be restored?

But his mind would contain it no longer. It was not for man's knowing. He put it from his mind, for it was a secret.

And then the white man Jarvis, and the inkosikazi that was dead, and the small boy with the brightness inside him. As his mind could not contain that other, neither could this be contained. But here were thanks that a man could render till the end of his days. And some of them he strove now to render.

He woke with a start. It was cold, but not so cold. He had never slept before on these vigils, but he was old, not quite finished, but nearly finished. He thought of all those that were suffering, of Gertrude the weak and foolish one, of the people of Shanty Town and Alexandra, of his wife now at this moment. But above all of his son, Absalom. Would he be awake, would he be able to sleep, this night before the morning? He cried out, My son, my son, my son.

With his crying he was now fully awake, and he looked at his watch and saw that it was one o'clock. The sun would rise soon after five, and it was then it was done, they said. If the boy was asleep, then let him sleep, it was better. But if he was awake, then oh Christ of the abundant mercy, be with him. Over this he prayed long and earnestly.

Would his wife be awake, and thinking of it? She would have come with him, were it not for the girl. And the girl, why, he had forgotten her. But she was no doubt asleep; she was loving enough, but this husband had given her so little, no more than her others had done.

And there was Jarvis, bereaved of his wife and his son, and his daughter-in-law bereaved of her husband, and her children bereaved of their father, especially the small boy, the bright laughing boy. The small boy stood there before his eyes, and he said to Kumalo, When I go, something bright will go out of Ndotsheni. Yes, I see, he said. Yes, I see. He was not shy or ashamed, but he said, Yes, I see, and laughed with his pleasure.

And now for all the people of Africa, the beloved country. *Nkosi Sikelel' iAfrika*, God save Africa. But he would not see that salvation. It lay afar off, because men were afraid of it. Because, to tell the truth, they were afraid of him, and his wife, and Msimangu, and the young demonstrator. And what was there evil in their desires, in their hunger? That men should walk upright in the land where they were born, and be free to use the fruits of the earth, what was there evil in it? Yet men were afraid, with a fear that was deep, deep in the heart, a fear so deep that they hid their kindness, or brought it out with fierceness and anger, and hid it behind fierce and frowning eyes. They were afraid because they were so few. And such fear could not be cast out, but by love.

It was Msimangu who had said, Msimangu who had no hate for any man, I have one great fear in my heart, that one day when they turn to loving they will find we are turned to hating.

Oh, the grave and the sombre words.

*   *   *   *   *

When he woke again there was a faint change in the east, and he looked at his watch almost with a panic. But it was four o'clock and he was reassured. And now it was time to be awake, for it might be they had wakened his son, and called him to make ready. He left his place and could hardly stand, for his feet were cold and numb. He found another place where he could look to the east, and if it was true what men said, when the sun came up over the rim, it would be done.

He had heard that they could eat what they wished on a morning like this. Strange that a man should ask for food at such a time. Did the body hunger, driven by some deep dark power that did not know it must die? Is the boy quiet, and does he dress quietly, and does he think of Ndotsheni now? Do tears come into his eyes, and does he wipe them away, and stand up like a man? Does he say, I will not eat any food, I will pray? Is Msimangu there with him, or Father Vincent, or some other priest whose duty it is, to comfort and strengthen him, for he is afraid of the hanging? Does he repent him, or is there only room for his fear? Is there nothing that can be done now, is there not an angel that comes there and cries, This is for God not for man, come child, come with me?

He looked out of his clouded eyes at the faint steady lightening in the east. But he calmed himself, and took out the heavy maize cakes and the tea, and put them upon a stone. And he gave thanks, and broke the cakes and ate them, and drank of the tea. Then he gave himself over to deep and earnest prayer, and after each petition he raised his eyes and looked to the east. And the east lightened and lightened, till he knew that the time was not far off. And when he expected it, he rose to his feet and took off his hat and laid it down on the earth, and clasped his hands before him. And while he stood there the sun rose in the east.

* * * * *

Yes, it is the dawn that has come. The titihoya wakes from sleep, and goes about its work of forlorn crying. The sun tips with light the mountains of Ingeli and East Griqualand. The great valley of the Umzimkulu is still in darkness, but the light will come there. Ndotsheni is still in darkness, but the light will come there also. For it is the dawn that has come, as it has come for a thousand centuries, never failing. But when that dawn will come, of our emancipation, from the fear of bondage and the bondage of fear, why, that is a secret.

List of Words

Afrikáans

> the language of the Afrikaner, a much simplified and beautiful version of the language of Holland, though it is held in contempt by some ignorant English-speaking South Africans, and indeed by some Hollanders. Afrikaans and English are the two official languages of the Union of South Africa.

Afrikáner

> "a" as in father. The name now used for the descendants of the Boers. Some large-minded Afrikaners claim that it has a wider connotation, and means white South Africans, but many Afrikaans-speaking and English-speaking South Africans would object to this extension of meaning. It is used here in its usually accepted meaning.

Ingéli

> The first "i" as in "pit," the second as "ee." The "e" is almost like "a" in "pane."

Inkosána

> The "i" as in "pit," the "o" midway between "o" in "pot," and "o" in "born." The "a" as in "father," but the second "a" is hardly sounded. Approximate pronunciation "inkosaan." Means little chief, or little master.

Inkósi

> As above. But the final "i" is hardly sounded. Means chief or master.

Inkósikazi

> As above. The second "k" is like hard "g." The final "i" is hardly sounded. Pronounce "inkosi-gaaz." Means mistress.

Ixópo

> The name of a village. Its Zulu pronunciation is difficult, and would be considered affected in English speech. It is pronounced in English, "Ickopo," with "o" as in hole.

Johánnesburg

> An Afrikaans word, but pronounced in English as it is written. It is the centre of the gold-mining industry.

Káfferboetie

> Pronounce "boetie" not as "booty" but to rhyme with "sooty." A term of contempt originally used to describe those who fraternized with African natives, but now used to describe

any who work for the welfare of the non-European. Means literally "little brother of the kaffir." Afrikaans.

Kloof

An Afrikaans word now as fully English. Pronounced as written. Means ravine or even a valley if the sides are steep. But it would not be used of a great valley like the Umzimkulu.

Kraal

An Afrikaans word now as fully English. Pronounced in English "crawl." An enclosure for cattle, where they come for milking, or where in the early days they were kept for protection. But it may also mean a number of huts together, under the rule of the head of the family, who is of course subject to the chief.

Kumálo

"u" as "oo" as in "book." "a" as in "father." The "o" midway between "o" in "pot" and "o" in "born."

Lithébe

Pronounced "ditebe," "e" approximately as in "bed."

Msimángu

The word is pronounced with the lips initially closed. Therefore no vowel precedes the "M." Pronounced approximately as written.

Ndotshéni

> Approximately "Indotsheni." "o" midway between "o" in "pot" and "o" in "born," "e" almost as "a" in "pane," "i" as "ee." Last vowel hardly sounded.

Nikosi sikelél' iAfrika

> Means "God bless Africa," though in the book it is taken to mean "God *save* Africa." This lovely hymn is rapidly becoming accepted as the national anthem of the black people. At any mixed meeting therefore, where goodwill prevails, three such anthems are sung at the conclusion, "God Save The King," "Die Stem Van Suid-Afrika," and "Nkosi Sikelel' iAfrica." This is co-operative, but very wearing. But such meetings are rare. Pronunciation, "Nkosi" almost as "Inkosi," "sikelele" with "k" as hard "g," and "e" approximately as in "bed," "iAfrika" with "a" as in "father," "i" as shortened "ee."

Odendaalsrúst

> Pronounced by English-speaking people as written.

Pietermáritzburg

> Pronounced by English-speaking people as written. A city founded by the Voortrekkers Piet Retief and Gert Maritz. Capital of the Province of Natal.

Pretória

Pronounced by English-speaking people as written. A city named after Voortrekker, Pretorius. Capital of the Union of South Africa.

Siyáfa

"i" as "ee," "a" as in "father." Means "we die."

Titihóya

A plover-like bird. The name is onomatopoeic.

Tíxo

I rejected the Zulu word for the Great Spirit as too long and difficult. This is the Xosa word. It is also difficult to pronounce, but may be pronounced "Teeko," the "o" being midway the "o" in "pot" and the "o" of "born."

Umfúndisi

The last "i" is hardly sounded. Pronounce approximately "oomfóondees," the "oo" being as in "book," and the "ees" as "eace" in the word "peace." Means parson, but is also a title and used with respect.

Umnúmzana

Pronounced "oomnóomzaan." Means "sir."

Umzimkúlu

Pronounced by English-speaking as "Umzimkóoloo," but the "oo" is very long as in "coo."

Veld

An Afrikaans word now as fully English. Pronounced in both languages as "felt." Means open grass country. Or it may mean the grass itself, as when a farmer looks down at his feet, and says, this veld is poor.

Xósa

The pronunciation is difficult. English-speaking people pronounce it "Kosa," "o" midway between "o" in "pot" and "o" in "born," "a" almost as "u" in "much." A native tribe of the Eastern Cape.

Zúlu

The great tribe of Zululand, which overflowed into Natal and other parts. Both "u"s are long as in "coo."

In all cases where such words as "umfundisi," "umnumzana," are used as forms of address, the initial vowel is dropped. But I thought it wise to omit this complication.